# Praise for Sharon Lynn Fisher

"Fisher has a fantastic voice—crisp, magical, and crystal clear."
—Darynda Jones, *New York Times* and *USA Today* bestselling author

"Magical and brilliant! A fast-paced romp that expertly weaves two different worlds into an adventure not to be missed. Sharon Lynn Fisher crafts clever dialogue and creates characters to fall in love with."
—Lorraine Heath, *New York Times* and *USA Today* bestselling author, on *The Absinthe Earl*

"The environment is lush and imaginative, with everyone appearing to hide their own seductive, dark secrets. It's a world that comes alive with mysterious, foggy moors, dangerous peat bogs, and gorgeous green hills . . . Irish mythology and folklore are where Fisher's writing shines."
—*Kirkus Reviews* on *The Absinthe Earl*

"Readers will be drawn in from the very first word of this fantasy romance . . ."
—*Booklist* on *The Raven Lady*

"This is quite a wonderfully dizzying mash-up of a historical setting, time travel of a sorts, and the fae. If you're a reader drawn to historical fantasy and magical Regencies, definitely give this series a try."
—*Book Riot* on The Faery Rehistory series

"This is a really fun sci-fi romance . . . Very cool setup and characters that I couldn't put down . . . the twist at the beginning will really hook you in!"
—Felicia Day, actress and producer, on *Ghost Planet*

"An absorbing and exciting story full of science, sex, and intriguing plot twists."

—*Publishers Weekly* on *Ghost Planet*

# SALT
# &
# BROOM

# *OTHER TITLES BY SHARON LYNN FISHER*

## The Faery Rehistory Series

*The Absinthe Earl*
*The Raven Lady*
*The Warrior Poet*

## Science Fiction

*Ghost Planet*
*The Ophelia Prophecy*
*Echo 8*

## *Erotic Fantasy Shorts*

*Before She Wakes*

# SALT & BROOM

SHARON LYNN FISHER

This is a work of fiction. Names, characters, organizations, places, events, and incidents are either products of the author's imagination or are used fictitiously. Otherwise, any resemblance to actual persons, living or dead, is purely coincidental.



Published by 47North, Seattle

www.apub.com



ISBN-13: 9781662515699 (paperback)
ISBN-13: 9781662515682 (digital)

Cover design by Alison Impey
Cover illustration by Colin Verdi

Printed in the United States of America

*For Charlotte B. and Mary S. and every witchy and wise woman I've ever known*

# *Author's Note*

Please note, dear reader, I am a novelist, not an herbalist, and this is a work of fiction. I have used some very old texts, along with newer ones, as references in writing this book. If you are interested in creating your own herbal remedies, please do your own research using modern, authoritative sources. I hope you enjoy my witchy Jane!

Her coming was my hope each day,

Her parting was my pain;

The chance that did her steps delay

Was ice in every vein.

*—Jane Eyre by Charlotte Brontë*

# *Prologue*

## *(Edward Fairfax Rochester)*

***Thornfield Hall, North of England—October 1, 1847***

Nearly midday, and still I tarried at my bedchamber writing desk, gazing out over the grounds of my ancestral home. Beneath the window, a maid dug quick fingers into the rich soil of the kitchen garden, harvesting some variety of root vegetable that would no doubt make its way to the dinner board. Her birdlike voice lifted to the window as she spoke with Thornfield's cook, the earthier-toned Mrs. Glenn, who stood closer to the house and out of view.

Off to the northeast, where the great oak wood wrapped around one corner of the estate, crows jagged and dived like my own unquiet thoughts, harrying the gilded treetops. Beyond the wood, and in all other directions, stretched rolling green hills and swaths of fading-purple heath. Bruised-looking clouds hung oppressively over all.

The nearest village was Hay, but the orientation of my bedchamber gave me no view of it; Thornfield might have been the only house for miles.

The estate came to me from my father, Osborne, and to Osborne from *his* father, and so on in an unbroken line all the way back to the first Rochester, who had married into it in the sixteenth century. Since the death of my father, I'd been the sole Rochester upon the place, except for the very brief period when there'd been a mistress of Thornfield.

If I continued in my procrastination, I might very well find myself the only soul still haunting the old hall by Christmas.

Sighing, I gazed down at my littered desk. I gathered up the crumpled, half-written sheets; carried them to the fireplace; and tossed them in, watching as they bloomed and hissed into yellow flame. I'd meant to complete this task days ago but had so far found it impossible to word a request for a thing I simply did not believe existed.

Yet I must do *something*. Else the servants would certainly desert me, and I could hardly blame them. For myself, I cared little if the old place fell derelict, but they deserved better. Thornfield's tenants deserved better. And I had a duty to my father to preserve the estate—though at this rate I might very well be the last Rochester to inhabit it.

*Blast.*

I returned to the desk, sank down, and took out a clean sheet of paper. With a long breath for clarity of thought, I dipped my pen into the inkwell and wrote with determination. When I lifted nib from paper, I did not read what I'd written but quickly blotted the letter, then folded it and applied my seal, addressing it finally to Mr. Simon Brocklehurst of Lowood School in Lancashire.

# *The Letter*

***Lowood School, North of England—October 11, 1847***

"Miss Aire."

It was a fine October day, the sun bright and warm, sky crisply blue, and a snap in the air that roused both mind and body. For this reason, the door to my apothecary stood half-open, letting in the fresh breeze off the herb garden—and also allowing Mr. Brocklehurst to steal in among us.

Slowly, I let my hand fall to my side, hoping the poppet I held would be concealed by my skirts.

"Sir?" I replied faintly.

Lowood School's trustee and superintendent, a fingernail-thin shade of a man, moved fully into the room. My six students also held poppets, all in various stages of completion—some armless or eyeless, others naked or bald. The girls stared at him wide-eyed, needles held aloft.

I cringed. As Lowood's mistress of cures, I was tasked with teaching herb healing and no more. The making of poppets, even if only to be used for healing spells, would certainly fall into Mr. Brocklehurst's category of "infernal witchery." It was a familiar old hypocrisy. In the burning times, folk were eager enough to be healed by cunning women, yet sometimes just as eager to cry "witch" when they needed someone to blame for their troubles. We thankfully lived in more enlightened times, but those fears still echoed.

"Come to the house when you've finished your lessons," said Mr. Brocklehurst.

I swallowed. "Yes, sir."

He left us, and I let out a breath. The girls eyed each other nervously. I smiled to reassure them, though my heart was beating fast.

Was this to be my last act of defiance? Was I finally getting the sack?

I moved distractedly through the rest of the class, until finally the girls collected their things to go. When my younger students arrived for their instruction, I set them to quizzing each other on the healthful effects of various kitchen herbs and went to find my mentor, retired Mistress of Cures Maria Temple.

I didn't have to go far. She sat on a bench in the herb garden just outside the old potting shed that served as my home, classroom, and apothecary, her eyes softly closed and sunlight washing over her face and neck. Even in this restful pose, she smiled, and it crinkled the corners of her eyes. Her thick brown hair, streaked with silver, had been pinned back neatly, but as usual, a few unruly curls had sprung free to frame her cheeks. Maria was close to Mr. Brocklehurst's age and still a beauty.

Her smile deepened as I approached. "What a glorious day, Jane." Her fingers gently brushed the purple-and-gold blossoms of a bunch of wild aster that had sprung up next to the bench. I'd been intending to collect and dry it for salve, but it was so lovely that I kept putting it off.

"Indeed."

Up to now, she hadn't opened her eyes, but the hesitation in my voice drew her gaze. "What has happened?"

I shook my head and moved to sit beside her. "Mr. B walked in on poppet-making earlier. I've been summoned to his lair."

Our superintendent resided on the grounds of Lowood, actually in a very charming little house. The man himself was a miserly beast, though. A blight on an otherwise excellent institution. His heart, if in fact he possessed one, was pinched at the edges. But his ancestress had built and endowed the school, so we were stuck with him.

"Oh dear," said Maria, brow furrowing. "Did he seem angry?"

"Strangely, no. Not a single baleful look. Maybe we've worn each other out."

No one liked Mr. B, and I was sure there was no one *he* really liked, but it seemed I was the only one with whom he engaged in open warfare. According to him, because I'd been left at Lowood as a babe and raised too indulgently by the staff, I had grown up willful and spoiled.

"Maybe there's news of some kind."

Maria had the Sight (my own was spotty at best), so this statement caught my attention. "You don't think he intends to send me packing?"

Her expression had returned to its normal state—tranquil, with glints that suggested mirth or joy might burst forth at any moment. "If he does, you'll be the happier for it. That's all I can tell you."

I tried to glare at her but couldn't. I tried taking her words to heart, but that failed too. What good could come of me losing my position? Lowood was the only home I'd known. If indeed I was finished here, where would I go? Girls who graduated from Lowood did thankfully have options. The school produced governesses by the sackful, as well as shopgirls, teachers, cooks, housekeepers, and office workers for factories. Like the governesses and other household staff, those who studied herb healing might go on to serve a wealthy patron. But I had no prospects beyond Lowood, despite fanciful dreams of one day opening a true school for witches—one where the craft was neither stifled nor scorned.

Still, Maria's sunny outlook was kindly meant and at least somewhat reassuring. Her Sight rarely failed her. Though sometimes her predictions manifested in odd ways.

I sighed and said, "We shall see."

She reached for my hand, closing her brown fingers around my pale ones. "Go on along and get it over with, Jane. I'll sit with the girls until you're finished."

I squeezed her hand. "Thank you. I'll be back as quickly as I can."

Passing through the herb garden's rickety gate—always open because there was no real need to close it—I resolved to accept my fate. Yet by the time I reached the gravel drive that led to the main school building, I was fretting again. While Lowood came with its challenges and frustrations, I truly had nothing else. My blood relations had left me in a basket at the school's gate without even a name, forcing the staff to give me one—"Jane," as plain as *I* was, and "Aire" after the great Yorkshire river, because Pharaoh's daughter had found Moses in a basket on the Nile. The staff and students had been my only family. After nearly thirty years, I found it hard to imagine myself anywhere else.

A modest limestone edifice, oblong and two-story, the school was homely and dun, but its lines were familiar and dear to me. A cluster of rosebushes obscured the entrance, and I could hear the *snip-snip* of the groundskeeper's shears, removing spent flowers.

A head popped out of the shrubbery. "Good day, Miss Jane."

"Good day, Mr. Ross."

Our groundskeeper was a good-natured Scot with a shock of red hair now softening to orange with age. He'd been at Lowood since my early school years and addressed me as though I had never left them. In my teaching and apothecary work, I made use of almost all the plants and herbs on the premises. Mr. Ross had been a helpful ally—and occasionally a querulous adversary. He and I sometimes differed over the categorization of "weed." Unlike with Mr. B, we always ended up laughing over our differences.

"I've saved them all for you," called Mr. Ross, holding up a bloodred rose fruit between a thumb and forefinger. "I'll leave them by your door."

I bowed my head genteelly. "I thank you, sir."

He chuckled. "Thank the missus. She does swear by your tonics."

Noticing me veering toward the tree-lined walk that wound around to Mr. B's, the groundskeeper raised a bushy brow. "God keep you, child."

My contentious relationship with the superintendent was not a secret. I think Mr. Ross himself would have been shocked at the word *witch*, and at some of the things I taught my pupils, but he and I enjoyed a comfortable friendship that trusted to good intentions—and didn't ask too many questions.

"Give my best to Mrs. Ross," I said as he went back to work.

Behind the school, a vegetable and flower garden had been planted, nestled into the L shape formed by the main building intersecting a north wing. Outbuildings obstructed my view of the garden, but I could hear the bright voices of students working—most likely our cook's and housekeeper's apprentices, digging potatoes and carrots and gathering the last of the season's flowers for drying.

Just beyond the garden was the picturesque caretaker's cottage, reserved for the use of Mr. B. Like me, he existed on the edge of things. I hesitated before the door. Woodbine rioted on a trellis above the doorframe, a lovely, bushy mound of red-tipped leaves. It struck me that this exuberant specimen—whether sweetly perfumed in summer or wearing its bright autumn raiment—was quite a contrast to the severe superintendent.

Taking a deep breath, I knocked on the whitewashed door. The maid appeared and let me in.

The house was sparely furnished—everything with squared edges and straight lines—yet filled with books, small piles of stones, birds' nests, animal bones and skulls, and various other items Mr. B had collected over the years. Thoughtfully curated, tidily (and I had to admit, artistically) arranged. He considered himself an amateur naturalist. It was a short slide into witchery from there, but I'd never be the one to tell him so.

I found him ensconced in his dark-paneled office, behind his great mahogany desk, a large magnifying glass in one hand. He'd been examining a gold butterfly with black-spotted wings, which rested on a white handkerchief in front of him. He set the glass down and gestured to the chair on the other side of the desk. A large casement behind him offered a view of the vegetable garden and the bare, sunlit Three Peaks in the distance.

Mr. B's hair had once been the same dark chestnut brown as my own but was now more the color of a wood mouse. Always carefully combed at breakfast, it stood wildly on end by luncheon. That hour was nigh, but it remained subdued, and I thought he must have combed it before our interview. His eyes were the rich brown of roasted coffee beans, though his tendency to narrow them often hid the fact. They drooped a little at the outer corners.

As I took my seat, he offered me something I might have called a smile, had his squint not suggested he might be in pain.

"I must inform you that you will be leaving Lowood, Miss Aire."

My heart dropped like an anchor into icy depths.

I managed to choke out, "May I ask why, sir?" He could easily name a hundred reasons.

"You might, or you *might* wait until I've finished speaking. But we don't number patience among your virtues, do we?"

I pressed my lips together, an angry heat creeping up the back of my neck. My fingers clenched in my lap. *Wait, Jane.*

Mr. B picked up a paper from his desk. Had he documented my misdeeds?

"About a week ago," he said, "I received a letter from a Mr. Edward Rochester, a gentleman with an estate near Leeds. He is not in fact a stranger to me; I grew up in that area, and my parents knew his."

*I'm not getting the sack.* It was the only significance his words held for me in that moment. My hands relaxed. I pressed my damp palms against my skirt.

He continued. "Mr. Rochester has requested to hire a person with your particular skills."

*I'm getting the closest thing* to *the sack.*

Heart in my throat, I replied, "I already have a job, sir."

He eyed me over the edge of the paper. "The posting is temporary."

I took my first deep breath since arriving in his office. "Mr. Rochester wishes to hire a herbalist?"

Mr. B's thin lips formed a tight frown. I waited for him to continue, but he seemed to be waiting for *me* to speak. I stared at him in confusion.

Finally, he handed me the letter.

The words *a Lowood witch* jumped out at me from the first line.

> I wish to engage the services of a Lowood witch. The specifics of the services to be rendered are of a delicate and confidential nature and will only be revealed to your employee. With regard to payment, I am prepared to make a sizable donation to your institution—half upon your agreeing to these terms and half upon successful completion of the task. If for any reason other than neglect of duties your employee is unable to complete the task, you shall retain the advance payment for your employee's labors, and the second payment shall be forfeit.

I looked at Mr. Brocklehurst. No wonder he'd suddenly lost his voice. It was a very large thorn in his side that Lowood was known to produce "witches" despite his ban on the teaching of any practices that delved deeper into cunning craft than herbal healing. Possibly because it was too fine a distinction for the general public to comprehend. Possibly because I (and Maria before me) had continued, secretly, to provide a thorough education anyway. And possibly because Lowood graduates, once out from under the superintendent's stern eye, were less committed to secrecy. (If they could earn a shilling for a charm or tea reading, why shouldn't they?) I once asked Maria why Mr. B kept the instruction going at all, and she told me that his grandmother, who had endowed the school, had insisted upon it. So witch education proceeded at Lowood, while Mr. B delivered severe looks, censures, and even threats when he detected me crossing his arbitrary-seeming line. And he constantly grumbled that the rumors hurt the school's ability to attract patrons.

Now this Mr. Rochester had asked him *directly* for a Lowood witch. I fought not to laugh in his face.

"I have written to the gentleman and confirmed the request is genuine," said Mr. B. "Mr. Rochester's family is an old one, and he himself is both wealthy and respectable. So obviously I have consented."

"I'm afraid it's not obvious to *me*, sir." My amusement took a sudden dark turn. Why should I do this for him? His disapproval had plagued me my entire life. Had Maria and I not persisted in defying him, he would not be in a position to profit off this gentleman.

Mr. Brocklehurst glared at me.

A voice in my mind tried to warn me. Such voices had never met with much success. "There are no witches at Lowood," I said. "The teaching of witchcraft is prohibited."

Mr. B folded his arms on the desk and leaned toward me. With ice in both his tone and gaze, he replied, "I am well aware you think yourself cleverer than I, Miss Aire."

Belatedly, as usual, I realized that I had gone too far. I clenched my teeth and held my tongue.

"Do you imagine an endowment to be an endless source of funds?" he continued. "Like a tree producing fruit every summer?"

I shifted in my seat. "No, sir."

"And when ours runs out, what do you think will happen to Lowood?"

I knew that much of Mr. B's work at the school revolved around preserving or raising funds. Our meals had always been thin and our classrooms cold. There were never enough candles, nor slates, nor slate pencils. We were minimally staffed, with the students doing much of the work themselves. And we teachers were paraded out for formal dinners with potential patrons. I had always resented it, viewing Mr. B as a mean and grasping sort of person—even imagining that he was accumulating wealth at our expense. The idea of the money "running out" . . . it had honestly never occurred to me. Had I been prejudiced by my personal dislike of him?

"You've fallen silent," he said, "so I will tell you what will happen. Our doors will close, Miss Aire. You, having already benefited from Lowood's generosity, would no doubt find your place in the world. But what of your students? What of other orphaned girls? I know you've lived a sheltered existence here, but how do you think they generally fare with no one to take them in?"

My chest had gone tight. While I couldn't quite overlook his hypocrisy, I could hardly fault him for snatching at a chance to make the school more secure. Moreover, wasn't this an opportunity to show him the value of what I was teaching my students?

"I understand you, sir," I said finally.

He took a deep breath, and he reached for the letter. "Excellent," he said crisply, igniting another little flare of rebellion that I quickly stamped out.

"Who will take over my classes?"

"I'm sure that Miss Temple will step into the breach." Scowling across the desk, he said, "Have I overcome all your objections, Miss Aire?"

"Yes, sir." Briefly, I wondered why he hadn't asked my mentor to take this assignment. Though equally headstrong, her temperament was far more agreeable. Possibly he knew as well as I did that she would refuse. She rarely left the school grounds. Like witches of old, she had faced persecution in the small Scottish village where she grew up.

Mr. B's gaze fixed on my face like a brand, and when he spoke, I felt like he'd been reading my thoughts. "It will not do for you to speak to Mr. Rochester as you speak to me. Your behavior reflects on the school and will also directly impact the ability of your students to make their own way in the world. I expect you to comport yourself as if your actions have consequences, because I assure you they do. Do we continue to understand each other, Miss Aire?"

I backed down from the challenge in his eyes, possibly for the first time ever. "Yes, sir."

With a short nod, he set the letter aside and picked up the magnifying glass. "Then go and pack your things. See Mrs. Phillips first; the school will loan you trunks."

I sat up. "When do I go, sir?"

He returned his attention to the butterfly, replying, "Tomorrow morning."

*Tomorrow morning!*

# Leaves of Tea

I left the cottage, thoughts racing. I had never spent a single night away from Lowood since the day I'd been left here, and tomorrow night I would sleep in a strange bed. Take my meals at a strange table. I would go heaven knew how long without seeing the face of a friend. It hardly felt real.

I walked directly back to the apothecary. My younger students were outside, weeding the beds of the herbs I'd set them to studying earlier—rosemary, thyme, sage, marjoram. I waved at them and went inside, where I found Maria making tea on my little coal stove. She had lived in the apothecary before me and, after retiring, had moved into another small house on the grounds, one kept up specifically for retiring staff with no family to take them in. She currently shared the house with the retired French teacher, whose nonstop chatter would wear on the nerves of a saint. I had told my friend she was welcome in her old home at any time.

Eyeing me with worry, Maria said, "So you're being sent away after all."

"Correct, as usual. Though it's only to be temporary."

"Come and sit down."

The apothecary was a rectangular outbuilding constructed of wood. The stove in the middle divided it into two halves, with my bed and dilapidated wardrobe on one end and the apothecary on the other. Next to the stove sat two worn armchairs and a tea table. A longer table nearly filled the other half of the building. My students sat there during class, and I used it for apothecary work. Shelves of dried plant matter; tinctures, tonics, and salves; and empty bottles and jars lined the walls around the table. Large windows at either end of the building faced east and west.

Plain but cozy, albeit drafty, it suited me perfectly.

I went to one of the armchairs and sank down, letting out a sigh. Maria poured a cup of tea and handed it to me. "Leave a little in the bottom."

She was going to read for me. *Thank heaven.*

Instead of fishing out the floating leaves, I avoided them as I drank. When I'd almost drained the cup, I took hold of the handle and spun the cup three times clockwise, murmuring the spell: *"Leaves of tea, reveal to me, whatever I most need to see."* Then I covered the cup with the saucer and flipped it over, draining the remaining liquid. The leaves would stick to the cup's sides, and hopefully Maria would learn something from them. It would have been futile to read for myself while feeling so agitated; a cool mind was needed to properly identify and interpret the symbols.

Righting the cup, I handed it to Maria.

Perched on the edge of her chair, she studied the pattern. I held my breath as lines formed and smoothed across her forehead.

When I could stand it no longer, I said, "Well?"

She tipped the cup toward me, pointing at a dashed line of leaves. "Here is your journey. It looks as if all will go smoothly enough, except for some slight trouble near the end. But see here below the line—a horse head. Possibly a lover, Jane! Although with part of the body outlined too . . ."

"It probably just indicates the journey."

Maria frowned. "We shall see."

I laughed at myself over the way this made my heart thump. After thirty years living among women and girls, along with mostly married and elderly men, I had resigned myself to the fact that romantic love was a thing that happened to other people. But I had read the novels that circulated clandestinely among the teaching staff, including those of Mrs. Radcliffe, and I could hardly say the thought had never entered my mind.

Maria pointed to another clump of leaves near the edge of the cup. "Here is clearly an *R*." *Rochester.* "And below, an *E*. Then a forked line. Some decision to be made." A cloud passed over her features.

"What else?"

She pointed to a shape near the cup's bottom. "What does that look like to you?"

My breath caught. "It's a dagger." *Danger.* I had worried about losing my position. About being away from home and leaving my students. The idea that there might be something to fear in the posting itself had not even occurred to me.

"I think you had better tell me about this journey of yours," said Maria, lifting her gaze from the cup.

I explained about the letter from Edward Rochester and the gentleman's request for a witch's services. I expected her to share my annoyance over Mr. B's hypocrisy, but she fixed on something else.

"This man has given no details about what he is expecting you to do?"

I shook my head, feeling a prickling up my spine. "He indicated it was a private matter. I was curious, of course, but didn't think much of it, as he's a man Mr. B both knows and trusts. You think whatever his trouble is might relate to the dagger?"

"It might," she said, frowning. "A dagger can also indicate power. Yours or . . ."

"Someone else's." I sank against the chair back with a sigh. "What am I to do, Maria?"

Her frown deepened. "I confess this worries me, Jane. Yet my sense is that you must go."

I feared she was right. The last thing I could do was go to Mr. B and ask to be excused based on a vague warning in a tea leaf reading. Even if there hadn't been the question of the money for Lowood.

"Can you see whether I will succeed?"

She hesitated, turning the cup this way and that. "The signs are so mixed . . . Here a triangle but there a cross. Multiple trees, normally fortuitous, and also a mountain—a powerful friend."

"Or enemy."

She nodded. "A rat here but there a rose." Finally she took a deep breath. "I have never in my life seen so many conflicting signs in one cup."

This was hardly comforting, and I covered my face with my hands. "And what does *that* tell us?"

She set the cup down with a clink. "I think, my dear, it tells us that you are approaching a crossroads. Good things may happen, or bad. Both, very likely. You will have to trust your own inner wisdom. You will have to trust your instincts."

If one theme had repeated itself in my instruction at Lowood, this was it. Confident as I was in my training, and my accomplishment through hard work and dedication to my craft, I sometimes questioned my inner knowing. I could not always distinguish between the voice of fear and the voice of my own guiding spirit. Maria said I overthought things, and it stunted my Sight. I wondered at times whether it came from having no parent to guide me and build me up. Yet, as Mr. Brocklehurst had been only too happy to point out, I had been fortunate. Far more fortunate than some.

I let out another sigh.

Maria refilled my cup and poured one for herself. "I believe in you, Jane."

Having extracted a promise to write her as soon as I could, Maria left me to prepare for my journey. I finished the morning's instruction and then went to Mrs. Phillips, Lowood's housekeeper, for my trunks. I hardly knew what to take with me, and after an hour or so of anxious packing, removing, and rearranging, I gave it up to resume in the evening. Then I returned to the main building to take my leave of the staff and my other students.

I hoped that afternoon to get a glimpse of the white-bellied hare that often came to a grassy patch beside my stoop, where I left twigs of herbs or carrot tops when I could get them. She always ate what I left and never disturbed any plant in the garden. Witches sought wisdom from animals, and sometimes one chose a witch for a companion. The hare was the closest thing I'd ever had to a familiar. Before sunset I put out slices of apple, hoping to lure her, but she did not appear.

Instead, that night she visited me in a dream. I saw her drinking from a forest pool, so dark that nothing reflected in its surface. As I drew closer, she jumped into the pool. I watched the ripples spread to the water's edge, hoping she would resurface, but she never did. A dream occurring the night before a journey had special significance. Much as Maria had read in my tea leaves, I read this as a sign I was venturing into the unknown.

And it wasn't the only dream I had that night. For as long as I could remember, I'd occasionally dreamed of a fairy woman with long, loose, fiery hair and a dress made of white flowers. She came at times when the veil between worlds was thin, such as Hallowe'en or Yule. In-between times, like this night before my journey. Though I sometimes glimpsed fairy creatures through the hedge behind my shed or when I wandered into the brambly wilds beyond Lowood (long-limbed, twiggy folk, barely distinguishable from the foliage), never had I seen this lady outside of dreams.

The dream was always the same. I approached a large hawthorn tree, where she sat in a V between branches, hanging her head so that her hair covered her face. As I drew closer, she would look up at me, hair shifting aside, and smile. In all the earlier dreams, she had vanished before I could reach her. This time I got closer, and just before I woke, she held out a twig bearing a few yellow autumn leaves and a cluster of red berries. Hawthorns were protective, magical trees strongly associated with fairies. I wondered whether the spirit meant to wish me a safe journey.

Rising before dawn the next morning, I checked my trunks and made my final preparations. A kitchen maid appeared at my door with a tray from Mrs. Shaw, our cook. She had sent scones, eggs, and even a little ham—a feast by Lowood standards. Mrs. Shaw had known me since infancy, and both of us shed a few tears when I told her I was leaving on a journey of unknown duration. Nervous about the travel and new post, I could hardly give the hearty breakfast the attention it deserved.

My carriage was to leave during Lowood's required morning prayers. It would be one of only a handful of times in my life I had been allowed to miss them, the other times due to illness. Mr. Brocklehurst was a devout Anglican (would have been a clergyman, had his grandmother not appointed him to oversee the school), and his charges were expected to be as well.

I did not anticipate meeting anyone except the groom, who carried my trunks—filled with my few humble belongings along with spell books, many small jars of dried plant matter, and other tools of my trade—down to the rickety old carriage and its equally rickety driver, Mr. Whitcomb. But as I approached the gate, drawing my wool cape tight against the morning chill, I saw a slender, dark figure waiting for me there.

*Mr. Brocklehurst.* Since he *led* morning prayers, I hated to think what had brought him out to meet me.

"Good morning, sir," I said neutrally, stopping before him.

"Good morning," he replied in the same tone. "I've come to see you off."

Why on earth would he bother? It became clear when he spoke again. "Don't fail to make the most of this opportunity, Miss Aire."

Of course what he really meant was *Don't fail.* The admonishment was unnecessary. He had put the fear in me already, and I was determined to succeed for the sake of the school, my students, and all the people I loved.

"Sir." With a stiff bob of my head, I stepped up into the carriage.

He next spoke a few words to Mr. Whitcomb. Mr. Whitcomb replied, and then he clucked to the horses. The carriage jolted forward.

I stared straight ahead as we got underway, but something made me look back. I suppose it was a morbid thought, but the tea reading had rattled me, and I wanted one last look at my home in case I didn't return. I missed my chance, however, as my eyes found Mr. B instead. He had not left the gate but stood watching us drive away.

The morning warmed and brightened, and for a while I enjoyed watching the countryside pass before the carriage window—heath, mountain, copse, picturesque bridge over sparkling stream, and the occasional village. Now nearly two weeks into October, the autumn scenery was very fine. The leaves had begun to turn golden and fiery, and bright-yellow whin blossom dotted the landscape. We passed carts full of squashes, cabbages, apples, and barrels of cider. Hunting parties, too, as the London season had ended, and the "quality" had retired to their estates.

It wasn't far to Kirkby Lonsdale, and there Mr. Whitcomb helped me transfer to the coach that would carry me most of the rest of my journey. It was some sixty miles to Leeds, where I'd trade coach for carriage again.

Though I'd soon traveled farther from home than ever before, the novelty of it quickly faded. The scenery outside the window grew dull for long stretches. I tried reading, but the rocking and jolting over the rutted roads made me nauseous. Finally I put away my book and closed my eyes. Mercifully, the old gentleman and two ladies who joined me at different stages of the journey felt no compulsion to make conversation.

Upon reaching the outskirts of Leeds, I felt extreme relief on leaving the coach, despite the fact it was a great, smoking industrial town. I stepped down with stiff and sore limbs, and when the driver had removed my trunks, I went inside the inn to await the carriage that would take me on to Thornfield, Mr. Rochester's estate. Happily, a warm fire awaited me in the inn's dining room. Though the day had been clear and dry, the traveling sickness left me with chills and little appetite. But I managed to eat some of the bread and cheese the innkeeper brought me, as well as drink a cup of tea.

All too soon, the carriage driver came to the dining room looking for me. Food, drink, and rest had made me more comfortable, but not long after we got underway, I was as miserable as ever.

We arrived in Hay, the village nearest Thornfield, in the early evening. The driver stopped briefly on some errand, and I got out and stood beside the carriage, which had drawn up in front of a public house.

With my feet on solid ground, breathing the cool, clear air, I began to feel better.

A few minutes later, the driver returned, and I asked, "How much farther, sir?"

He eyed me with sympathy. "It is not two miles, miss."

I turned and looked out. Hay was situated on a hill, with higher hills behind and a wide valley below. The setting sun washed the hills and heath in golden light, while a slight haze blanketed the fields below. Crows darted and dove over a tract of woodland a short distance to the south, and just beyond the trees, I could make out the lines of a large house.

"Is that Thornfield there?" I asked, shading my eyes from the sun's last slanting rays.

The driver squinted. "Indeed it is."

The scene was romantic in the extreme. The old manor house, nestling among the low hills of the valley, partially veiled by mist. The crows calling and cowbells tinkling in the distance. This was a more pastoral beauty than the wilds around Lowood, and I found myself enchanted and eager to examine it more closely. Indeed, the little valley *tugged* at me.

Yet I was *not* eager to return to the carriage.

I turned to face my driver. "I shall walk the rest of the way, sir."

His mouth twisted up in a frown. "How now, miss? Walk, you say?"

"You may go on ahead with my trunks and deposit them at Thornfield."

He stared. "But it's going on dark, miss. I'm to carry you to Thornfield, and I—"

"My mind is set on it, sir. I will easily make it there before dark."

The driver did not know me. If he had, he would not have continued his protests. I had resolved not to arrive at my new post both weak and ill. The evening was clear, and the road had no turnings. The walk would revive me as nothing else could, and no one would talk me out of it.

At last the driver saw he was beaten. Shaking his head, he climbed up to the seat; pointed me to the road, which stretched plainly before me; and drove on ahead.

I breathed a great sigh of relief and started after the carriage.

The road gradually descended into the valley, and soon I walked among the heather and whin. With the sun now gone, everything around me lay in gray-purple shadow. Tiny birds flitted in the foliage, foraging seeds before going to their rest. From somewhere close by came the sibilant murmur of a stream. A beautiful eventide indeed. My spirits rose to be moving in the fresh air again.

Still, doubts crept in. I remembered Maria's reading, and I began to wonder whether I'd been too willful about this walk. Obviously the carriage driver had thought so, and Mr. Brocklehurst reminded me regularly that it was my greatest fault. Opposition tended to strengthen my resolve.

Yet I wasn't really worried for my safety; I'd covered nearly half the distance already, and dark had not overtaken twilight. My trunks would by now be at Thornfield, so the house had notice of my coming and no doubt would send out a rider should I fail to appear. But it wasn't quite the right way to begin.

With a churning in my stomach, I recalled Mr. B's warning. "Your behavior reflects on the school and will also directly impact the ability of your students to make their own way in the world."

Lifting the hem of my dress an inch or two, I increased my pace. Soon the clopping of horse hooves sounded behind me, and having frightened myself with doubting, I moved quickly to one side of the road and hoped the rider would pass without noticing me.

Then a scream tore a hole in the night.

# *Otherworldly*

Spinning around, I half expected to find some fiend at my heels.

"What the *devil*?"

In fact, the scream had come from a great black horse rearing on the road, and the rider—the source of the unfamiliar voice—had apparently been thrown into the heather.

"Sir!" I tried to get to him, but his terrified mount danced and snorted in my path.

"Catch him, will you?" called the man.

*Catch him?*

The animal and I sized each other up warily. I hadn't much experience with horses, though as a girl I'd sometimes taken pilfered carrots to the stable. But no horse at Lowood could compare with this large, spirited beast.

I held out a trembling hand. "Easy, it's all right . . . easy . . ."

"Phoebus," said the man. His voice was coarse, like he was in pain.

I took a step, and the frightened horse tossed his head. My heart hammered. "It's all right, Phoebus."

He flinched as I reached toward him, but I murmured soothingly and tried again. Gently I slid my fingers up the velvet muzzle and lightly grasped the bridle. Phoebus's ears flicked toward me, and he snorted.

"Easy," warned the man. "He's not sure what to make of you."

Before leaving Lowood, I had tucked a few sprigs of fresh yarrow into my pocket for protection. Yarrow was also soothing to the spirit. I took out the sprigs and held them under Phoebus's nose. While he snuffed at the herb, I traced my fingers up his rein and then grasped and slowly lifted it over his head.

"Good boy," I said quietly, leading him from the middle of the road toward his fallen rider.

Slowly extracting himself from the heather, the gentleman rose to his feet, and I got my first look at him.

A tall man, dressed all in black. Not a fiend, yet with twilight's haze thickening to mist around his boots, I could not but question whether he was *some* otherworldly creature. He'd lost his hat, and dark, wavy hair framed his face, which was almost luminous in the low light. The coloring of his eyes was so slight that they, too, seemed to glow—not like fire but like the cool light of the stars. His expression was bleak.

He gave me the impression of a ghostly king. A specter who could only return at the thin time of year around Hallowe'en. I shivered and took a step back, forgetting Phoebus, who blew a warm puff of breath into my hair.

The man stepped forward—and stumbled, letting out an oath. *Mortal after all.*

"You seem to have been injured, sir," I said, moving toward him again.

His head lifted, eyes moving over me. "What on earth are you doing on the road at such an hour?" His voice was as imperious as everything else about him.

"I'm on my way to Thornfield Hall, sir. I'm so sorry for—"

"Thornfield! Whatever for?"

I began to feel annoyed by his brusque manner, which reminded me of Mr. Brocklehurst. What business was it of *his* where I was going or why?

"I am expected there," I said coolly. "It's nearly dark, as you see, so if you're fit to ride, I, too, will be on my way."

"Expected?" He hesitated, and I tried to think how I might get away from him without being rude. As I held his horse's reins out toward him, his eyes went wide. "Surely you can't be the witch."

The witch! How could he know? Then, with a sinking feeling in my chest, I realized how. "Might you be Mr. Rochester?"

He frowned. "Indeed, I might."

*Oh, Jane.* This was worse than even Mr. B could have imagined. I had caused injury to Lowood's new patron *before we'd even been introduced.*

I took a deep breath. "And I am indeed Jane Aire from Lowood School, sir."

"Has there been some other accident?" He looked around, muttering, "I suppose at this point it should hardly surprise me. But where is your carriage?"

Heat crept into my cheeks. "No accident, sir. It being a fine evening, and feeling ill from the motion of the carriage, I chose to walk from Hay."

He stared at me, apparently at a loss for words. Finally he said, "To *walk*. And what of your luggage?"

"The carriage will have left it at Thornfield by now and presumably gone on its way." Heavens, was there any recovering from this?

Mr. Rochester was shaking his head, but before he could follow with more questions, I said, "Please let me apologize for startling your horse, sir. I fear that you were injured in the fall. Can I help you in any way?"

He looked doubtful, but he reached out to me. "Just allow me to steady myself. Let us hope you're more substantial than you appear to be, or we'll both go tumbling into the heather."

This mental picture raised another blush, and I was grateful for the gathering darkness. Adjusting my grip on the reins, I stepped forward and took his hand. The leather of his glove was fine and soft against my skin. My own gloves had remained in my carpetbag throughout the journey. Unaccustomed to carrying both, I'd forgotten them in the carriage.

I stiffened my arm as Mr. Rochester's hand tightened around mine, and he stepped carefully out of the heather and back onto the road. He uttered a short groan, and Phoebus gave a conciliatory nicker.

"It appears I've turned an ankle."

"I'm very sorry to hear it, sir."

While he tested the ankle, then retrieved his hat and riding crop, I continued my study of him, noticing a streak of nearly white hair at one temple. He was certainly older than me, but I thought by no more than ten years. As he limped back toward Phoebus and me, I had an odd thought. Was he ensnared in something? A gossamer net, like the web of a giant spider? It was something I felt rather than saw with my eyes.

*The night air has made you whimsical, Jane.*

Yet I recalled what Maria had told me before I left: "You will have to trust your instincts." It might not be whimsy. Mr. Rochester had asked specifically for a witch. Perhaps he suffered from some malady of the spirit.

Taking the reins from me, he said tersely, "Your surname is Scottish. Are you indeed a Scot, Miss Aire?"

Unwilling to disclose my unusual history to my new employer, I could only think to reply, "I believe my name comes from the river, sir."

Mr. Rochester moved to his horse's side, muttering, "A water sprite, then. It explains much."

I sighed quietly and held my tongue. Before I could think of a way to smooth his ruffled feathers, he said, "Come, Miss Aire of Lowood School, I'll not have you out wandering the countryside alone, witch or no. I am willing to shoulder some of the blame, having concealed from Mr. Brocklehurst the recent mysterious and unsettling events in the neighborhood. Though it would never have occurred to me that a woman of sense might set out walking over remote countryside in the dark."

I overlooked the insult, and the exaggerations, for what he'd said before that—"mysterious and unsettling events."

"We shall ride back together," he continued, motioning me closer.

I froze on the spot. Both of us on the one horse?

"It can't be helped," he said, reading my thoughts. "The ankle's not bad, but it won't be improved by walking the rest of the way. Nor will my temper."

Finding my voice, I said, "Please don't trouble yourself, sir. I am happy to walk alongside your horse."

"Yet I am *not* happy, Miss Aire. I am tired, sore, and hungry, and I wish to reach Thornfield before midnight." He gestured again for me to come forward, and this time I complied.

"Now, Phoebus has spirit, as you may have observed. Are you a competent horsewoman?"

Rarely had I felt so lacking as I had in the last quarter hour. "No, sir."

He laughed dryly. "An honest one, at least. In that case, I shall go before. Once I'm in the saddle, I want you to lift your foot into the stirrup and then give me your arm."

He mounted, and I did as he'd instructed. Taking my arm, he hauled me up behind him like I weighed no more than a sack of grain.

"I suggest you hold on to my coat to help keep your balance."

As I gripped his coat on either side of his waist, he clucked to Phoebus, and we got underway. My thoughts spun dizzily. I had never in my life sat in such proximity to a man. My forward leg and hip pressed snugly against his back, and mere inches separated our upper bodies. The situation felt like something out of a novel. Except that I was . . . well, *me*, and not some gentlewoman in distress. And the spiny Mr. Rochester had more the flavor of villain than romantic hero. Yet the sudden intimacy caused heat to course through me and rendered me silent.

Mr. Rochester scooted slightly forward in the saddle and then broke the silence. "I had expected someone more advanced in years, Miss Aire. But perhaps you are a prodigy."

"I wouldn't say that, sir," I replied lightly, ignoring the patronizing note in his tone, "but many people, when thinking of a witch, may picture a crone."

In the pause before his answer, I heard the distant screech of a barn owl. Then a nightingale warbled from a nearby hedge. The first could be a warning; the second suggested a mystery or . . . love. *Or just a bird singing in the hedge.* Reading signs was rather an imprecise art.

"The truth is I have hardly thought of witches at all up to this point," he said finally. "But you may be right." He glanced over his shoulder. "I will tell you plainly that it was not my idea to bring you here."

Now *this* was a clear omen—of a rough road ahead. Of course Mr. B wasn't the only person in England who disapproved of witches. The practice had survived for centuries behind closed shutters and bolted doors, until our less fearful—and more curious—age had made it possible for it to come into the light. While rural cunning folk had always peddled herbal cures and simple charms, now even society ladies consulted spirit mediums and card readers. But there would always be those who feared witches, believing them ungodly. Or those who were bothered by the fact that, unlike in the Church, the tools of witchcraft were mostly being taught and wielded by women.

"I see," I replied in a voice that failed to hide my disappointment.

"I forbid you to take offense, Miss Aire. The truth is that I am indifferent to witches. Actually, I'm not sure that I believe in them at all, and I suppose you *will* take offense at that. But my servants have all threatened to desert me. I have no faith that it is within your power, or anyone's, to lift the shadow that hangs over Thornfield. So you see it is only a last resort that you are here."

He fell silent after that, and I left him to it. What could we have to talk about now that I knew he had no respect for my profession, didn't really want me here, and assumed that I would fail?

In truth, his feelings about me didn't much matter. I had been hired to do a job, and for Lowood I must give my best effort. Moreover, the sooner I completed my task, the sooner I could go home.

Still, my pride had been wounded. "You consider yourself a skeptic, sir?"

He shrugged. "It neither serves nor disserves me to believe in witches and their craft. I don't waste much thought on things I can't see or ever hope to understand."

A thing happened then that I could no more control than the beating of my heart. It was my natural response to what I took for arrogant disdain, which again reminded me very much of Mr. Brocklehurst.

In the barest whisper—so bare I believed he wouldn't hear—I said, "Then I suppose you have never been in love."

Phoebus halted. I could feel Mr. Rochester's body go rigid as a standing stone. The horse's ears flicked back nervously, and my heart faltered.

Mr. Rochester turned to look at me. It was now full dark, but by the light of the stars and the sickle moon, I saw the cold fire in his eyes.

"Never again speak to me of love, Miss Aire, do you understand? It is not your place."

My throat was tight and hot. *What have I done?*

"Miss Aire," he said icily, "I require an answer."

My voice trembled as I said, "I understand, sir."

# *Inquiry and Investigation*

The next few minutes were torture. We didn't speak, and the air around us—even the contact between our bodies—buzzed with anger and regret.

*Mr. Brocklehurst is right about me.* I had always justified my willfulness as a natural result of his controlling nature. And maybe that was fair, but in this particular moment it came as cold comfort.

We soon reached the old iron gates to the estate. They stood open and apparently had for some time, with one gate mostly overtaken by traveler's joy. The bunches of long, feathery seeds glowed white and trembled in the evening breeze.

Though preoccupied with the wording of my apology—and with the fear there could be no recovery from this—I noticed a change as soon as we passed through the gates. I could *feel* the shadow Mr. Rochester had mentioned, and a shiver ran through me. A kind of shroud that draped lightly over everything, reminding me of winter days when the clouds hung low enough to walk through.

"What is it, Miss Aire?" asked Mr. Rochester. His tone had moderated slightly.

"Sir?"

"We are sitting far too close for you to hide your reactions. Tell me what made you shiver just now. Was it only the chill in the air?"

This reminder of the intimacy of our position set my stomach fluttering. I sat up straighter.

"The shadow you mentioned," I said, loading my tone with all the respect and mildness I could. "For a moment, I felt it. Like a shroud of magic."

"Mm. Do you know what would cause such a thing?"

Sensing I was being given another chance, I paused, choosing my words carefully. "There are many possibilities, sir. It would require some inquiry and investigation."

I held my breath, waiting for his answer. All he said was, "Very well."

Encouraged, I ventured, "You've perceived it yourself?"

"I feel . . ." He sniffed. *"Something."*

A small creature flitted over our heads. Likely a bat—I could hear its wings caressing the still night air. Phoebus tensed, and Mr. Rochester murmured reassurance.

"Miss Aire, I must beg your pardon for my temper earlier. I've been under a strain, but it's no excuse. I should not have spoken so sharply."

My chest at last unlocked and allowed in a full breath. "There's no need, sir. *I* should not have spoken so *rudely.*"

He made a soft sound, almost a laugh. "Well, my hunch is you never meant for me to hear the remark—which I confess was quick-witted and not entirely undeserved—but pray let's both forget it. Though it was not my idea to bring you here, I intend for you to do the job you were hired to do. You must feel free to speak your mind. And I must ask you to tolerate my prickly nature."

"Yes, sir," I replied wholeheartedly. I was used to dealing with prickly patrons, and I could tolerate anything except being sent back to Lowood in disgrace. Freedom to speak my mind was no small boon either—though I suspected there were limits to what Mr. Rochester would tolerate, and I must do better.

I could see the lamps on the drive now, and I looked forward to being on the ground again—not to mention a more comfortable distance from my employer. But I had one last question before we found ourselves surrounded by servants.

"Sir, might I ask who suggested a witch be consulted?"

He reined in Phoebus, who, perhaps anticipating his bucket of oats, had picked up a slow trot that knocked his uneasy riders against each other.

"That was Mrs. Fairfax, my housekeeper." He again glanced over his shoulder, shifting in the saddle and causing my hand to graze his waist. "I half suspect her of witchery herself."

"Oh? On what grounds?"

"Small bundles of weeds. *Everywhere.* I've complained on more than one occasion, but it makes no difference."

For once I was grateful to be mounted on the horse, as he couldn't see me smiling at the exasperation in his tone. Him having a witch in his household didn't surprise me. There were certainly many more of them than the ones I knew personally. Few witches were fortunate enough to receive formal education; it was more typically passed down in families.

"They sound like protective charms," I said.

"I don't think they're working."

He muttered this reply grimly, but the existence of Mrs. Fairfax gave me hope. I might find an ally in her. She would be knowledgeable about the house, and she couldn't help but be easier to talk to than our employer. Recalling that his full name included Fairfax, I wondered whether she might be related to him.

What I could see of the old hall's facade was impressive, though the long shadows cast by servants moving around the lamps lent it an otherworldly quality. *Like its master.* At this time of year, could I be sure of what was real? Mightn't the ghostly king have stolen me away on his fierce black steed to his castle in Fairy? The fanciful thoughts brought another smile to my lips, though a subtle feeling of unease remained.

Thornfield had two stories, battlements, a north and south wing, and a towerlike entrance whose stonework was probably centuries old. I would have to wait for morning to see the gardens, which were of particular interest to me. I'd brought my own stock of dried plants, but I had no idea how long I might be here, and fresh herbs were preferable when you could get them. The hint of rosemary on the breeze was another cause for hope.

At the entrance to the hall, Mr. Rochester gave me a hand down before dismounting. Domestics came filing out, and a groom who'd been waiting on the drive took Phoebus away. There were murmurs of surprise and welcome, the staff clearly confused by our arriving together. I soon gathered from their talk that Mr. Rochester had been away, and his arrival itself was a surprise.

An older woman wearing a white cap and apron came out onto the drive to meet us.

"Mr. Rochester," she said, smiling, "I see you've recovered Miss Aire. I wish you'd sent word you were coming, sir. Cook is beside herself about supper."

"She needn't be, Mrs. Fairfax," he replied, taking no notice of the gentle scolding. "Something simple will do; I'll dine in my rooms. Give the best of what we have to Miss Aire. She will be famished after her march across the heath."

I winced. Before I could protest that no pains should be taken on my account, the housekeeper addressed me. "I'm afraid I've been worrying about you, dear. At this time of year there is sometimes ice on the road."

"I apologize for causing anxiety, Mrs. Fairfax. I'm very pleased to meet you."

"Rest and restore yourself, Miss Aire," said Mr. Rochester. "Then please join me in the blue drawing room. Let us say an hour from now."

"Yes, sir," I replied, taking out my pocket watch. "At half past eight."

"I'll see you then."

I had hoped to escape further conversation with him this evening. Fatigued from the journey and used to the early hours at Lowood, I knew the later it got, the more likely I'd blunder again. It might even be worse next time, if that were possible.

But after such a disastrous first meeting, I didn't dare deny him.

# *Interlude*

## (Rochester)

Inside the hall, I dropped my hat and gloves on a table and wove among bustling servants toward the stairway, attempting to flee the howling ghosts that had been flitting through my head for the last half hour. What on earth had summoned them? The return to Thornfield? Trips to London—with its pointless bustle, desperate poor, and surface gaiety—had always made me quite happy to return to the lonely old hall. I doubted the fall from Phoebus had so unsettled my mind, for I'd taken far worse. Nor the injury itself, for that was slight (though I now felt all my thirty-eight years as I climbed the stairs to my rooms on the sore ankle).

*It's the woman.*

When I first glimpsed her on the road, I'd honestly thought her a spirit of some kind, a sentiment Phoebus had obviously shared. With everything else that had happened recently, it hardly seemed out of the question. What flesh-and-blood woman would promenade upon a deserted country road at such an hour?

It had only very belatedly occurred to me she might be the witch. She was quite right that I'd imagined someone older. Someone less kempt, and admittedly, more ill-favored. I was rather ashamed of myself for it now.

Yes, she was youngish, with large, round eyes. Her hair a deep glossy brown, I thought, though it had been nearly dark, and only a few locks had escaped her bonnet. Her face was more rounded than long, its bones delicate and even elfin, bolstering my earliest theory about her. She had proven quickly enough that her faculties were well in order. I wasn't entirely sure she hadn't gotten the better of me in our first exchange.

But all of this was beside the point. What about her had dredged up this mood?

Crossing the ancestral gallery above the hall without acknowledging a single painted gaze, I pushed open the door to my bedchamber. I tossed my coat onto the bed, sloshed a little whiskey from a bottle on the mantel into a glass, and sank into the chair before the fire.

*Open your eyes, man; it's quite obvious.*

Miss Aire, simply by virtue of being a lively young woman, reminded me too much of all I had lost. Of the things I could never have, because Thornfield had become a house of death.

# *Thornfield Hall*

When Mr. Rochester had gone into the house, I said, "Allow me again to apologize for my tardiness, Mrs. Fairfax."

"There's no need, dear," she said kindly. "An old woman will worry, you know. Did you meet Mr. Rochester on the road? I hope there's been no accident." Her keen eyes moved over me, searching for damage.

"There was, in fact," I confessed. "I'm afraid I startled Mr. Rochester's horse, and he was thrown."

"Thrown!" Her gaze found its way back to the door, though Mr. Rochester had disappeared inside. "Has he been injured?"

"He turned an ankle but claims it's not serious."

She nodded knowingly. "I'll send for the surgeon in the morning. I'm glad nothing worse befell either of you. The spirits make mischief this time of year." She looked suddenly flustered and added, "But I'm sure you know all about that."

Inhabitants of the spirit world—elementals, fairies, departed souls—were indeed more likely to be encountered in the days approaching Hallowe'en. But Maria had taught me how to counter their mischief. A talisman or a few sprigs of yarrow usually sufficed. If a more serious threat appeared, witches who had the knack for it could conjure a spirit-light for even stronger protection.

"They do indeed," I replied agreeably, hoping to reassure her I didn't expect to be viewed as more expert due to my training. "On the road, Mr. Rochester accused me of being one."

*A water sprite, then. It explains much.*

The housekeeper laughed. "No doubt he did, though he professes to be a great skeptic." She held out a hand to me, and I grasped it. "Come along to the house and have your supper."

We passed through a gothic arch into a shallow porch and then through the heavy entry door, ornamented with a lion's head knocker, into another world. My breath caught at the splendor of the place.

The entrance hall, spacious and open due to the high ceiling, had been furnished to reflect its medieval character while still providing comfort. A richly hued tapestry with a hunting motif served as the room's backdrop, and rugs warmed what looked to be the original stone floor. Dark wainscot covered the walls to my left and right, which also had doors that led to the north and south wings; the southern door stood open, and I could see into the corridor beyond. An enormous fireplace was recessed into the wall on my left, and a more modern staircase on the right side of the hall led to the upper floor. At the top, a gallery ran along the back wall, providing access to the upstairs rooms. Opposite the gallery, above the entrance, a series of narrow, vertical openings now fitted with windows would let in some natural light, especially in the afternoon.

Thornfield's servants were active for this time of day, probably due to the master's sudden arrival. One fed peat after peat into the fireplace, which already gave out a welcoming warmth. Iron candlestands throughout the room and a large iron chandelier lit the hall brightly, revealing it to be immaculate, despite the fact some of the furnishings must have been quite old. Ornately carved chairs rested before the fire, benches lined the back wall, and there was a display of ancient weaponry on the wall near the hearth. Obviously Mr. Rochester cared very much about the place, and Mrs. Fairfax was uncommonly good at her job.

Inside the hall, we turned right, toward the south wing. As we passed the staircase, polished to gleaming and with a beautifully carved newel, a candlelit portrait above an antique console table caught my eye. By the style of the subject's gown, the portrait was quite old—the time of Queen Elizabeth or even earlier. She had an arresting countenance, perhaps the effect of unsmiling black eyes in a luminous complexion framed by a wide white ruff. The artist had managed to render her ageless. I couldn't have said whether she was a girl of sixteen or a matron of forty. The only portrait in the hall, the lady seemed to be holding court. I imagined lively music and colorfully dressed ghosts twirling about the room.

"She is a Montagu," said the housekeeper, who'd turned back to see why I'd paused. "Her ancestors built this tower, and her father added the north and south wings. She married one of Mr. Rochester's ancestors."

"It's a striking image, isn't it?"

"If by 'striking,' you mean that it gives one a shiver, I would have to agree with you."

I laughed. "I suppose it does."

"There are all manner of stories about the lady. Some say she was accused of witchcraft—of murdering her husband, even—and that she paid with her life. Some even say she was the reason no master of Thornfield was ever made a peer."

I stared at the housekeeper. It was a harrowing reminder of how dangerous it once was to be accused of witchcraft. And in fact, many of those accused had nothing to do with the craft but had somehow become targets. Their husbands died young, or the neighbor's cows stopped producing milk, or a fever took hold in the community.

"My goodness!" I said. "It's quite a lot to lay at one lady's door."

Mrs. Fairfax nodded. "So it is, and I suspect the more shocking aspects of the tales may very well have been inspired by this likeness rather than any real family history. I don't think Mr. Rochester much cares for the portrait, though, and in point of fact, she is no relation of his."

"Oh?"

"According to the Rochester family Bible, the lady bore no children, and the estate was inherited by her stepdaughter." She looked again at the likeness. "But this was *her* hall, and the portrait has always hung there."

Curious that Mr. Rochester hadn't mentioned this lady earlier, when he was confessing an indifference toward my chosen profession. I wondered whether the family lore might have contributed to his skepticism.

Mrs. Fairfax turned from the painting. "Come, you must be hungry."

She steered me into the south wing, and we left the Old World behind for modern comforts like wood flooring, oil sconces, and papered walls. Along the corridor, several bow windows, each with its own window seat, faced out onto the grounds in front of the house.

A few doors down from the hall, the housekeeper let me into a small sitting room with a welcoming fire, candles on the table, and comfortable—if less opulent—furnishings.

The table had already been set for one, and she gestured for me to sit. The scent of herbs filled the room. A vase of dried lavender rested at the center of the table, and bunches of thyme, rosemary, and sage had been hung to dry on hooks in the room's corners. As she closed the door behind us, I noticed a sprig of holly hanging over the door. *Protection.* Mr. Rochester had been right about her.

"This is a cozy room," I said, laying my cape and bonnet on a chair before taking my seat.

Mrs. Fairfax moved to a wingback chair next to the fire. "This is my own sitting room, and you are welcome here at any time, Miss Aire."

"You're very kind."

She took up some knitting from a table beside the chair. "Eat your supper, and if you like, we'll talk a little and get better acquainted."

"I *would* like that, thank you."

A thick wedge of kidney pie sat in a shallow bowl, and suddenly I was famished. The housekeeper let me eat in silence for a few minutes before asking, "Your journey was uneventful, I hope?"

"Indeed," I replied and sipped from a glass of beer. "Until I unhorsed Mr. Rochester, that is."

She laughed. It had a warm and gentle rhythm to it. "I'm sure you gave him quite a fright."

I caught a sudden flash of dismay in her eyes, and her smile faded.

"Mrs. Fairfax," I began carefully, "would it be appropriate for me to ask why Mr. Rochester has brought me here?"

Her eyebrows lifted. "He hasn't told you?"

"Not very specifically. He spoke only of a shadow over Thornfield."

She sighed. "I see."

I gave my empty dish a nervous push and forged on. "Does it have to do with *him* somehow? I can feel the shadow over the estate, and I got the sense that Mr. Rochester might be caught in some kind of . . ." I looked at her. "Spiritual trouble."

The housekeeper nodded. "You are perceptive, my dear. While I don't feel it's my place to discuss Mr. Rochester himself, I'm happy to provide details on why you were called here, as I was the one who suggested it."

"I would be so grateful."

She took a deep breath, and she fidgeted with her knitting, which now rested in her lap. "I'm no expert, Miss Aire, but I do know a little of your craft, and to me, this shadow over us feels like a curse."

I rose partway from my chair, adjusting it to an angle more comfortable for conversation. "Could you tell me what you've seen that makes you think so?"

She gave me a look that I might have called grandmotherly, had I ever possessed that relation. "Are you sure it won't disturb your rest, dear? I would be happy to tell you tomorrow, in the light of day. And you must be fatigued from your journey."

I studied her, wondering how bad it was. But for a man who didn't believe in witches to hire one, it must be bad enough.

"I assure you I'm eager for the information, but I don't want to keep you from *your* rest."

Finally setting the knitting aside, she said, "Perhaps we'll begin with a few examples, and we can talk more tomorrow." She lifted a quilt from the arm of the chair and spread it over her lap. "Some of the occurrences have the characteristics of fairy pranks. We've had soured milk and blighted apples. Broken crockery. Laundry gone missing from the line." She looked over the top of her spectacles at me. "But there was also an unusual outbreak of summer fever among the servants. One of the maids nearly died. Another tumbled down a flight of stairs and broke her arm. She swore she felt something around her legs, but it could not be accounted for. And the groom's boy . . ." She shivered. "A few weeks ago, on his way home from the post and the grocer in Hay, he claimed he was chased by a shadow."

I frowned. "What did he mean?"

"We couldn't get much sense out of him about it, unfortunately. He was too badly frightened."

"Could it have been an animal? A tenant's or neighbor's dog?"

Once folk had begun to speculate about unnatural causes of their misfortunes, they sometimes began to *imagine* misfortunes. Even today, it could lead to false accusations. I doubted Mrs. Fairfax was about to accuse anyone of authoring Thornfield's troubles, but that didn't mean others on the estate wouldn't. English law no longer allowed a person to be charged with witchcraft (though if a person claimed to be a witch and defrauded someone, they could be prosecuted like any huckster).

But as witches grew more comfortable practicing in the open, who was to say we wouldn't find ourselves in dark times again?

"Indeed, a dog is the most likely explanation," Mrs. Fairfax admitted. "But it was one more thing, and no one feels quite safe anymore. Mr. Rochester is the only one not bothered. He seems to think us all feeble of mind."

Of course I didn't know Mr. Rochester, but I thought this unlikely. The shadow over his estate clearly troubled him. And I liked that he hadn't jumped to supernatural explanations, despite the fact there might very well be one.

"You've taken some measures yourself, I imagine?" I said, hoping to draw her out about her expertise.

"I've done what I can, and it isn't much. I learned charms from my mother. I know some herb healing too. But I'm afraid a case like this is beyond a simple country witch."

I wondered whether I was much more than that myself. Clearing my throat quietly, I said, "Mr. Rochester seems not to have much faith in our craft, and I wondered whether you could tell me how he's tolerated the measures you've taken?"

She chuckled. "He tolerates them, and that's about the extent of it. He complains about the bunches of herbs and sprinklings of salt I leave about, but he never disturbs them."

Well, it was something anyway. I got the sense she was fond of her employer, and I took the opportunity to ask, "Am I right in guessing that you're a relation of Mr. Rochester's?"

"My husband claimed a distant kinship to his mother, and his father was kind enough to offer me the position of housekeeper when the previous one retired. With my husband recently gone, rest his soul, and my children grown and married, I didn't quite know what to do with myself. It was a blessing."

"I'm happy his kindness has given me the opportunity to make your acquaintance."

She smiled. "As am I."

I checked my watch—a quarter past eight. "Could I ask you one more question before I join Mr. Rochester and leave you to your rest?"

"Of course."

"Has there been any recent trouble at Thornfield? I mean before all of this."

The change in her face was striking. Her cheeks hollowed, and her eyes widened. *There is something.*

"Any feuds with neighbors," I continued, "or servants let go? Deaths on the property?"

She stared at me in obvious dismay. "Did you not know, Miss Aire?"

I stared back blankly, shaking my head.

"Mrs. Rochester—his wife—she died."

# *Shadows and Ghosts*

Died! "Indeed, *no*, ma'am. I didn't know there *was* a Mrs. Rochester."

"I'm so sorry, dear. Mr. Rochester is not communicative, but I'd have thought you'd have heard it from *someone*."

Mr. Rochester, a widower. I don't know why it surprised me he should have a wife; he wasn't a young man. Yet he certainly didn't seem old enough to have a *deceased* wife.

Which could mean there'd been a tragedy. I recalled my careless comment on the ride to Thornfield and cringed. *Then I suppose you have never been in love.*

"It's been some months more than a year now," she continued, her face still very pale. "You don't think the curse, the shadow—whatever it is—has anything to do with that?"

I didn't know what to think, but a year wasn't all that long. "May I ask how she died?"

"It was a wasting illness that ran its course quickly. They had been married just two months."

Heavens! No wonder the man was subject to melancholy and fits of temper.

What I wanted to ask next was difficult but less so than if I had to ask our employer. "Was there a strong attachment between them, Mrs. Fairfax?"

She did look somewhat shocked, and I hastened to add, "I don't mean to pry; it's just that it could be important."

"Well, she was a beauty, to be sure. Sadly quite young. I do believe the master was fond of her, though he didn't know her well. She was a cousin on the Rochester side, you see."

"The union was arranged, then?" I couldn't have said curiosity played no part in my questions, but if there was deep love on either side, it could be relevant to the shadow over Thornfield. Such a shadow might be the result of a restless spirit.

"Yes, it was." She turned her gaze to the fire. "As I understand it, Miss Mason—Mrs. Rochester—had a great fortune and had already refused other offers. The marriage to Mr. Rochester was advantageous to both families."

I waited for her to say more, but I waited in vain. I respected her for preferring not to gossip about her employer.

Arranged marriages were often about money. Family estates were expensive to keep up. Mr. Rochester might have wanted to make improvements. He might have been in debt. Or he might have been wealthier than her other suitors. It could have been a case of consolidating family wealth.

"She was a lovely, sweet child." The housekeeper's eyes came to rest on me again. "*Everyone* loved her, and I'm sure Mr. Rochester did, too, in his own way."

*Fond of her. In his own way.* Clearly Mrs. Fairfax didn't believe her employer had been in love with his wife. The next question, which I judged best to save for another time: Had Mrs. Rochester loved her husband?

The housekeeper looked grave and unsettled, so I said, "Thank you so much for answering my questions, Mrs. Fairfax. The more information I have, the sooner we will be able to sort this out. Now I will leave you in peace."

"Of course. I will help you however I may, Miss Aire." She started to rise. "Let me show you the way to the drawing room."

I raised my hand. "Please don't trouble yourself. If you direct me, I'm sure I can find it."

"Well, it's easy enough. I'll be awake for a while yet, so come back here when you've finished. I'd like to show you to the cottage you'll be staying in."

She told me where to go, and I made my way back to the entrance hall with a few minutes to spare before the interview. I paused before the spacious hearth, rubbing a thumb against my hagstone talisman, a smooth stone with a hole through it that I always wore on a cord around my neck. I tried to imagine the master of Thornfield enjoying a glass of port here along with his guests, perhaps after a foxhunt or other sport, all high spirits and flushed from the autumn air and exercise. It was a fine old hall that I was sure had seen many festive seasons. Yet with no servants moving about, a heaviness had settled over it. I sensed it had been some time since Mr. Rochester had entertained—either guests *or* high spirits—if indeed he ever had.

*Nothing here but shadows and ghosts.*

Shivering, I finally went on to the door that led to the north wing and knocked lightly.

"Come," called a voice within.

I saw immediately why this was called "the blue drawing room." Dark-blue and gold damask covered the chairs and sofas, and the rug continued the same color scheme on a background of ivory. Above the wainscot hung floral-patterned paper. Candlelight picked up its gold accents and made them glitter. I had never seen so many candles burning all in one place. They rested on every horizontal surface and reflected from the room's ornate mirrors, suggesting at least an attempt on Mr. Rochester's part to chase out the darkness. As in the south wing's corridor, bow windows looked out onto the front of the property, though there was nothing to see at this hour.

"Miss Aire," he said in greeting. He stood at the fireplace mantel holding a glass of port—much as I had tried to imagine him in the other room, though quite alone here, not even a footman in attendance. The hearth was on the drawing room's south wall, sharing a chimney with the grander one in the entrance hall.

"Please take a seat." He motioned to one of a pair of chairs facing each other in front of the fire, eyes following as I moved to sit down. Mrs. Fairfax and I had been so cozy and comfortable together that I hadn't felt nervous about this interview—until now.

A door opposite the one I'd used opened, and a footman came in with a tray. He set it on a mahogany pedestal table next to my chair. On the tray were a coffeepot, a bottle of sherry, and a plate of biscuits. He poured two cups of coffee and one of sherry before bowing and leaving us alone again.

Mr. Rochester came closer, picked up one of the cups, and moved to sit in the chair across from me. I reached for the cream pitcher, glad to have an occupation while my employer examined me for the first time in a well-lit room. I wished I'd taken a moment to smooth my hair and inspect my dress for travel stains. My hand trembled slightly as I poured the cream; maybe I should have taken the sherry first.

*He's not going to eat you, Jane.*

"Now that we are safely indoors," said Mr. Rochester, "fed, warmed, and rested, allow me to properly welcome you to Thornfield."

"Thank you, sir. It is a very beautiful house."

He bowed his head, acknowledging the compliment, and something unexpected struck me: Mr. Rochester was a handsome man. His hair and brows were almost black, and the streak at his temple was the same shade as his pearl-gray eyes (which had seemed to shine like silver earlier, in the twilight). The effect was bewitching. Though he wore his hair smoothed back from his high forehead, the locks behind his ears curled at the ends, belying the stiffness of his countenance. The light could not completely do away with his otherworldliness, but I found this quality enhanced rather than detracted from his appeal. Perhaps not everyone would agree with me.

I became aware that Mr. Rochester was watching me examine him, and my face grew hot. Quickly I raised and sipped from my cup.

"I had intended for you to stay with us here at the house," he said, "but Mrs. Fairfax seems set on installing you in the cottage. It's private, of course, and might allow you more autonomy, but it's rather rustic."

It sounded like *heaven*. That I might be given private lodgings had never occurred to me. Now that I'd met Mr. Rochester, I believed the fewer opportunities I was given to annoy him, the better.

"I live alone in my apothecary at Lowood, sir," I said. "I'm sure I will be quite comfortable. Is it close by?"

He nodded. "In the herb garden, just north of the house. You may experience a change of heart when you see it. You must say so at once, and we'll have you moved to a room in the house."

While I would not have called his tone warm, I believed his consideration was genuine. "Thank you, sir."

Again I sipped my coffee. It *looked* like the same brew I drank each morning at breakfast, but the resemblance stopped there. It was flavorful, rich, and bracing.

When Mr. Rochester showed no sign that he would speak again, I said, "May I inquire about your injury?"

He shook his head brusquely. "Only a slight sprain. It will mend soon enough."

He finished his coffee and took up his port glass again. The silence grew heavy, and I wondered whether he was as uncomfortable as I was. Was it too soon to ask him about the events at Thornfield?

I opened my mouth, and we spoke in the same breath.

"Mrs. Fairfax tells me—"

"How is it that you—"

I laughed nervously.

"Go ahead, Miss Aire."

Yet I thought he looked cross, so I said, "Please, sir, my question can wait. What would you ask me?"

He adjusted in his seat. Then he got up and went back to the mantel. I began to hope we would see little of each other while I was here, if it was always going to be so awkward. Yet I would need his cooperation to do the job I had been hired for, especially in light of what Mrs. Fairfax had told me about his wife.

"I'm curious how you came to be—how you came into the study of witchcraft at Lowood."

I took a deep breath and set my cup on the tray. He had cut right to the heart of things, but I suppose it didn't surprise me. Inability to make small talk appeared to be a trait we shared. My answer would require some tact—also not a particular strength of mine.

"Lowood does not in fact offer a curriculum in 'witchcraft.' Officially, I teach—and was taught—the use of plants to treat both physical and mental afflictions."

His confusion was plain. "Yet everyone in Yorkshire knows of the 'Lowood witches,' and I have hired you with the belief you have been trained as such."

"Yes, sir. I'm afraid it's complicated."

"I think you had better enlighten me, Miss Aire, so I may know whether I've made a poor investment."

How I wished I had picked up the glass of sherry.

"While my colleagues, students, and I do not always use the term *witch*—historically it had a dangerous and ugly connotation—you may rest assured that's what I am. Despite the lack of official curriculum, my mentor at Lowood is a well-versed practitioner from a long line of witches."

He frowned. "This is all rather convoluted, Miss Aire, but I begin to suspect that what you are telling me is that Lowood—that Mr. Brocklehurst—does not sanction the training of witches, but that witches are being trained, and he is only too happy to hire them out if the price is right?"

He had hit the nail precisely on the head, despite my attempt to sugarcoat.

I forced myself to keep my eyes raised to his. "To continue operation, the school relies on its patrons, sir." It was not lost on me that I had picked up Mr. B's justification.

"Of course it does. I perceive you quite well. How fortunate is Mr. Brocklehurst to be able to have his cake and eat it too."

I did now reach for the glass of sherry. *Honest to a fault.* So much for tact.

"Miss Aire."

Cold gnawed my belly as I glanced up at him.

"I have very little interest in Lowood School," he said, "even less in its custodian. I am only interested in restoring Thornfield to order. I am only interested in whether you are up to the job."

I swallowed a sip of sherry. "I must confess that at this point I am still trying to *understand* the job, though Mrs. Fairfax has told me some. It would help me greatly to hear it from you, in your own words."

He drank the last of his port and set the glass on the mantel, then stood gazing into the fire. "I hope you will humor me a few minutes longer. I have endeavored to prevent the troubles on my estate from becoming the business of everyone in the county. I would feel better knowing something about you before I confide in you."

It was a reasonable request. "Of course, sir."

He returned to his chair, folding long-fingered hands in his lap. "Will you tell me about your family? What induced your parents to send you to Lowood for education?"

I raised my glass again to cover my surprise. It was clear by his conversational tone that he'd blundered into this unfortunate question, but how I wished it need not have been *me* who pointed out his error.

"Lowood is a school for orphaned girls, sir."

Color stole along his cheekbones, and his gaze lowered to the rug between us. "I beg your pardon, Miss Aire. I believe I knew that, but it had slipped my mind."

"It's quite all right, sir. You do not offend me."

He looked up. There was what I might almost call a *gentleness* in his expression. "That is kind, even if not entirely honest."

I sat up straighter. I would not have him pity me or treat me like I was fragile. "Lowood's students are permitted to choose a specialization when they reach their sixteenth year—teaching, housekeeping, or bookkeeping, for example. Our education is meant to prepare us to support ourselves in the world, since we cannot all expect to marry. There are few respectable occupations open to young women without family, and Lowood's founder hoped to address that deficiency."

A thin smile rested on his lips. "Not everyone is suited to be a governess."

"Precisely, sir."

"If I may ask, what made you choose . . . apothecary craft?"

I smiled at his tact. "I enjoyed learning about the healing properties of plants. My mentor, the woman I mentioned earlier, believed I had an aptitude. And I was quite keen to learn more about the deeper practices of which our superintendent disapproved. I have an inquiring and independent nature—not necessarily qualities one associates with governesses."

His smile broadened, and I felt strangely gratified. "It's good to be aware of one's limitations."

We then heard a light tapping on the door.

For the span of three heartbeats, Mr. Rochester held my gaze. When he looked up and bade the person outside come in, I discovered I was holding my breath.

The door swung open to reveal Mrs. Fairfax, carrying with her my cape and bonnet. "I'm sorry to disturb you, sir. I was about to retire and thought if you were finished here, I would show Miss Aire to the cottage."

"By all means," he said, rising. Then to me, "It's late, and you must be tired from your journey. We'll talk more tomorrow."

I stood up, setting the sherry glass on the tray. "Yes, sir. Good night, sir."

I followed the housekeeper out, glancing again into the room as I pulled the door closed. Mr. Rochester's eyes touched mine briefly, raising a flutter in my chest. Then he turned toward the fire.

Despite the awkwardness of our interview—and the fact he had *still* not provided any details about why he'd brought me here—it had overall been successful. I'd managed not to offend him again, and by the end, we'd found a better footing.

At the entrance, I took my things from Mrs. Fairfax, and she lifted an oil lamp from a table. Together we went out into the night.

Though it had come as a pleasant surprise that I would have separate lodgings, leaving the manor gave me a pang of regret. Even with the pall that hung over it, my curiosity had been piqued by both the history and mystery of the grand old place. And, truth be told, of its master. After the interviews with him and his housekeeper, I couldn't help feeling that moroseness was not native to his character. I wondered what he'd been like before his wife died.

We followed a bricked path north along the manor's facade, and Mrs. Fairfax told me the herb garden and cottage were situated between the house and the apple orchard. It was an ideal spot for a witch. Boundaries were where magic happened. More practically, I would have easy access for foraging, and I wouldn't be distracted by the servants.

"We'll be sure to keep the lamps lit along the path at night while you're here," said Mrs. Fairfax as we walked through a corridor created by the end of the north wing and a wall covered with vine roses.

Soon we came to a gap in the wall on our left, and we passed through it into the herb garden. The garden itself lay in darkness, but a lamp hung from a post next to the cottage, and I could see that the snug dwelling was picturesque. Certainly more of an intentional habitation than the potting shed at Lowood. Built of stone and thatch, I guessed it to be as old as the hall, and like the hall, it had been kept up by the family. The roof and chimney looked whole and the thatch fresh. Light glowed around the edges of the shutters and shone through the crack under the door.

"This cottage has likely been on the property longer than the manor," said Mrs. Fairfax, confirming my guess. "There have been improvements, of course, like the chimney and paned window. You'll want the lamp inside, I think."

I lifted the lamp from its hook on the post, and she opened the cottage door with a soft creak.

The interior was warm and welcoming, the light coming from candles on a table in the center of the room as well as a fire blazing away in the grate. A large, overfull basket of peats sat near the hearth, and more candlesticks rested on surfaces throughout the room. I placed the lamp on a small table next to the door as we stepped inside.

In addition to the sturdy dining table and two chairs, there was a bed in one corner, covered in quilts faded and softened by age. Some of the other furnishings—a damask chair by the fire, a wardrobe and rug by the bed, and the pair of gleaming silver candlestick holders on the table—were finer than the rest, though somewhat worn and dinged by time. Probably they had once belonged to the manor. I spied various useful implements about the room—baskets and iron pots on a worktable under the window, gardening tools on one of the mostly empty shelves along the back wall, and a broom propped near the hearth. As in the housekeeper's sitting room, herbs hung from the rafters, scenting the cottage pleasantly, and holly hung over the door.

"No one has stayed in the cottage for years," said Mrs. Fairfax, "and I dry flowers and things here. I thought you might not mind, but I can remove them if you like."

"Oh no, I shall feel right at home."

My skirts swished suddenly against my ankles, and I glanced down. A white shorthair cat had apparently come in through the open door and was rubbing against me, tail held high. She began to purr softly.

"This is Sybil," said the housekeeper, smiling. "She comes with the cottage, I'm afraid. If you don't like cats, you can make her stay outdoors. She mostly prefers it anyway. But she'll keep the mice out."

"Hello, Sybil," I said, and the cat looked up at me. "Thank you for sharing your home with me." A witch never chased away helpful creatures.

Sybil mewed. Then she strolled over to the bed, hopped up, and curled at the foot.

Mrs. Fairfax laughed. "I suppose that's settled, then."

I noticed my things—trunks, bag, and ash wood walking stick (which also served as a staff)—had been placed near the bed.

"I hope you have everything you require," she said, "but if not, you need only ask one of the maids."

I thanked her, and she turned to go. At the door, she said, "A bolt has been installed for privacy. Should anything disturb you in the night, the household servants will be easiest to raise. Their rooms are at the back of the manor, and you can access them by the kitchen door. You are always welcome at the house, by *any* door."

*Should anything disturb you in the night.*

"Come to my sitting room for breakfast," she continued, "and we'll talk about how best I can help you while you're here. Have a good night, dear."

When she'd gone, I took a deep breath and slowly turned, again surveying the cottage. I hadn't liked leaving Lowood, but my accommodations and the break from teaching responsibilities might almost make it feel like a holiday.

*If I didn't have a curse to deal with.*

If in fact it was a curse.

I went to the hearth and examined the broom—a birch besom, twigs bound with bark strips to a crooked but sturdy handle. *This will do nicely.* Though the cottage was neat as a pin, I opened the door and swept the floors thoroughly, giving careful attention to the corners. It wasn't dust I hoped to cast out but any dark or creeping spirits. Then I bolted the door, and I sprinkled salt mixed with dried mugwort and vervain flowers in each corner.

"Salt and broom, make this room
Safe and tight, against the night.
So mote it be."

Sybil mewed as if in response to my spell. I glanced up, and she held my gaze for a moment before adjusting herself on the bed and yawning.

I laughed. "I wholeheartedly agree."

At last I dressed for bed, blew out the candles and turned down the lamp, and crawled gratefully under the quilts, careful not to dislodge my new friend. The last thing I heard before drifting off was the haunting trill of a tawny owl in the trees beyond the garden.

Despite the unfamiliar surroundings and shadowy talk before bed, I slept soundly. Still, excitement and nerves—along with the unblinking green-eyed stare of a cat mere inches from my face—woke me before dawn.

"Well, good morning," I said, slipping out from under the quilts.

Sybil hopped down and stretched, and I dressed for the day before brushing my hair and twisting it up into a simple knot. Then I began to put my things away. Clothes in the wardrobe, jars of ointments and herbs on the shelves that lined the back wall, and notebooks, pen, and ink on the table. I'd almost finished this task when there came a tapping on my door.

Outside in the watery gray morning light, I found a young maid with a breakfast tray. Sybil took the opportunity to bolt from the cottage without so much as a glance in my direction. The maid gave a startled cry as the feline made her swift escape, almost dropping the tray.

"Sorry," I said, laughing a little at my new friend's antics. I took the tray from the maid, and I noticed she looked pale and anxious. Then I recalled I was supposed to breakfast at the house. "Is Mrs. Fairfax well?" I asked.

"Yes, miss," she said shortly. "There was some trouble she had to see to."

The maid was moving off, and I said, "Could I ask what sort of trouble?"

She stopped but didn't turn. Clearly she was eager to get back to the manor—or possibly away from *me*.

Finally she said, "The great thorn tree in back of the house was set ablaze afore sunrise."

# *Blackthorn*

"Set ablaze!" I stared at the maid, who had half turned toward me. "You're certain?"

"Yes, miss. Saw it myself."

I shook my head, still having trouble believing her. Who would set fire to a tree so close to the manor? And *why*? "Is it thought to have been an accident? A leaf fire left burning, or—"

"No, miss."

The maid's whole manner was one of discomfort. It might be the fire setting her on edge, but I'd seen this behavior before, sometimes directed at Maria and me by a Lowood student or staff member. It would have been worse had Maria Temple not been almost universally adored. I was no Maria Temple. Where she aggressively won people over, I avoided those outside my circle and hoped any problems would keep their distance. I couldn't afford to do that here.

Before the maid could escape, I said, "The tree was a thorn, you say?"

"Yes, miss. An old blackthorn."

This was indeed troubling. To destroy a thorn tree—especially a blackthorn—was ill-advised at best, and at worst might very well bring the spirits of the place down on your head. Thorn trees could often be found standing alone in fields, the farmers having been unwilling to risk removing them.

I bent my head to one side, trying to catch her eye. "May I ask your name?"

I saw her throat work as she swallowed.

"There's no need to be afraid of me," I said gently. "Mr. Rochester and Mrs. Fairfax have brought me here to help."

"You're a witch." She spoke the accusation faintly, then flushed to the roots of her hair.

"You may have a mistaken idea of what that means. I would never hurt you, nor anyone. In fact, I'm a healer."

I watched her think about this, hands gripping her apron so tightly that her knuckles blanched.

"My name is Jane," I said. "Will you give me yours?"

"Agnes," she replied in the same thin voice.

"Thank you, Agnes. Now, can you take me to see the tree?"

She took a step back. Her voice trembled as she replied, "Don't you want to eat your breakfast, miss?"

I glanced down at the tray—toasted bread and coffee, which would be cold by the time I returned. It was a fitting reminder that I had not, in fact, come here on holiday. "Give me one moment."

I went to the table and set down the tray, then took my cape from a peg near the door and stepped out onto the stoop. Agnes walked on, and I followed.

The trees beyond the herb garden's stone walls were no more than ghosts in the mist. Inside the garden, wilting leaves and stems and spent flower heads hung sodden with morning dew. I could smell their rich decay, mingling with the clean scent of the bolder and more resilient rosemary. The fairy woman from my dreams came unexpectedly into my mind. *Rosemary for memory, lavender to forget.* As the image faded, another one took its place: my housemate Sybil and her close inspection this morning. The two creatures' eyes were exactly the same color—the bright green of new leaves.

Agnes got ahead of me while I mused, and I hurried to catch up, treading over wet and glistening autumn leaves in hues of orange, yellow, and brown. The grounds were not exactly unkempt, but they did have a wildness that appealed to me. The vine roses had been allowed to entangle and droop over the path. The stone walls were under creeping assault by woodbine and bramble, the latter with a few dark berries still clinging to the prickly vines. "The fairies' portion," October fruit had been called by Mr. Ross. The state of things out here was all the more striking in comparison to the pristine condition of the interiors.

"Do the grounds always look like this?" I asked Agnes a little breathlessly.

She cut her eyes at a riotous clump of jasmine. "Mr. Hatcher did most of the tending. He went away some months ago. Since then, the others laze about."

The sharp-edged cries of crows suddenly pierced the soft morning air, and I looked up to see a trio of them swooping over the house, dropping low as they passed us.

*"Ach,"* cried Agnes, hunching away.

The antics were ill-timed. Rural folk could be superstitious about crows, and the maid was frightened enough of me already. "The birds come from the nearby rookery?" I asked, hopefully making it clear they had nothing to do with *me*. "I noticed it from Hay yesterday."

"Yes, miss."

I looked out toward the orchard. The mist was thinning, and I could make out many dark shapes winging in jerky circles above the trees. "Some say a family of crows brings luck."

"Not where I come from," muttered Agnes, walking on.

Letting out a quiet sigh, I followed. "Mr. Hatcher—he left Thornfield for another position?"

"No, miss."

"Retired, then?"

She ducked under an arbor whose rose vines had partially freed themselves from the lattice. They grabbed at her cap as she passed, and she let out a groan and tugged it back into place.

"I couldn't say, miss."

I ducked after her and stopped on the other side. "Agnes, please wait."

The maid slowed and turned. She looked harassed and wary.

"Thank you," I said earnestly. "I'm told the strange events at Thornfield have made everyone uneasy. I very much want to help, but as an outsider, I can't do it alone. My questions aren't meant to annoy or frighten you. I'm simply trying to gather information. Won't you help me?"

Her gaze fell away, shoulders hunching slightly. "They say he saw a spirit."

"The groundskeeper? He saw a ghost?"

She nodded.

"One he recognized?"

"I couldn't say."

"And what about you, Agnes? Have you seen a ghost at Thornfield?"

Pressing a hand to her chest, she said, "Hope not to, miss."

"I can't say I blame you. Have you seen *anything* unusual?"

She began to tremble, and tears pooled in her blue eyes. "I'm expected back at the house, miss," she said in a quaking voice.

It was hard not to press her, but the poor girl was terrified. *Patience, Jane.*

"All right," I relented. "Direct me to the blackthorn and I'll go on alone."

She nodded in the direction we'd been walking. "Follow the path. You'll come to it directly."

I watched her hurry away. The first thing I must discuss with Mrs. Fairfax was interviews with the servants. She could perhaps smooth the way for me and help avoid another situation like this morning.

Continuing along around the back of the house, I heard voices. The garden wall ended, and the way opened up before me onto a lawn of late-summer sere. There had been enough autumn rain that it had begun to green again in patches.

I approached a small gathering around a beautifully shaped but blackened and smoking tree at the back edge of the lawn. Thorn trees could grow again if even a small part remained green and living, but I thought it unlikely any part of this one would survive. Surprisingly, the tree still stood mostly upright, with a few heavy, charred branches littering the ground underneath.

Mrs. Fairfax was there, along with a couple of laborers and a maid. They were in animated conversation about who had seen what and when. The maid had made the discovery, noticing the smoke when she stepped out to the greenhouse at dawn. I glanced around, wondering why Mr. Rochester hadn't come out.

I kept back from the others while they talked, continuing to study the blackthorn. The trunk and branches all had a clockwise twist to them, like the tree had been picked up in a swirling windstorm and dropped again. Thorns could be bush-like—hedges of thorn kept cattle in and unwelcome visitors out—but this was a large, well-formed specimen. It must have been ancient.

*A tragic waste.*

"Miss Aire?"

I turned to find my employer approaching. "Good morning, sir."

"Is it?" He stopped beside me, looking at the ruined tree, his face pallid above his black coat collar and waistcoat. Lines creased his forehead, but there was a dreadful sort of resignation in his gaze. Sighing, he said, "Come along. I presume we have the same destination."

As we joined the others, my heart beat with an odd, stuttering rhythm. I felt less afraid of him than I had in our first meeting, but I was far from easy. He unsettled me, and I thought not only because of the risk of offending him again. Yet what other reason could there be?

"Have you gotten to the bottom of this?" Mr. Rochester asked his housekeeper.

"No, sir," Mrs. Fairfax replied mournfully. "There's been no violent weather, and no brush or leaf burning on the property in the night. It seems someone has set fire to it."

"And why on earth would *someone* do such a thing?"

She shook her head. "I wish I knew, sir." It wasn't hard to see what she was thinking. She'd lumped this in with the other disconcerting events on the property.

"What about the rest of you?" asked Mr. Rochester. "Did anyone see anything unusual?"

There were murmurs of "no, sir." Then he repeated some of the other questions Mrs. Fairfax had asked them, but he learned nothing new.

At last he said, "If we presume it to be arson, then my question is, *Why?* What was the point of it? Or was it merely a prank, like the others we've had lately on the grounds?"

Mrs. Fairfax's gaze floated a moment and then came to rest on me.

Mr. Rochester's eyes followed. "We suspect our witch, do we?"

"We do not, sir!" protested the housekeeper.

I knew he was not really accusing me. In his impatience, he was chiding her, probably understanding as well as I did why she was looking at me. She wanted me to be the one to invite his displeasure by suggesting this was anything more than an unfortunate accident.

Which was fair enough. She was really the one who'd brought me here, and the closest thing I had to an ally.

"Blackthorn is a strongly protective tree, sir," I said. "Likely it was planted here—or left standing when the house was built—for that reason."

The same could be said for hawthorn, but blackthorn went one step further. It would not only protect the manor and its inhabitants but cast a malevolent shadow over any enemies. Blackthorn was symbolic of confronting darkness.

"What are you suggesting?" asked Mr. Rochester.

"The possibility that some person—or some spirit—wished to deprive Thornfield of the tree's protection." If so, they must have been ignorant of the danger in destroying one . . . or powerful enough to counter the tree's magic.

The furrows in his brow deepened. "To what aim?"

"That I cannot yet say."

He stared at the tree, clearly baffled and dissatisfied.

"Make sure it's out completely," he said to the laborers, who were eyeing me warily now. If anyone on the estate was still in the dark about what I was, they wouldn't be for long. "When it's cooled enough," he continued, "remove it."

"I would wait, sir."

His gaze swung back to me, and my heart stumbled. "And risk it falling on someone, Miss Aire?"

*Courage, Jane. You've been summoned here for this.*

"Give me leave to perform a blessing. There may be beings associated with this tree. I'd like to appease them if I can and entreat them to remain on the grounds. Then it can be taken down, but I'd suggest letting it lie, or burying it on the spot."

As I spoke, the corners of his mouth dipped, and I felt the fearful paralysis of those around me, like they anticipated a bluster. Yet all he said was, "Very well." Then, abruptly, he was going.

"Sir?" I called after him.

He turned.

"Would this be a convenient time for me to ask you a few questions?"

"I will see you at the house for dinner. We can talk more then."

He continued toward the manor, and I held back a sigh of frustration. I was to spend an entire day at Thornfield still mostly in the dark about what I was up against.

The servants began to drift away, casting more wary glances in my direction, but Mrs. Fairfax came over to me.

"Good morning, dear. I hope you slept well."

"I did, ma'am, thank you."

"I'm sorry you've had so little time to adjust. Can I offer my assistance with your blessing?"

Tempted as I was to take her up on the offer, I didn't want to risk annoying Mr. Rochester, who was paying her to keep house. "That's very kind of you, ma'am, but it's not necessary, and I don't want to keep you from your duties."

"Very well. But you must promise you will let me know how and when I may best assist you. I am yours to command at a moment's notice."

"Thank you, Mrs. Fairfax. I'll want to interview the rest of the staff at some point, but I'd like to speak more with Mr. Rochester first. Perhaps tomorrow?"

"I'll arrange it."

"Another thing you might help me with—I spoke briefly with Agnes this morning, and it was clear that I made her uncomfortable. I don't know if there's anything you could say to the staff, to prepare them and help put their minds at ease?"

The housekeeper gave a knowing nod. "I'll be sure to let them know you are here at my request and that I trust you. I'm sorry Agnes was difficult. She is rather a nervous girl, especially since her mistress's death."

"Was she close to Mrs. Rochester, then?"

"She was Mrs. Rochester's maid. She came with her to Thornfield."

Her maid! What a shame she had such a strong aversion to me. She might have saved me having to ask Mr. Rochester difficult questions.

"When the mistress died," continued the housekeeper, "Mr. Rochester—or maybe it was Mr. Mason, I can't recall—left it to Agnes to decide whether she would stay or return to Thrush Hall."

"Did you think it odd she remained, after such a short time here?"

Mrs. Fairfax's gaze drifted to the blackthorn. "I had observed her to have a particular affection for her mistress. Perhaps she found it too painful to return without her."

After my interaction with Agnes, her showing anyone "a particular affection" wasn't an easy thing to imagine. But the loss of her mistress could help account for her gloom and anxiety.

Mrs. Fairfax returned to the house after that, and I went back to the cottage to collect the things I would need—my ash wood staff, a fresh candle, and a small iron pot from the hearth, to which I added a few hot coals. Going to the shelves now stocked with my supplies, I tied up one of Mr. Rochester's "small bundles of weeds"—sage, yarrow, and mugwort, for healing, dispelling evil, and communicating with the spirit world. I also packed my salt, for courage and protection, and a bottle of rosewater for an offering. When I had everything ready, I spared a few moments to break my fast on toast and cold coffee before leaving the cottage again.

Returning to the tree, I spread my cape on the lawn, arranging my tools on top. I took hold of my hagstone talisman, curling a finger around the edge to keep it steady, and peered through the hole. A hagstone could serve as a tiny window into the spirit world, and I had glimpsed fairies through it before. Once, at yuletide, I'd heard music on the other side of a hedge and looked through in time to catch the tail end of a fairy procession.

Now I studied the blackened remains of the tree, searching for damage beyond the obvious. I wasn't prepared for what I found.

Beneath the twisting branches, at the base of the ridged trunk, a slender figure was curled—arms folded around legs, hair fanning out over the ground. My breath caught, and slowly I moved closer.

She looked peaceful, like she was sleeping. Dark, leafy veins ran beneath her bare, greenish skin. Both her willowy form and the color of her skin reminded me of the fairy woman from my dreams. Unlike the dream fairy, her hair was the dusty blue of sloes, the fruit of the blackthorn. *A dryad.*

To my knowledge, I had never been this close to a fairy; for the most part, they avoided men. I was getting a long look at this one for a reason. She had died with her tree.

If there was no curse before, there would be now. This attack would be viewed as a murder by the spirits around Thornfield, even if it was a careless accident or prank. Fairy folk rarely interested themselves in the "why" of things. But I couldn't help feeling this had been deliberate.

Going back to my cape, I picked up my staff and walked a blessing circle around the tree, dragging the staff's tip along the coarse grass. Next I placed the pot on the ground in front of the tree, and I dropped a handful of loose herbs on the coals. Whorls of fragrant smoke rose and formed a cloud, representing the element of air and also clearing the space of any remnants of ill intention.

Taking up the candle, I lit it from the coals and worked it an inch or so into the ground next to the pot, representing the element of fire.

Again using the hagstone to guide me, I laid the herb bundle close to the dryad as part of my offering. *Element of earth.*

Then I dripped rosewater in a circle around her body. *Element of water.*

I had never before been called on to perform a blessing for a slain creature, either mortal or immortal, so I had followed my instincts. Still, something felt lacking, and I asked myself what I would counsel another witch in the same circumstances to do.

*Show respect. Express regret. Promise to make it right.*

Kneeling before the dryad, I began, "Gentlefolk and spirits of Thornfield, my heart is heavy over this loss. This untimely death of one of your own. If any of you knows who or what is responsible, I humbly ask that you reveal it to me. I pledge to do everything in my power to remove this shadow, and I pray that you will work no vengeance upon the master of this house or those servants who are innocent of this crime."

I sat in quiet vigil a few minutes, studying the dryad's ageless features—the loose, lustrous hair and flawless skin taut over sharp-angled bones. She was a heart-achingly beautiful creature.

Finally I lowered the hagstone and sprinkled a few more herbs on the coals. When the smoke had thinned, I blew out the candle and slipped it in a pocket to finish burning back at the cottage.

As I dragged my staff widdershins to open the circle, goose bumps ran up my arms. The hagstone grew hot and heavy against my breastbone. Straightening, I looked up at the manor—a figure watched from a window on the upper floor. *Mr. Rochester.*

My heart bounced, though of course it was natural for him to observe me at the work he was paying me to do. Just as I was looking away, the palm of his hand came to the glass with a thump, and his eyes went wide.

I spun to look behind me. Tugging the hagstone out of my bodice, I held it up with trembling fingers.

I gasped and staggered backward—the dryad was *on her feet.*

# *Baneful*

Had I been mistaken about her death? *This is no living creature*. Cold fear seized me, anchoring me there.

Gone was the peaceful, sleeplike expression. The dryad's lips twisted in a grin of pure menace, and her wide-open eyes had heavy black rings around them. Her complexion had turned so sallow that the leafy-green veins stood out starkly, and her blue-black hair floated strangely about her head, like tendrils of water weeds caught in an eddy.

Her mouth gaped, and I flinched as she let out a wail—long and high-pitched, like I would imagine the keening of a banshee. Then, with a jerk, she moved toward me, flinging her slender arms forward. I scrambled back, giving a cry of alarm.

A white blur burst into the space between us, leaping at the creature with an angry yowl. Suddenly the dryad vanished, and the blur—Sybil—landed lightly on the grass. She watched the ground where the dryad had stood, tail twitching as she stalked a circle around the spot. When she'd made several circuits, she came and sat at my feet, looked up at me, and mewed.

Still trembling, I knelt and scratched her soft head. "You're a brave one."

She purred under the attention a moment but then darted away. Rising, I turned to find Mr. Rochester approaching.

"Are you all right, Miss Aire?" he asked, breathless, as he crossed the swath of lawn. His gaze darted between the tree and me.

"I am, sir," I said. But I was confused. It had been *his* reaction that warned me about the dryad. "May I ask what you saw from the window?"

His eyes finally settled on me, his features rapidly composing. "Only a shadow, apparently."

*That won't do, Mr. Rochester.* "What did you *think* you saw, sir? It could be important."

He stood perfectly still—with one notable exception. His hands hung at his sides, and one thumb tapped lightly at the seam of his trousers. I doubted he was even aware of it.

"I thought the tree was falling," he answered. "You were in its path. I realize now that I was mistaken. Forgive me for frightening you."

"You were not mistaken."

His thumb stilled, and he looked again at the tree.

"What I mean to say is there *was* a threat, though it looked very different to me."

He frowned. "How so?"

"Whomever set fire to this tree has also killed its dryad. A dryad is—"

"A tree spirit. I do *read*, Miss Aire. Are you about to tell me you've actually seen one?"

"On this very spot, sir."

He folded his arms, studying the charred ruin with a doubtful expression. "I suppose since our young queen claims she was visited by fairies as a child, I must accept their reality."

Queen or not, plenty of people had laughed at Victoria, and I wouldn't be surprised to find Mr. Rochester had been one of them.

"The blackthorn's dryad appeared to be resting peacefully," I said. "Yet by the time I finished my blessing and turned away, she had transformed into something menacing. I mightn't have noticed had you not warned me."

His eyes came back to me. "But that's not what I saw at all."

"Not everyone can see fairies. Perceiving the spirit world requires the Sight. But you *did* perceive a threat. That tells me you have at least a little of it."

He hesitated, considering. Then he said, "You're mistaken, Miss Aire."

It wouldn't do to argue with him. Instead I closed my hand over my talisman and said, "I would give much to have it myself. I'm forced to compensate with other tools."

He looked surprised. "You don't profess to have it?"

"Maybe a touch, but it comes as it chooses. So I must thank you for the warning."

Our exchange had unsettled him, that was clear. It would be a hard thing for a skeptic to hear. But the Sight didn't care who believed in it.

Finally, he said, "Well, no harm has come to you, thank goodness. The thing went away, I suppose?"

"It does seem she's gone. It may have simply been a warning."

"A warning. So the measures you took"—his eyes found the tools of my trade, gathered on my cape—"they've had no benefit?"

I thought about that. It was a fair question. "It's hard to know, sir. Until I discover the source or cause of your troubles here, my small magics may not be of much use. A bee balm and honey infusion might soothe a cough but have no lasting effect if there is serious underlying disease. Yet a creature has been slain, and I think it is never a waste of time to try to make amends."

He offered a faint smile. "Quite right." His hands came to the edges of his coat. "I have some business to get back to at the house. I'll look forward to continuing our discussion at dinner."

"Yes, sir."

I watched him walk back toward the manor, still favoring his right leg. I wondered whether he'd accept a salve to soothe the swelling and pain, then remembered that the surgeon had been sent for.

*It's not your place, Jane.* No, indeed.

A sudden stiff breeze blew his coat open, causing it to flap behind him like a crow's wings.

He was a strange and brooding gentleman, and the tinge of otherworldliness never quite left him. At first I'd compared him to Mr. Brocklehurst, but the similarity really ended at the stern exterior. Elementally speaking, Mr. B was as earthy as they came, while Mr. Rochester was all air and fire. And there was a mystery about him I was keen to unravel.

Arriving back at the cottage, I was surprised to meet Agnes coming with another tray.

"Mrs. Fairfax bid me bring you something more to eat." She looked composed, and I wondered whether the housekeeper had spoken to her about me.

I opened the door for her and then paused outside to fold back the shutters. When I went inside, I found her pouring my tea. Then she moved to the hearth to build up the fire. She moved stiffly as she worked, casting furtive glances about her.

Her earlier behavior toward me had stung, and it was tempting to let her finish in silence and go. But wounded pride was never a good reason for doing anything. I had learned that lesson more times than I cared to remember. Now that I knew Agnes had been Mrs. Rochester's maid, I must try to make an ally of her—however hopeless the case might be.

Walking over to the shelves to find my nettle-and-burdock tonic, I said, "Mrs. Fairfax told me that you were Mrs. Rochester's maid, Agnes. I'm so sorry for your loss."

She straightened and turned from the fireplace but kept her eyes lowered, palms pressed against her apron. "Thank you, miss."

I returned to the table with the tonic and added a few drops to my teacup, along with some milk and sugar. The herbs and sweet tea would help restore my strength after the eventful morning.

"She made it sound like the two of you got on well. You must miss her."

The maid's eyes widened and met mine for a moment before flitting away again. *Some secret there. Tread lightly.* "Yes, miss."

"Mrs. Fairfax speaks highly of Mrs. Rochester. I got the impression she was a kind mistress."

The line of Agnes's shoulders relaxed slightly. "Yes, miss. The kindest there ever was."

I sipped my tea. "I understand you chose to stay on at Thornfield. I can imagine it would be hard to go back, with all the memories."

Agnes looked up, her eyes shining with tears. "Yes, miss," she repeated faintly.

My heart softened toward her. Despite my lack of family, I had known the pain of loss. "I could make a charm for you if you like. Something soothing, to help heal a hurting heart."

Fear clouded her brow, and she glanced at the shelves.

"I make them with garden herbs and flowers," I said lightly. "Only if you like."

I returned my attention to my tea, giving her a private moment to think. Hungry and chilled, I quickly drank the rest of the cup.

"I—I don't know, miss." She clasped her hands together in front of her. "You said you're a healer?"

"That's right. How about this: you can watch me make the charm, and then you can take it if you think it might help you."

Without waiting for a response, I went for a box of apothecary supplies and jars of dried herbs. I carried a candle to the hearth and lit it, placing it in the center of the table. Then I fished a small cloth bag out of the box.

"First," I said, "motherwort and hawthorn flower for heart healing." I opened each jar and lifted out a few leaves and flowers, adding them to the bag. Next I opened a jar of blue flowers and another of red berries. "Borage for courage and lifting the spirits and rowan berries for protection, in case the recent troubles at Thornfield have you feeling uneasy."

I took a scrap of thin blue ribbon from the box and tied the bag closed, murmuring a spell.

> "Blessings upon Agnes, bearer of this charm.
> Tree, herb, and berry, keep her from harm.
> So mote it be."

I set the charm on the edge of the table, then deliberately turned my attention to the tray she'd brought. Lifting the cover on the dish revealed eggs, scones, and clotted cream. My mouth watered.

"Dear Mrs. Fairfax," I murmured.

I sat down, but before I could pull the tray closer, Agnes came and moved it for me and also refilled my teacup. "I'll be going back to the house now, miss."

"All right, Agnes, thank you."

She gave a quick curtsy and started for the door.

*Ah well, it was worth a try.*

But as I glanced at the edge of the table, I noticed the charm was *gone*. It wasn't on the floor below either. Agnes must have pocketed it as she moved to serve me.

I smiled and picked up my fork.

Two days in a row now, I'd enjoyed an unusually hearty breakfast. Meals at Lowood usually consisted of weak tea or coffee, toasted bread, and porridge or soup. On special occasions, there might be scones and jam. I tried to make the everyday fare more satisfying by adding mushrooms, nuts, or berries I gathered in the woods, and I taught my students to do the same. The other teachers used what they saved from their meager salaries to add variety to their diets. Maria had squirreled away tins of biscuits all over her room. Anyone who was really hungry could go to the kitchen, as Mrs. Shaw hated Mr. Brocklehurst's miserly ways and would always give a slice of bread and jam if she could spare it. Between the kindnesses of Cook and Maria, I'd developed a fondness for anything baked.

When I finished my meal, I consulted my pocket watch and found that the early part of the day had flown. But through the window, I saw that the clouds and fog had cleared, and there was still plenty of time to inspect the herb garden and possibly even venture out to explore the grounds. I set the tray of dishes on the table next to the door and put on my cape again.

Outside, I was greeted by the brilliancy of the midday sun, which had transformed the garden. Formerly lank foliage came vividly alive, the dewdrops rendered to glistening jewels by the light. I stepped back inside and grabbed an apothecary bottle.

I would have liked to spend at least a few minutes familiarizing myself with the garden before harvesting anything, but sun-ripened dew was a rare opportunity. While regular dew would carry the essence of the plant it was collected from, *this* dew would make a powerful restorative. The sun's warmth would soon dry up all the precious resource, so I moved quickly, identifying yarrow, thyme, rosemary, and Saint-John's-wort. I tipped leaves and gently pressed fronds, collecting the droplets into my bottle. These herbs were most potent in spring and summer, but the dew and the sun would restore and amplify their properties. And because in October the plants were preparing to rest and gain strength for the next growing season, this essence could be used to encourage a healing sleep.

When I finished with the herbs, I wound round to the stone wall behind the cottage, collecting more dew from the few blooms left on the rose vines. As I tipped the moisture from a final red rose, I pricked my finger on a long thorn. I flinched, and a bright drop of blood dripped into my bottle.

Straightening and holding the bottle up to the light, I groaned—to have spoiled it after all my careful work! It felt a sad waste of an unexpected gift. As I was about to empty the bottle onto the ground, it occurred to me the essence might *not* be spoiled. Perhaps I'd simply created a different tonic from the one I intended. It would require some thought, so I corked the bottle and slipped it into my pocket.

I was turning back to the cottage when something caught my eye: the overgrown rose vines had almost completely concealed an old wooden gate. Carefully shifting some of the tangled mess aside, I found the door handle. I tried it, and the door moved a little, but some work would be required to free it.

This task could certainly wait for later, and I might save myself the trouble by asking Mrs. Fairfax what lay beyond the door. But my time was my own until dinner, and curiosity got the better of me. I went back to the cottage and returned with pruning shears and gardening gloves. Then I went to work, trimming the overhanging vines and cutting through the ones that stretched across the gate. By the time I finished, sweat coated my brow, and I'd torn a hole in my dress sleeve.

The gate, constructed of a heavy, dark wood, was surprisingly free from rot. I removed the gloves and reached again for the iron handle, pausing as I noticed this time that it had been forged in the form of a grimacing imp. Gripping my talisman in one hand, I grasped the handle with the other.

I suspected the gate might be blocked on the other side as well, but with a loud protest of hibernating hinges, it swung free.

A dramatic change of atmosphere occurred just beyond the threshold. This smaller, walled garden had clearly not been tended in a very long time, and the overgrowth created a closeness that trapped pockets of mist. Various types of vining plants clung to every inch of the old stone walls, and the branches of a tree that sprawled in the center of the garden reached horizontally over the planting beds.

I stepped out from the arch onto the brick path, stopping to inspect the vines closest to the gate—not roses but a plant with large drooping leaves and shiny, bright-red berries. A similar plant with black berries grew in a nearby planting bed, and the pungent odor of henbane filled the air. Moving among the beds, I quickly identified belladonna, hemlock, wolfbane, and the lovely hellebore, or Christmas rose, among the first plants to bloom in the New Year. One bed even had a small patch of fly agaric mushrooms, looking like something out of a fairy tale with their alluring red-and-white caps.

*A poison garden.* Or what was more typically called an apothecary garden. In the hands of a novice—or someone motivated by ill intent—these were baneful herbs. I had used them only in salves or in flower essences, like I had collected in the herb garden but greatly diluted. Taking an essence allowed a sufferer to work with the spirit of a plant rather than directly with its strong medicine. I had found them quite effective for persistent pain, both mental and physical, and chronically disordered sleep.

The beautiful old tree at the garden's center was some variety of elm. It had a stout trunk and branches like outstretched arms. Elm trees possessed both strong protective qualities and dark associations. Used in spells, elms could be harnessed for either good or ill. There was said to be an elm at the entrance to the underworld, and elm trees often dropped branches without warning. I supposed it made sense to design a poison garden around one. The great boughs blocked much of the light, though, so I had to wonder at the apparent hardiness of the plants underneath. The leaves on the tree should have been brilliantly colored at this time of year, but instead they were a ruddy brown.

*Like old blood.*

As I was puzzling over all this, I heard something—voices speaking in hushed tones.

"Is anyone there?" I called.

The voices silenced, and nothing moved but the slowly shifting mist. I raised my hagstone but still saw no one. No sounds from the house or grounds reached me here, nor even from small creatures moving in the foliage. Only the whispers of my own shortened breaths.

Then I did detect movement—in the shadows on the far side of the garden. A figure emerged and came toward me. Goose bumps pricked my flesh, and my body went cold.

"Hello there," called the figure—an ordinary flesh-and-blood man, it seemed. "I apologize if I've startled you."

I let out a breath. "Good day to you, sir."

I laughed at myself for thinking him a spirit for even a second. He was quite solid in form—healthy and handsome, about my own age or a little older, with intelligent brown eyes. His clothing marked him as a gentleman.

He removed his hat and extended his hand. "I'm George Poole, Thornfield's physician."

"Ah." I grasped his hand. His fingers felt cold even through his glove. "You've come to examine Mr. Rochester's ankle?"

"Indeed, I have."

Dr. Poole must be Mrs. Fairfax's "surgeon." Advances in the field of medical education seemed to be blurring the lines between surgeons and physicians these days. I had observed the two to have little respect for each other and thought this evolution would likely benefit their patients.

I glanced down the brick path in the direction the physician had come. "Is Mr. Rochester with you? I thought I heard voices."

He shook his head. "I've left him resting in his study. Pardon me, but you are . . . ?"

*Charming, Jane.*

"Forgive me," I replied, laughing. "My name is Jane Aire. I've just arrived at Thornfield."

"Ah, you must be the Lowood witch. I overheard a couple of the servants discussing your arrival."

I could only imagine. The physician's expression was carefully neutral. Historically, relations between physicians and women who practiced herb healing were about as cordial as between physicians and surgeons. We were called on to treat many of the same ailments, but it went deeper than professional rivalry. We were often viewed by physicians as quacks.

"Yes," I replied, thinking the less said about it the better. "I hope Mr. Rochester's injury is not serious?"

"A minor sprain. If he can stay off it, he'll be right as rain in no time."

"I'm relieved to hear it." I couldn't help being curious about what Dr. Poole was doing in this garden, not to mention *how* he had gotten in. "I confess you did give me a fright, Dr. Poole. I had not expected to meet anyone here. It's rather a gloomy spot."

He glanced up into the branches of the elm. "I suppose it is. But I always come here when I visit Thornfield. I find it peaceful."

This struck me as odd. From what little I'd seen of the grounds, I imagined there were many more inviting places to wander, especially on such a pleasant autumn day. I was of course interested in the plants, but few others would be. Even over the course of my brief visit, the cold had managed to creep into my bones, and I was quite ready to take my leave of it.

"Opening the gate behind my cottage required some sweat and determination," I said. "I wish I'd known there was another entrance to the garden. It would have saved Mr. Rochester's roses."

He smiled. "It's a very small door, and well hidden. I'd never have known this garden was here had Mrs. Fairfax not shown it to me once.

None of the staff come here, not even the groundskeepers, as I suppose is apparent. When I first heard your voice, I confess I wondered whether you might be a . . ."

"A ghost?" I said when he trailed off.

"Quite right. I know it's ridiculous."

"From all I've learned since I arrived, I don't find it ridiculous at all." Too late, I recalled how Mr. Rochester had been worried about neighborhood gossip. Although, the physician would certainly have been called to attend to the illness and injury Mrs. Fairfax had described.

He sobered. "Ah yes, the strange events at Thornfield. It's why you were asked here, I believe?"

"Yes," I said, relieved. I studied him. His expression wasn't exactly open, but I thought it at least neutral. I needed information, and Mr. Rochester, as of yet, had not been very forthcoming. Did I dare consult the physician without permission from my employer?

*I might not have such an opportunity again.*

"You could be of some help to me, sir, if you're willing."

A frown tugged at his lips, but he replied, "Happy to, of course, though I don't know how. I've seen nothing here myself that I wouldn't put down to plain old bad luck."

"You may be right. But if you'll indulge me, I have a few questions that, as Thornfield's physician, you are uniquely qualified to answer."

He nodded.

"Did you happen to attend the late Mrs. Rochester?"

This question obviously took him by surprise; he blanched, then quickly blinked a couple of times. I could understand it being a painful subject for him, having lost such a young patient, and I regretted having to ask.

"Indeed I did attend Mrs. Rochester," he said, "though mostly when she was still Miss Mason. I was her family's physician for a time, and after her marriage, I came to Thornfield to care for her in her illness. She didn't survive much beyond that."

"So I understand. Her family estate is near here, then?"

He shook his head. "Thrush Hall is in Norfolk."

I frowned, confused. "You currently attend the Rochester household from *Norfolk*?"

He turned his hat in his hands, letting his gaze move around the garden. "After Miss Mason—Mrs. Rochester—died, I chose to remain in Yorkshire until I saw how Mr. Rochester got on after her death. He felt it quite keenly, you see, though they hadn't been married long. A year later, I still find myself here."

Now this struck me as *very* odd. It made a kind of sense for Agnes, whose mistress had become part of Thornfield through her marriage, but Dr. Poole would likely have left a practice behind. And he'd given me another interesting piece of information: *He felt it quite keenly, you see*. Perhaps I had gotten a wrong impression from Mrs. Fairfax. Perhaps Mr. Rochester *had* loved his young wife.

"Did you not have a practice in Norfolk?" I asked.

"I did, actually. But the elderly physician who had served Thornfield and the surrounding estates died soon after Mrs. Rochester. I found the wild country had grown on me, so I moved my practice."

Having grown up in an untamed corner of Lancashire, this country felt quite civilized in comparison, but I took his meaning. Despite the tidiness of the village and valley, there was a wildness to the woods on the estate, with its raucous rookery, as well as in the surrounding heathland and dark hills. I sensed the presence of old spirits.

"And this garden as well?" I asked on impulse.

He smiled faintly. "Yes, I suppose so. Many of the plants have medicinal value, and I'm something of a hobbyist apothecary. But mainly I enjoy coming here to think."

So he knew his baneful herbs. It was unusual; few physicians would sully their hands beyond the ink stains resulting from writing prescriptions.

"It's been very nice meeting you, Miss Aire," he said, replacing his hat on his head. "I'm afraid I must dash off now. I've a call to make in Hay. But perhaps I'll see you again."

I had barely gotten started with my questions, but the physician seemed suddenly in haste. "I won't keep you, sir, but might I just ask what was Mrs. Rochester's diagnosis?"

He studied me, and I supposed he must have wondered why I was so interested in Mrs. Rochester. But all he said was, "She died of consumption." Which I had suspected, based on Mrs. Fairfax mentioning "a wasting illness." Helen, my dearest girlhood friend at Lowood, had died of consumption a year before completing her studies.

He touched the brim of his hat. "Good day, Miss Aire."

"Good day to you, Dr. Poole."

He turned and walked back the way he'd come. I watched him, hoping to discover the location of the other entrance. A few beams of sunlight had found their way into the garden, thinning the mist enough for me to see that the door was set low in the west wall. It had been completely concealed by a stand of spent foxglove, whose tippy stalks the physician had to part with both arms. He stooped to open and pass through the small arched door. It struck me that the garden didn't particularly want visitors.

Poole had seemed a pleasant enough fellow. He'd made no trouble over my profession, and he'd answered my questions. Knowing how Mrs. Rochester had died was useful, as well as having confirmation that her husband had been attached to her. Yet something about the interview left me feeling vaguely troubled. For one, he had never acknowledged or offered explanation for the voices I'd heard. Which could be because he hadn't heard them. But there was something more, related to his fondness for the strange garden, or to his decision to remain in Yorkshire, or possibly both. I couldn't put my finger on it.

I shivered. I was ready to return to the cottage's warm fire. As I started back toward the gate, there came a scratching, scurrying sound. Likely a squirrel or rat, but I stopped to listen. Then came a loud crack overhead—on instinct, I flung myself toward the gate.

I felt a rush of air and turned in time to see a thick bough crash onto the path right where I'd been standing only a moment ago.

# *A Troubled Spirit*

I stood panting, heart pounding. The accident had been so near that twigs from the fallen branch had caught in my skirt.

Drawing a spiral on the palm of my hand with the tip of a finger, I murmured, *"Light within, shine without,"* and my spirit-light flickered to life—a cool white flame, gently undulating above my hand. The magic welled up from low in my belly, filling my mouth with the taste of spring water flowing over smooth stones.

I backed slowly to the gate. Sybil met me there, mewing energetically and pacing. When I'd made it safely to the other side of the wall, she crouched down in front of the doorway and hissed. Eyes fixed and tail twitching, she seemed to be watching something in the garden. I raised the hagstone and looked but could see nothing.

As I lowered the stone, I caught movement on the edge of my vision—a shifting shadow.

"Dr. Poole?" I called.

Sybil was now purring loudly, and her small body pushed against my skirt. I stood listening for an answering voice, eyes sweeping the garden. A ray of sunlight warmed my face, and I was struck again by the contrast between the atmosphere inside and outside.

Still purring, Sybil began circling my legs. "All right," I said finally, taking hold of the door and swinging it closed. *Creak. Thud.*

Sybil uttered a sharp sound that was more like a bark than a meow, then dashed around to the front of the cottage. I dropped my hand, letting the spirit-light go out, and followed her. Instead of joining me inside, the mysterious little beast sat down on the threshold, preventing me from closing the door. There was a scone and a small pitcher of milk left on my breakfast tray by the door. Picking up the scone, I poured what was left of the milk onto the dish and set it on the stoop. Sybil gave a satisfied mew and lapped at the offering. *Nothing mysterious about that.*

Nibbling on the leftover pastry, I went back inside. I lit a candle from the fireplace coals, set it on the table, and retrieved a bottle of brandy I'd noticed on a shelf when putting away my things. Taking the dew bottle out of my pocket, I filled it the rest of the way with brandy to preserve it. I dripped wax from the candle to seal the cork, wrote "Thornfield dew" and the date on a slip of paper, then used more wax to affix the label to the bottle. Finally, I placed it on a shelf with my other tonics.

Returning to the table, I went through the stack of notebooks I'd brought from Lowood. Half of them were entirely filled with scrawl—remedies, spells, crude illustrations, and notes—while the others were mostly blank. I chose a spell book that still had some blank pages and jotted down the name and date of the tonic with a list of its ingredients, both accidental and intentional. Beneath that, I wrote "Use: ?" The tonic was meant to be restorative; would the drop of blood increase its power or change its nature altogether? I would consult Maria when I was home again.

Setting the journal aside, I rose to add peats to the fire. There were kitchen things on the table in front of the window, and I was pleased to find a kettle among them. I'd seen a well in the herb garden, so I went out for water, then filled the kettle and heated it on a hook over the fire.

When the water had boiled, I brewed tea in a charming pot with a pattern of pink and cream roses, which I'd found on a shelf together with the tea tin. The spout was chipped, and the cups and saucers were of different patterns, which made me feel quite like I was at home in my apothecary.

The tea warmed and revived me, and I began thinking over the day's events. The fallen branch, along with the earlier destruction of the thorn tree and its dryad, did seem to fit into the catalog of occurrences on the estate that Mrs. Fairfax had given me. What shadowy thing was at work here?

I got up and relit the candle I'd used for the dryad blessing so it could burn the rest of the way and complete the spell. The more I thought about it, the more the menacing spirit that had appeared after the blessing seemed to me like a warning. Maybe even an answer to the plea I'd made . . .

*If any of you knows who or what is responsible, I humbly ask that you reveal it to me.*

Did the apparition suggest that a troubled spirit was responsible for Thornfield's curse?

My curiosity had been greatly aroused by this mystery, along with my concern for all the folk on the estate. And of course I had strong personal motivation for getting to the bottom of it. Payment for my success would help to sustain the school, and it might even persuade Mr. Brocklehurst that his "Lowood witches" were more asset than liability. If not, well . . . maybe it would be motivation for me to think more seriously about striking out on my own.

*First things first.*

I poured another cup of tea and opened a blank notebook. Taking up my pen, I began to write down everything I could remember from my conversations with Mr. Rochester, Mrs. Fairfax, Agnes, and finally Dr. Poole. I had an excellent memory, but I wanted to be sure not to lose even the smallest details of expression or manner. Anything might be important.

Among these details, I found myself dwelling particularly on the ones pertaining to my employer. I wished to know him better. Did he have siblings? What had his family life been like? What were his interests? I had begun to suspect there was some deep wound at the heart of his melancholy. What, or who, had inflicted that wound? *Was* he still mourning his beautiful young wife?

Though answers to these questions could turn out to be useful, I had to remind myself that Thornfield was my true patient. Mr. Rochester had not confided in me; he had in fact seemed determined to tell me as little as possible. He had not asked me to help him. Yet he was too young to spend the rest of his life wasting away from grief, and I couldn't help hoping that in healing the estate, I might also heal its master. It was, after all, what I had been educated to do.

It was more than that, though. I had a strong desire to know him as he'd been before this shadow descended.

I had a strong desire to hear him laugh.

*But why, Jane?*

Sighing, I picked up my cup and finished my tea. I turned to the next blank page and started a list of the questions I hoped to have answered, either at this evening's dinner or in interviews with the household staff in the coming days.

*Have any ruins, barrows, or ancient trees (other than the blackthorn) been recently disturbed?*

*Has anyone on or around the estate claimed to have seen a spirit or anything they can't explain? (Ask Mrs. Fairfax about the old groundskeeper.)*

*What was Mrs. Rochester's state of mind at the time of her death?*

*Was Mrs. Rochester in love with her husband?*

*Was Mr. Rochester in love with his wife? (Mrs. Fairfax seems to believe not; Dr. Poole believes so.)*

I was interrupted by a knock on the cottage door, and I took out my watch on the way to answer it. Lowood's dinner hour—five o'clock—had come and gone!

Opening the door, I found Agnes on the stoop. "Am I late for dinner?" I asked.

She shook her head. "Mrs. Fairfax asked me to see if you needed help dressing."

Relieved, I held open the door for her.

At Lowood, our dinners were far from formal occasions. In fact, unless it was a feast day or Mr. Brocklehurst was playing host to a patron, I rarely changed my dress. I could manage it on my own, and I preferred to. But it would go quicker with the maid's help, and I could continue my efforts to win her trust.

I went to the wardrobe for my dinner gown. Though of better quality than what I wore by day, it was still quite plain, and I found myself wishing for something finer. At least it was a dark forest green instead of my usual brown or gray.

I laid it across the bed, and Agnes came to help with the buttons of my day dress. Her fingers were practiced and quick; the dress was soon shed and the gown lowered in its place.

Knowing Mr. Brocklehurst would want me to look as smart as possible, I took off my talisman and left it along with my pocket watch on the nightstand. I didn't like going without some protection, though, so I opened my trunk and fetched the one item of material value that I possessed—a brooch left to me by my friend Helen. Having first belonged to Helen's mother, the cameo depicted a white stag on a dusty pink background in a gold filigree mount. Though skillfully carved and quite pretty, the brooch was dear to me only because Helen was. The stag likeness, and Helen's love in giving me the gift, also instilled the piece with protective magic.

After watching me fiddle clumsily with the brooch for a moment, Agnes reached for it and carefully pinned it at the lowest point of my neckline.

With my dress complete, there was nothing left but to neaten the low knot I wore in my hair. As I started taking it down, Agnes said, "I'll do it, miss."

Our situations had reversed. I had never been tended to by a lady's maid, and Agnes had waited on the lady of Thornfield before me. I was far out of my element, and I felt it.

Agnes pulled the knot free, picked a few twigs from my hair, then brushed and plaited it efficiently, arranging the plaits behind my ears and at the base of my neck. As she worked, I noticed a leather cord went round her neck and down into the bodice of her dress. I didn't recall seeing it before and wondered whether it might be attached to the charm I'd made for her.

She stuck in the last hairpin and stepped back to survey her efforts. I gave her a nervous smile. "Shall I pass muster?"

"You look very pretty, miss."

Though spoken in a businesslike tone, the compliment touched me. I never had felt that I was pretty and certainly never had been told so. Mr. Brocklehurst didn't hand out compliments, and Maria was more concerned with a young lady's mind than her person. I had a recollection of Mrs. Shaw long ago referring to me as "a pretty child," but then what child wasn't?

"Thank you, Agnes," I said. "I would have bungled it on my own."

While she didn't quite smile, I thought she looked pleased. "I'll take you on to the house, miss."

Clouds had gathered in the twilight, and the air was cool and still. I had half expected Agnes to take me around back, to the kitchen entrance, which would be the one most used by household staff. But I was dining with the master of Thornfield, and I supposed that wouldn't look right. As we rounded the northwest corner of the house, I glimpsed the dining room through a window, aglow with candles and firelight.

We found Mr. Rochester in the hall, standing just as I'd seen him in the blue drawing room the previous evening—in front of the great fire, holding a glass of spirits this time. He made quite a figure in his evening coat with tails and dark-red cravat. I couldn't help feeling it a pity he was so isolated here. It seemed unnatural for a man still in the prime of life. Again I wondered about his family. I wondered whether he'd marry again.

He looked up as we approached. "Here you are."

Agnes curtsied and left us.

"I'm sorry if I've kept you waiting, sir."

"It wasn't long," he replied, putting out his arm.

For a moment, I was stunned to stillness. Of course offering his arm was perfectly proper, as well as a very gentlemanly thing to do. But I lived among women, and this was a first for me.

"Is anything wrong?" he asked.

"No, sir," I said, propelling myself forward and taking his arm.

He led me through the blue drawing room, my heart skipping along nervously. This would be my longest opportunity yet to offend him. How was I to get through a whole evening without mishap?

We passed through another door into the dining room, and he guided me to the nearer end of a long table, where two settings had been placed. A footman approached, but Mr. Rochester waved him away and pulled out the chair next to the table's head himself.

"Thank you, sir," I murmured as I sat down.

My eyes moved over the table—spotless white linen adorned with china and silver, everything gleaming brightly in the candlelight. Vases of greenhouse roses rested down the length of the dining table and on smaller tables throughout the room. Above the dark wainscot, a continuous fresco covered all four walls, interrupted only by the fireplace, the two doors, and the north- and west-facing bow windows. The fresco depicted a tree-lined river at twilight, with various waterfowl in the foreground and a pale-blue sky tinged with pink fading into the distance. It was so realistic, I could almost hear the mournful call of a loon.

Opposite the table from me, a healthy fire blazed. Above the mantel, a ceiling-high mirror with ornate gilded frame reflected the bright opulence of the room. Despite all this, the overall effect was one of rustic comfort rather than fussiness.

Yet I felt anything but comfortable.

My employer's eyes had remained steadily on me, and I now looked at him. He gave me a puzzled smile. "One might almost think you'd never dined before, Miss Aire."

Warmth rose to my cheeks. "In fact I haven't, sir. At least not in this way."

"I suppose by *that* you mean dining at Lowood is a dreary affair. I can well imagine."

While this was true, I didn't like him to think I was complaining. "What I meant is that Lowood is frugally managed. I am unused to finery and society manners."

His eyes glinted. "'Frugal' is a tactful description of your administrator."

Unsure how to respond to this playful baiting, I attempted deflection. "Mr. Brocklehurst mentioned he'd grown up near here and that your two families were acquainted. Do you know him well?"

He shook his head. "Really only by reputation. But yes, our families attended the same church, in fact. A devout lot, the Brocklehursts."

"Indeed, sir."

"Do you not find him rather severe?"

I gave him a baffled smile. "It is most ungallant of you, sir, to invite me to speak ill of my employer."

To my relief, he returned the smile. "So it is."

He continued to study me, and I sipped from my water goblet to cover my uneasiness. How simple I must seem to him—a nervous country mouse at his grand table. I wondered whether I was sitting in Mrs. Rochester's place. I wondered whether he was comparing the two of us.

*For pity's sake, Jane.*

Finally, he picked up a bell that had rested on the table and rang it once. The footman, who'd remained standing unobtrusively next to a door beside the fireplace, left the room.

"You're rather sober this evening," said Mr. Rochester, "but you look well. That color suits you."

I couldn't help staring at this second—and even more unexpected—compliment. He cleared his throat and added, "I'm sure you won't mind an old man telling you so."

Two footmen came in with the first course, giving us something else to focus on. As soup bowls were placed before us and wineglasses filled, I rallied my faculties and said, "While I'd hardly call you old, sir, I thank you for the compliment."

A thin smile appeared, and he raised his wineglass. "To your health, Miss Aire."

"And yours, sir." In addition to being miserly, Mr. Brocklehurst generally did not approve of drink, and wine was available only on special occasions. Though I did keep a bottle of brandy for making tinctures—and occasionally calming my nerves after a confrontation with Mr. B. Still, I wasn't used to it, and I took a very small sip.

Picking up his soupspoon, Mr. Rochester said, "So you do not dine with your colleagues at Lowood?"

"Not formally, except on feast days or when important people visit. Generally we take our meals in the school's dining hall with the students."

"Well, I hope I haven't made you uncomfortable by summoning you here."

"No, sir," I lied. "I'm eager to hear more about my commission, and to discuss the things I've observed on my first day at Thornfield."

"Straight to business, then."

Thinking perhaps I'd offended him, I added, "When you're ready, of course, sir."

He rested his spoon on the rim of his bowl and looked at me. "Miss Aire, your manner has changed since our first meeting on the road, and I'm not at all sure for the better."

Potato soup curdled in my stomach. Before I could attempt an apology, though I wasn't sure what for, he said, "Do *not* tell me you're sorry. Stop being so deuced polite."

I closed my mouth and looked down at my bowl. Angry tears started in my eyes. *Heaven above, not* now.

Mr. Rochester uttered a groan and dropped the handle of his spoon with a clinking noise. "The fault is my own, and I know it. My churlishness has made you skittish of me."

Clearing my throat and blinking back the tears, I lifted my gaze and spoke up at last. "I don't find you churlish, sir. But I do find you . . . intimidating. I want more than anything to be useful to you, but—"

"But I was unhelpfully honest when I said I haven't much faith in your craft."

I let out a sound somewhere between a sigh and a nervous laugh. "Perhaps, though I would not have preferred that you lie to me."

"So here we are, both wanting to be told the truth but with no promises we'll be gracious about hearing it." He drank from his wineglass and fixed his eyes on me. "Know this, Miss Aire. Whatever my feelings about witches in general, I *do* wish for you to succeed. More than you can imagine. Do you believe me?"

"I do, sir."

"Good. Henceforth I will try harder to support your efforts, and you have my pledge not to heckle you. In exchange, you will worry less about offending me. Do we have an accord?"

I barely suppressed a smile. "We do."

He gave a short nod and continued with his soup.

"May I ask you a question, sir?"

"Our brief acquaintance notwithstanding, I require no tea leaves to divine there will be *many* questions in my future."

"That borders on heckling, if I may say so."

He let out an honest-to-goodness laugh, and it dropped years off his features. The mirthful sparkle in his pale-gray eyes, and the laugh lines at their corners, brought his haunting good looks somewhat down to earth.

"Right you are, Miss Aire. Please ask your question."

"I believe you saw your physician this morning?"

He dipped his head. "I did."

"A physician must question a patient to arrive at a diagnosis, yes?"

A cloud passed over his brow. "I haven't much faith in physicians, either, but your point is taken. You cannot do your job if I avoid topics that may be unpleasant to me."

Before I could reply, the second course arrived, and for the next quarter hour we gave our attention to the roasted pheasant. Unfortunately, my nerves dampened my enjoyment of what was quite possibly the best meal I'd ever eaten.

At one point, I caught his gaze drifting from his plate to my bodice. Heat singed my cheeks, and I resisted an urge to raise a hand to my chest.

"I hope you'll excuse me for admiring your brooch, Miss Aire," said my employer. "It's very fine."

*Of course.* "Yes, thank you, sir."

"It looks to be a valuable piece."

"I believe it is. It was left to me by a dear friend."

His eyes fixed on me. "*Left* to you? I'm sorry. You seem very young to have lost a dear friend."

"It's been many years now." Seeing a way that I might naturally steer the conversation around to where I needed it to go, I added, "She died of consumption when she was only sixteen."

He looked down at his plate and repeated, "I'm sorry."

"I understand—that is to say, Mrs. Fairfax mentioned—that you lost your wife a short time ago, and that she, too, was quite young."

His jaw clenched. "Yes. Far too young."

"That must have been very difficult for you."

"Not as difficult for me as for her."

His mood had slumped, and how I wished I could do as my heart urged me and let the subject drop. But this was not a social engagement.

"On the contrary," I replied, "it's incredibly difficult to watch a loved one fade and be powerless to stop it. It was sudden, I understand."

His eyes came back to my face, and I glimpsed the rawness of his grief. "Yes. We had been wed only two months."

He had slightly misunderstood me. I meant to say the onset of illness was sudden, if she'd been well enough to marry only two months before. But the distinction seemed unimportant.

"How tragic, Mr. Rochester. I'm very sorry."

"Thank you, Miss Aire."

I sipped my wine and screwed up my courage again. "I met your wife's physician this morning."

He laid down his fork and wiped his mouth with his napkin. "Poole."

"Yes. Strolling in the apothecary garden after he had been to see you. He said he enjoyed the solitude of it."

My employer looked confused. "Apothecary garden?"

"Through the gate behind the cottage? I discovered it this afternoon. I must tell you that the gate was overgrown by vining roses, and I pruned them enough to gain entrance. I hope that was all right."

His expression loosened. "Ah yes. No one goes there, and I had all but forgotten it. Indeed, I believe Dr. Poole employed some of the plants when Antoinette's suffering was greatest."

My breath caught as a dark thought suddenly bloomed in my mind. I recognized it as the source of the unease I'd felt immediately after my conversation with the physician.

*I'm something of a hobbyist apothecary.*

The plants in that garden were dangerous. Might Dr. Poole have accidentally *poisoned* Antoinette Rochester? However ill she may have been, death from unnatural causes could explain a restless spirit on the estate. Spirits sometimes lingered because they'd not had enough time to put their affairs in order or they'd left important things unsaid.

"Dr. Poole told me Mrs. Rochester died of consumption," I said.

"That's what they called it, yes, though I suspect physicians attach that label to any affliction of the lungs they don't understand and cannot cure. She saw specialists in London, but none could help her. In the end, she asked to be left alone. She died here in the house."

*In the care of her family physician.*

Mr. Rochester pushed his plate away and took up his glass. He stared into the fire.

"I hope you'll forgive me if my questions have caused you pain, sir. I did have reason beyond curiosity for asking."

He looked at me.

"The disturbances on your estate—they could indicate a troubled soul. Occasionally, a person who dies will fail to move on from our world to the next. This stasis can change them, though it sounds paradoxical. They may take on qualities they never had in life. They may even become a threat to the living."

Mr. Rochester was staring rather fixedly, and I felt an uneasiness in my stomach. "Do you suggest, Miss Aire, that my late wife is *haunting* Thornfield?"

"It is but one possible explanation, sir. It wouldn't be the first time such a thing had happened. But there are more questions to be answered before I can make any real headway with your case."

He stiffened, and I feared an angry reply. But he said, "What else do you wish to ask me?"

Now came the test of all he had asserted—that he wanted me to be honest with him, and that he intended to support and assist me.

"Might I ask, sir, whether there was strong attachment between your wife and yourself?"

His frozen expression didn't fool me. I had dropped a glowing coal into a hay crib.

*Never again speak to me of love, Miss Aire, do you understand?*

Yet when he spoke, his tone was cold rather than hot. "We hadn't the luxury of knowing one another well enough for that. She was the granddaughter of a cousin of my father's, but we met only a short time before the wedding."

This did not seem to fit with the concern Dr. Poole had expressed for Mr. Rochester, nor with the grief I had observed myself. But I suspected Mr. Rochester felt things deeply, and whether or not he loved her, he would certainly feel the tragedy of such a death.

"The marriage was arranged, then?"

He nodded. "To keep Thrush Hall—an estate in Norfolk—in the control of my father's family. Antoinette was her father's only child."

The vagaries of inheritance were far beyond my experience, but I knew heiresses were not common, nor always approved of. Marriage to a family member might help protect her interests, or bolster her standing in society, or both.

A wine bottle rested on the table, and Mr. Rochester lifted it and refilled both our glasses, though I'd drunk only half my glass. "And now, Miss Aire, having had the temerity to ask such a question, *you* must submit to interrogation."

My heart missed a beat. "Sir?"

"Why do you ask whether I loved my wife?"

He had stripped the question bare of my careful wording, and though I believed I had good reason for asking, I now felt somewhat ashamed.

"I ask because sometimes a very strong attachment can hold a person's spirit in the living world beyond death."

His skepticism was plain. "It has been more than a year since Antoinette died."

"Spirits may remain restful for a time. They may initially be confused or unable to get our attention."

The footmen came in with dessert, and Mr. Rochester raised his fingers in a silencing gesture; he understandably didn't want to talk of ghosts in front of his servants. They poured coffee and placed slices of apple tart before us, and then he released them for the evening.

"You've experienced other hauntings?" asked Mr. Rochester when they'd gone.

"Until this morning, I had but once seen a spirit," I admitted. "My friend Helen, who gave me the brooch, appeared to me the night she died." She had stood in my doorway and smiled, all traces of the ruin wrought by her illness smoothed from her face. The memory was very precious to me. "But I've read accounts of hauntings written by those who have helped such spirits find their way to the other world."

He eyed me over the rim of his coffee cup. "And now that you've pried from me that my wife and I were not madly in love, will you withdraw your initial hypothesis?"

I shook my head. "There could be other reasons." I recalled what he'd told me about Dr. Poole and his remedies, but I judged it best to keep that particular line of inquiry to myself for the time being. "Mrs. Rochester was very young," I said. "She might have trouble letting go of her life for that reason alone."

Yet another possibility occurred to me. I must have shown some sign of it outwardly, because Mr. Rochester asked, "What is it, Miss Aire?"

*This is going too far, Jane.*

We had, however, just agreed that I was to worry less about offending him, and he was enduring the questioning tolerably well. He hadn't erupted or ordered me to pack my things.

"Tell me," he persisted.

I dug at an edge of the apple tart with my fork. "To your knowledge, was your wife expecting?"

No answer came, and finally I glanced up. No crack appeared in the stony visage. No blink came to relieve me from the silver-eyed stare. "She was not."

He exchanged his coffee cup for his wineglass, and I managed to breathe again. I couldn't help wondering how he could speak with such certainty. She might not have told him; she might not have been sure. Then I realized there was one way he *could* be sure. The couple had barely known each other. Mr. Rochester might be stern, but he was not inconsiderate. And she had quickly fallen ill. *There was no opportunity for her to conceive.*

"Tell me, Miss Aire, do you have any theories that don't involve my dead wife?"

He sounded more weary than angry, but still I didn't like being the cause of it.

"I will need to interview your staff," I said, "and I hope to have the opportunity to witness more of these events for myself. But in answer to your question, yes, there are other possibilities. Someone might have angered a powerful spirit on the estate, perhaps by disturbing an old grave or ruin. Or someone might have cursed the place intentionally. These would typically be the first stones I'd unturn. However, I could not but look into the particulars of a recent death."

He let out a sigh and pushed his tart away untasted. "I understand you. Or I'm trying to, at any rate. With regard to 'these events,' do you include what happened with the blackthorn tree?"

Finally I took a bite of my own tart, giving my thoughts a moment to settle. Desserts were a rarity at Lowood, and this was a more sophisticated specimen than anything good Mrs. Shaw had served—identical slices of apple arranged in perfect symmetry, a light dusting of snowy sugar, a hint of brandy, and a spice I couldn't quite identify.

"Yes," I said. "I do believe the burning of the tree—and what happened with the dryad after—along with the later dropping of an elm branch in the apothecary garden, are most likely related to the other events."

He stared at me, suddenly aghast. "You've been attacked by another tree?"

"'Attacked' might be overstating it, sir." I was discovering my employer had a tendency to exaggerate. In the context of his concern for me, it was rather endearing.

Mr. Rochester's eyes blazed. "But it's the second time you've been threatened since you arrived. Were I a reader of signs, I'd call that a fairly clear one."

He wasn't wrong, and it was something that should have occurred to me. But it would do no good to alarm him. "I employ various protections, sir. You needn't worry about me."

"You yourself admit that you don't know what's happening at Thornfield, which means you also don't know the extent of the danger." He shook his head. "I will ask Mrs. Fairfax to move you to the house immediately."

It was my turn to be horrified. "Mr. Rochester, please—the cottage suits me very well. It's what I'm used to. I assure you I can take care of myself." I had never expected the cottage, but that didn't mean I was willing to give it up.

"That may be, Miss Aire, but I am unwilling to take the risk. While you're at Thornfield, you are my responsibility."

I sank against my chairback, composing myself—sensing that the more agitated I became, the tighter the net would close. *Give me the right words.*

"Recall, sir, that you have hired me to help you. You must have faith that I know what I'm doing. You must allow me to do my job." I paused, then added, "As you would *any* employee on your estate."

An odd thing happened then—a deep flush spread over his face. He took a breath and let his gaze drift to the bow window on the opposite end of the room.

"You're right, of course," he said at last. "I would rest easier if you came to the house, but I shan't insist on it."

"Thank you, sir."

Helen had sometimes chided me for stubbornness and for having such a high opinion of my own way. Yet I couldn't help feeling I'd be more effective if I stayed where I was, without the distractions of a busy manor. Without the distraction of my employer himself, who in addition to making me "skittish" was becoming far too interesting to me.

He eyed my empty dessert plate. "Have you finished? I don't want to keep you too late."

It felt like a polite dismissal, and my spirits sank a little. I realized I had been enjoying his company. Not asking him uncomfortable questions but finally hearing him laugh. I had *made* him laugh, and it had shown me a whole other side of him.

It struck me that I had never felt this kind of exhilaration in talking with . . . well, *anyone*.

*Far too interesting, indeed.*

"Of course," I said, moving to rise. He stood up and scooted my chair back.

"I'd rather not raise any of the maids at this hour," he said.

I glanced at him in surprise but quickly nodded. "I can easily find my way, sir."

While I wasn't enthusiastic about the idea of walking back to the cottage alone, especially without my talisman, neither would I want Agnes or any of the others to have to return to the house unaccompanied.

"Certainly not," he replied with a snort. "You are alarmingly independent, Miss Aire. I'm afraid you must accept *me* as your escort."

# "Take Care, Miss Aire"

"Oh," was my articulate reply. Whatever was wrong with my *heart*? The beat was so frantic, I worried he would hear it.

Again I took his arm, and together we left the dining room. I'd set my shawl on a table in the entryway, and Mr. Rochester picked it up and settled it over my shoulders. I felt the light weight of his fingers a moment before he turned and opened the door.

The fresh night air wafted in, carrying with it a scent—a blend of rosemary, lavender, spirits, peat smoke, and something sharper I could not place. Saddle leather? My first thought was that it was one of the best things I'd ever smelled. My second, that it had come not from outside but from *him*. From the evening breeze moving through his hair and clothing.

I flared my nostrils trying to capture the scent; it was both soothing and invigorating. *Magical.* I wanted to hold on to it.

We stepped outside, and the next breeze swept the scent away. But in the apothecary of my mind, I was already combining ingredients. *Juniper has a hint of leather, and birch tar for smoke . . .*

A greeting from Sybil, who joined us as we stepped onto the path, brought my attention back to the living world. Her milky form practically glowed in the light from the lamps along our way.

"I see you already have an escort," said Mr. Rochester. "Tell me, is it true what they say about witches and cats?"

"What do they say, sir?" Of course I knew very well what he meant.

He cast a sidelong glance at me. "Toy with me, then. I far prefer it to your walking on eggshells."

I smiled but didn't meet his eye.

"*They* say," he continued, "that a cat is a witch's servant."

"Have you ever met a cat who was anyone's servant?"

He laughed. "So it's only a myth?"

"Not entirely," I admitted. "A cat—or any creature—may sometimes choose a witch for a companion. Sometimes an animal may be of service to a witch."

"And has this one chosen *you*?"

Sybil mewed, and we both laughed.

"I wouldn't presume to speak for her, but she sees things I don't, and she has warned me of danger twice today."

"Then we must see she is well treated so she will continue to do so."

I stole a glance at him. His countenance was easy and open. There was even a gentleness to his expression.

*He's warming up to me.* And it had happened rather easily, without the concerted effort I had made with Agnes. Just by being myself. *Warts and all.*

As we stepped into the herb garden, the clouds parted, revealing the sickle moon adrift in a river of stars. By their light, I noticed a white shape against the thatch of the cottage, just above the door. Sybil uttered a low, feline growl. The gleaming thing gave an eerie screech and erupted into flight—a barn owl.

*Not exactly subtle.* Owls were messengers between the worlds of the living and the dead. Sometimes they carried warnings from beyond the grave.

Mr. Rochester and I had both frozen in place. "Another friend of yours?" he asked.

"Only a visitor."

My tone was uncertain, and he looked at me. "Is there some significance?"

I didn't need to give him another reason to move me to the house, so I forced a smile. "I think he's looking for his mate."

"Ah," he said, laughing softly.

We went on to the cottage. I let go of his arm as he opened the door, and Sybil darted inside. He stood a moment on the threshold, surveying the interior. In my absence, a servant had built up the fire. Orange light danced over the walls, deepening the shadows.

"Cozy and snug," he said. "I do see the appeal. No leaks or vermin?"

"None that I've noticed."

"And you won't reconsider moving to the house?"

"I promise you that if I become truly afraid, I will come."

He nodded, resigned. "What is your plan for tomorrow?"

"I'd like to speak with the servants about what they've seen and heard. I believe Mrs. Fairfax was going to arrange it."

"I'll check with her in the morning."

"Thank you, sir." A sudden urge possessed me, and I said, "Will you wait a moment?" *Trust your instincts,* Maria had said.

He gave another short nod.

I went inside for a small bag of odds and ends that I'd tossed into a trunk at the last moment. I never knew what materials I might need on any given day, and it had been hard to leave anything behind. Finding a thumb-size stone, black and unusually smooth, I went back to him.

"Will you take this, sir?" I said a little breathlessly. "Respecting your feelings about 'small bundles of weeds,' I thought this might do instead. I hoped you might carry it for protection, especially walking alone on the grounds at night."

His keen eyes darted from the stone to my face, causing a flash of heat. He reached out and took the stone from me, his fingers grazing mine.

"What makes it protective?"

"I found it on the edge of a fairy pool—a sacred pool fed by a natural spring—in the hills behind Lowood. The color black, too, is protective." *As is a gift given with affection.*

He ran his thumb over the stone's smooth surface. Then he looked at me, brows slightly lifted. "I wouldn't like to take away anything that's helping to keep you safe."

This statement was made without a hint of irony, and his effort to overcome his skepticism, along with his concern for me, touched my heart.

"I have my own talisman. Sometimes when an item with magical properties comes to me, I don't know right away how I will use it. I hadn't thought of the stone in years, but suddenly it seemed right for you to have it."

He closed his fingers over the gift and slipped it into his pocket. "It's very kind of you to think of me."

He was going, but after a few steps, he looked back. "Please take care, Miss Aire. If you feel you must embark on another dangerous adventure, for heaven's sake come to me first and I'll accompany you."

Small moths flitted in my stomach. "If you like, sir."

"I insist. Going forward, I shall expect a report from you every evening at dinner." He waved me inside. "Now close and bolt the door."

I crossed the threshold and turned. "Good night, sir."

"Good night."

When he'd gone, I moved around the cottage lighting candles, then sat down at the table. I had work to do before bed, but at first I could only stare into the fire and think back over my evening with Mr. Rochester. He and I had grown more comfortable with one another, which was a tremendous relief. But it had gone further than that. I felt we had established a rapport. And he had shown a concern for my welfare that seemed to go beyond the surface.

I recalled how the muscle of his arm bunched beneath my hand as we walked. I recalled our fingers brushing as he took the stone. I recalled the hypnotic scent that had wafted over me in the hall.

*Jane, don't be a fool.*

Sighing, I took up my pen and forced my attention to my work. A key question had been answered this evening. Mr. Rochester had certainly cared for his wife, but as for love . . . *We hadn't the luxury of knowing one another well enough for that.* Though I couldn't allow him to speak for his wife. Agnes might know something of her mistress's feelings, and tomorrow I would find a way to ask her.

My thoughts turned to the "hobbyist" apothecary. It wasn't a word that inspired confidence, especially when connected to the dispensation of baneful herbs. Yet I hated even to consider the possibility of such a tragic accident—one that, if uncovered, could freshly inflict the pain of loss on the lady's family—and resolved to go into the interviews the following day with an open mind.

Once I had the evening's findings documented, I took a moment to scribble a few notes about the perfumed oil I hoped to create. It had properties that could make it effective for sleep disturbances and possibly dream travel. *And it will remind me of him when I'm gone.*

I snapped the notebook closed and got up to feed the fire and blow out most of the candles. Then I dressed for bed, brushing some loose soil and dry grass from the hem of my gown before returning it to the wardrobe.

I climbed under the quilts, careful not to disturb Sybil, who woke only long enough to slowly blink at me. Despite my resolve to banish such thoughts, the last thing that came to my mind before sleep was the keen attention in Mr. Rochester's gaze when I'd offered him the fairy stone.

I was not naturally an early riser, but morning prayers at Lowood had gotten me in the habit. Also Mr. Brocklehurst believed nothing wholesome could happen after evening prayers, so everyone generally retired by eight. I did sometimes sit up later at apothecary work or preparing lessons, and morning would come all the harder. Last night, I had sat up *much* later than usual, but Thornfield's rhythms were more forgiving, and I allowed myself to sleep in.

I had just completed my simple toilet when Agnes arrived to fetch me to breakfast with Mrs. Fairfax. The maid seemed uneasy again this morning and hardly spoke, but she still wore the leather cord around her neck.

I joined the housekeeper in her sitting room. Her pleasant table was set for two.

"Good morning, Miss Aire," she said, smiling kindly but looking weary. "I'm happy to see you. How are you adjusting?"

"Very well, ma'am, thank you."

"I'm pleased our troubles haven't frightened you away. Nor Mr. Rochester, which was just as likely."

I laughed. "No, ma'am. Mr. Rochester has been very kind."

"I'm glad to hear it. He's a good soul but can take some getting used to." She gestured to the table. "Won't you join me?"

We sat down to heaping plates of ham, eggs, and potatoes. Mrs. Fairfax poured cups of the excellent coffee, and I saw there was also a basket of scones with a saucer of blackberry jam. I could easily get used to eating like this.

"I hope you'll relay to the cook that her scones are heavenly," I said.

She brightened. "You'll have a chance to tell her yourself. I've made arrangements for you to interview the staff today."

"Ah, thank you," I replied, tipping cream into my coffee.

"May I let them know the nature of the questioning, to dispel any anxiety they might feel about meeting with a stranger?"

*Who also happens to be a witch.*

"I'm mostly interested in anything unusual or worrisome they may have seen but not reported to anyone. For example, Agnes mentioned to me that Thornfield's head groundskeeper had left the estate after seeing a ghost."

"A ghost!" Mrs. Fairfax stared. "Mr. Rochester told me Mr. Hatcher was retiring."

I frowned, but it didn't surprise me. "Perhaps he was uncomfortable giving the real reason to Mr. Rochester." Or perhaps Mr. Rochester was uncomfortable giving the real reason to his staff. "I hope there may be other stories we've not yet heard. Even small details and observations could be helpful."

"Yes, of course."

I could see she had received a shock. Pulling apart a scone, I took my time spreading jam over it, giving her a few moments to recover.

"I was very grateful for your help with the old thorn tree," she said finally. "Such a sad business. I hate to think anyone on the estate would do such a thing."

I eyed her, wondering how much I should say. Though she was elderly and kind, I didn't get the sense she was frail or easily shaken. And it had been her concern about Thornfield that had brought me here.

"There's more than you know, Mrs. Fairfax."

"Indeed?"

I told her about the dryad and the specter that had appeared after the blessing.

"How dreadful, Miss Aire! In all my years at Thornfield, I've never seen such a thing. I'm so glad you weren't harmed!"

"It was quite a shock, but I'm not sure that harm was intended."

Her brow furrowed. "What do you make of it, then?"

"I think it may have been a communication from the spirit world about what's amiss at Thornfield. I don't yet understand the message."

She let her gaze drift to the hearth, perhaps seeking comfort in the cheery blaze. But I judged she was weathering the new information well enough for me to continue.

"After performing the blessing, I spent some time in the herb garden. Someone has taken excellent care of it."

Her gaze returned, and she smiled. "I enjoy tending it when I can. The kitchen has its own garden, so it's not strictly necessary, but the cottage garden supplies herbs for cleaning as well as for my own humble cures."

"It contains a great many useful herbs and is also a very pleasant spot. If I lived at Thornfield, I think I might spend all my time in it."

We both laughed, lightening the mood.

"I also discovered the smaller garden in back of the cottage," I continued.

She frowned. "Do you mean the old apothecary garden?"

"I do. I hope I haven't gone against any orders you may have given in cutting back the roses and opening it up."

"No indeed. I had all but forgotten there was a gate on that side. It's a peculiar garden. Rarely tended or even visited. I fear you found it quite overgrown."

"It was rather, but that only added to its interest. I encountered Dr. Poole there, after he had attended Mr. Rochester."

It seemed to me that her expression darkened, though it was subtle. She reached for the coffeepot, but I took it up first. "Please let me." I filled both our cups.

"Thank you, dear," she said, adding cream and a lump of sugar. "The apothecary garden is a bit of a relic. I showed it to Dr. Poole when he was staying here, attending Mrs. Rochester. He hoped to formulate a tea that would relieve the lady's chest spasms at night, so she might sleep."

Belladonna could do that. Or henbane. The dosage would be critical.

"It surprises me you found him there," she said.

"Does it?"

"I wouldn't have thought . . ." She glanced out the window, which offered a view of the back lawn and the hills and heath beyond. The morning fog was clearing, penetrated here and there by streamers of pale-yellow light. "It's only that he seemed to be very fond of her. I wouldn't have thought he'd like to be reminded."

This was unexpected. The physician had not seemed much affected by my questions about Mrs. Rochester. He had remained professionally cool. But he *had* abruptly exited soon after I'd asked about her.

"He said he found the garden calming. Do you know if he did in fact use any of the plants?"

She gave a small shrug. "I'm afraid I don't. I wasn't directly involved in Mrs. Rochester's care." Then I caught a glint of dismay. "It was all right, wasn't it? Showing him the garden. Him being a physician, it never occurred to me . . ."

I quickly nodded. "Of course, Mrs. Fairfax. Please don't let my questions alarm you. I'm only trying to gather as much information as I can."

She raised an eyebrow. *Don't try pacifying an old lady,* her expression seemed to say. "You believe our troubles are related to Mrs. Rochester's death."

"Not with certainty. I have yet to learn of anything else that I might point to as a possible cause, but that could easily change after I've spoken with the servants."

This seemed to satisfy her. She lifted her coffee cup to her lips.

"You mentioned that Dr. Poole was fond of Mrs. Rochester?" I ventured.

She smiled, but I could see she was uneasy. "It did seem so to me. We all were, in fact. She was a sweet-tempered girl."

"He had been her family's physician?"

"I believe so, though he is too young to have been so for long."

I waited to see if she'd say more. Though even from my short acquaintance with Mrs. Fairfax, I thought it unlikely she would gossip about her former mistress.

"Dr. Poole had seemed quite . . ." She sat very still, thinking. "To me he seemed quite desperate to help her."

*Desperate* was an interesting word choice. Poole and his patient were closer in age than Mr. and Mrs. Rochester. They had a longer association, and because he was her physician, there would be a certain degree of intimacy. Might Dr. Poole have been more than "fond" of Antoinette Rochester? Desperation could cause a person to make mistakes.

"Has Mr. Rochester been able to help you at all?" asked the housekeeper, moving on from Dr. Poole.

"He *has* been helpful. His wife's death still seems to pain him a great deal."

She nodded. "Indeed, he hasn't been the same since it happened."

On the surface, this was hardly surprising. But the more I thought about it, the more I wondered. She had died more than a year ago. He hadn't known her well, or long, and professed not to be in love. I could understand a lingering regret, but why did it still weigh on him so heavily?

I could think of one thing to account for it. *Guilt.*

"Are you well, Miss Aire?"

I looked up.

"A dark cloud settled on your forehead for a moment," she said. "I hope this won't be too much for you, my dear. We live under a kind of pall here. I'm very glad to have you, of course, but I don't think it's healthy for a young person, so bright and full of life." She reached toward me and covered my hand with hers. "I hope you'll take care, Miss Aire."

"Thank you, Mrs. Fairfax, I will."

She squeezed my hand and rose from the table, and I started to do the same.

"You keep your seat," she said. "A maid will come to clear the dishes, and then I'll start the servants in to speak with you."

When she'd gone, the thought that had clouded my brow unfurled before me. Could *Mr. Rochester* be somehow responsible for his wife's death? He could be said to have one of the oldest motives in the world—a wife he wasn't attached to, whom he had married for her father's estate. Antoinette's death would not be required for her husband to inherit, of course, but it *had* freed him to marry someone he might like better.

I hardly knew him, yet I couldn't think it of him. He might feel responsible for his wife's death without having caused it. He might feel she would have lived had she not come to Thornfield. And he would certainly have questioned whether more could have been done to save her; at dinner he had hinted at dissatisfaction with her physicians. He might even feel guilty for not loving her.

All of it was enough, surely, to leave him a changed man.

# *The Lady's Maid*

When breakfast had been cleared away, the first of the servants came in—Thornfield's groom. The man was obviously frightened of me, and I had my work cut out for me putting him at ease. I asked him questions about his work and his children, keeping my manner as light as I could. It had been his boy who'd been chased by "a shadow" on his way home from Hay, but he couldn't tell me much besides his son having been badly frightened. Maybe Mrs. Fairfax could arrange an interview with the boy himself.

I spoke with two maids after that—one who had been very ill with fever in August and one who had been injured falling on the stairs. Mrs. Fairfax seemed to have first sent the servants who were known to have experienced troubling events on the estate. Even so, the only useful information that came out of these interviews was that the injured maid was certain someone had tripped her—"felt as if someone was grabbing at my skirt." She would no longer work alone on the upper floor. Neither of them had much to say on the matter of Dr. Poole and his patient, though I felt comfortable asking them only the vaguest of questions. They expressed their regret that their kind mistress had died so young and little else.

Next to join me was a familiar face.

"Good morning, Agnes," I said brightly as she came in.

"Morning, miss." She still looked uneasy, and I guessed she had been anxious about this interview.

"Come and sit down." I gestured to Mrs. Fairfax's chair. "How are you today?"

"Well enough, miss." She touched the charm hidden in her bodice—if indeed it was the charm—as she took her seat.

"I'm glad to hear it. We've already talked a bit about Thornfield's troubles, but I have a few other questions for you, all right?"

She adjusted herself in the chair. "Yes, miss."

"I know it saddens you to speak of your mistress, so I will try to keep that part of our discussion brief. As Mrs. Rochester's maid, you likely had some dealings with Dr. Poole?"

Pink bloomed in her cheeks. She nodded.

"Can you tell me about that?"

Shifting again in the chair, she said, "I took instructions about meals and special teas. Sometimes I helped the nurse with the mustard plasters."

I must remember to ask Mrs. Fairfax about the nurse. "Did you brew her medicines yourself or . . . ?"

Her chair was angled toward me, and I could see her fingers clenching together in her lap. "Dr. Poole would give me the herbs, and I would steep them."

"I see. Do you know which herbs he used?"

"Thyme was one; I know because Cook sometimes asks me to pick it from the kitchen garden. But I don't know as to the others."

"That's all right. Did Dr. Poole's therapies appear to help Mrs. Rochester?"

She thought about this. "At times they did. She slept better some nights. But mostly her coughing fits got worse."

I weighed my next words carefully, trying to sound as casually interested as possible. "How *was* Dr. Poole with Mrs. Rochester? Did he seem kind and attentive or stiff and impersonal? Gentle or hard?"

Agnes cleared her throat. "Gentle," she said, and her chin lifted slightly. "Kind and attentive, too, especially to her."

"Especially to her? I suppose you mean that because he was her physician and had known her for some time, they had a warm relationship?"

Agnes frowned. "I suppose so."

"Tell me if I've got it wrong," I said, smiling. "Sometimes I'm not as clever as I think I am."

She rubbed her lips together, thinking. There was something working its way out, if I could only stay out of its way.

"Well, 'course he'd be fond of her. Everyone was. Ill as she was, she was still so bonny and always spoke soft and kind."

Had I caught a note of resentment? Slight as a grain of salt in the sugar dish, but I felt sure it was there. Had Agnes been *jealous* of Antoinette Rochester? Dr. Poole was a handsome and, as far as I knew, unmarried gentleman. Yet the maid seemed genuinely devoted to her mistress.

"I don't know why Dr. Poole didn't send her down to London again," she went on. "There are all kind of doctors there, an't there? *Someone* might have done something for her."

Clear resentment this time. But as for my jealousy theory, this wasn't very complimentary of Dr. Poole.

"I understand from Mr. Rochester that it was his wife's wish to remain here," I said.

Agnes's face softened, and her eyes moistened. "Someone might have done something," she repeated quietly, "if he would've just let her go."

My heart, rabbitlike, gave a thump of alarm. "You think it was Mr. Rochester who didn't want her to go to London?"

Agnes frowned in confusion. "Dr. Poole."

*I've got it backward.* The insight struck me suddenly. Agnes was jealous of *Poole*.

"You grew very attached to your mistress in the time you were with her," I said in the gentlest voice possible.

Agnes's bottom lip quivered. "She was an angel from heaven, miss. It was a terrible shame what happened to her."

"Indeed it was. You seem to wish Dr. Poole had made different decisions about her care."

She swiped a tear from her cheek, and her features tightened. "I'm no one to say, miss."

"Well, no, I understand that. What I meant is that it's very hard to lose someone we care about, and it can make us second-guess. I know Mr. Rochester wishes Dr. Poole had been able to do more for her."

Agnes's gaze drifted to the vase of lavender in the center of the table. "I suppose he wouldn't have liked her being away, in case she got worse and he didn't see her again. But that was selfish of him, wasn't it?"

"Do you mean Mr. Rochester?" By this point, I knew she didn't.

She looked at me. "Dr. Poole."

*Poole was in love with Antoinette.*

Taking a long breath, I lifted a pitcher of water from the table, filled an empty glass, and pushed it toward her. She picked it up and drank, then curled a hand around it and held it against her chest.

"We can move away from that now, Agnes. Thank you for answering my questions. I have only one more thing to ask you. When we first met, I got the feeling that you had seen something at Thornfield that frightened you. I know such things are hard to talk about, but it is exactly the kind of information I need if I'm to be of any help here. Will you tell me what you saw?"

Agnes's features went chalky. Despite her naturally pale complexion, it wasn't subtle. She took another sip of water and set the glass on the table with trembling fingers.

"One day last week, I was walking through the hawthorn wood at eventide, and I heard a woman singing."

I waited for more but in vain. "One of the other maids?" I prompted.

"No, miss. It started out a sweet voice, the sweetest voice there ever was. But then . . . well, the voice went harsh and . . . and sort of crackling."

She closed her mouth. Her whole face closed up. *Full stop.*

I forged on. "Could you make out any of the words?"

She raised her hand to her charm. "I'll not repeat them for anything. Not one of them."

Well this was a new puzzle, likely an important one. "You're certain it wasn't anyone you—"

"No, miss. No one who would speak like that." She sniffed and sat up. "I've work to do, miss. May I go now?"

I could tell it would be useless to press her, and it might even risk the ground we'd gained. I'd have to wait to make another attempt.

"You may. Just tell me where I may find the hawthorn wood."

Her eyes widened, but she said, "It's just beyond the drive, between the groom's lodge and the orchard."

"Thank you for your help, Agnes."

As she was going out, one of the maids from the earlier interviews came in with tea and bread and butter. She conveyed from Mrs. Fairfax that there would be no more interviews until the afternoon. I would have two hours to myself, which would give me time to see more of the grounds and think over all I'd heard.

We'd been blessed with another golden autumn day, the kind that makes you almost prefer it to midsummer. An invigorating freshness to the air, the smell of a cider press somewhere on the grounds, and the lovely burnished leaves. As I strolled down the drive toward the iron gates, I made up my mind that Thornfield was a charming old estate, despite the spiritual pall that currently hung over it. It might even be this contradiction that captivated me—and made me all the more determined to unravel the mystery.

I stopped on the drive and turned, taking in the manor itself for the first time in daylight. Stern gray facade and battlements whose lines had been softened by time, as well as by shrub, moss, and vine. The many rosebushes that cozied up to it, fading now, but still dotted with the occasional bloom of coral, red, yellow, or white—bright pops of color against the dark stone. The fiery autumn foliage surrounding the property and the busy rookery to the north.

As I stood feeling the warmth of the sun on my face, my thoughts returned to Mrs. Fairfax's sitting room and the interview with Agnes. I felt sure now that there had been something between Dr. Poole and Mrs. Rochester. An illicit love, even if never acted upon, could be a reason for Mrs. Rochester's spirit to rest uneasily. Of course, it might have been one-sided, but then there was still the question of whether Dr. Poole's desperation to save the woman he loved had accidentally caused her death.

Yet I had no more evidence against Poole than I did against Mr. Rochester. And if I believed Mr. Rochester less likely to have had any connection to his wife's death, it was only because I liked him.

*There. Best to be honest with oneself.*

Also best not to put the cart before the horse. I had yet to even confirm there *was* a haunting at Thornfield. Though there had certainly been ghostlike activity, no one claimed to have seen the specter of Antoinette Rochester. Only the former groundskeeper was believed, at least by Agnes, to have actually seen a ghost.

But Agnes herself—*she* had heard something that disturbed her so much that she would hardly talk about it. From where I now stood, I could see the groom's lodge and the hawthorn wood she'd spoken of. I thought about the singing she'd described, and something suddenly came to me.

*The sweetest voice there ever was.*

This phrasing—both the wording and reverential tone—reminded me of the way Agnes talked about Mrs. Rochester. In fact, the maid had said something very similar about her mistress yesterday.

*The kindest there ever was.*

Had Agnes recognized the voice in the woods as that of Mrs. Rochester and been unwilling to say so? I remembered how she'd said the song turned dark and then refused to repeat the words. *She doesn't want to believe it was her mistress.*

I would have to question her again the next time she came to the cottage. Maybe the privacy there would make her more comfortable sharing her secret. In the meantime, I could see the hawthorn wood for myself.

As I was stepping off the drive, something made me glance back at the house. I saw Mr. Rochester walking on the path that led around the north wing toward the cottage. It reminded me of his final words to me last night.

*If you feel you must embark on another dangerous adventure, for heaven's sake come to me first.*

"Looking for a ghost" was likely to fall squarely into the category of "dangerous adventures" as far as my employer was concerned, so I thought it best to follow and speak to him. He also might very well be on his way to see me.

He had a long, quick stride, and I hurried to catch up with him. He disappeared from view as he took the turn into the herb garden. I almost called out but decided he might not approve of an employee shouting after him. If he was going to the cottage, we'd meet up soon enough.

As I followed him into the garden, I was disappointed to see him continuing on to the orchard through the arch in the garden's north wall. Apparently, his errand had nothing to do with me.

At this point, I decided I might as well go back to the cottage to make notes about my morning interviews and save the visit to the hawthorn wood for later.

But that's not what I did.

# *Stones*

I couldn't have said why I followed him. Simple curiosity or the impulse of the moment. *Trust your instincts.*

I had every intention of making my presence known, but he walked purposefully and with a preoccupied air. I hesitated to the point that it became awkward. What reason could I give for intruding on his privacy? The only sensible course was to turn back. Yet still I followed.

The estate's orchard had a fine collection of storybook apple trees, leaves burnished red and gold by the changing season. The heavy-sweet, slightly alcoholic aroma of past-ripe fruit filled the air. Mr. Rochester's brisk footsteps hissed through the leaves that had fallen along the path, covering the smaller sounds I made as I walked—scurrying steps, followed by waiting and watching. Periodically, a crow or squirrel scolded him for his intrusion. Me, they thankfully ignored, perhaps deeming one warning sufficient for the pair of us.

At the outer boundary of the orchard, we passed through another arch and entered a wilderness of fine, stately old oaks. Had I come here on my own, I would have gathered acorns and hen-of-the-woods mushrooms. I would have run my fingers over the emerald moss that covered the great rounded stones. I would have used my hagstone to try to peek beyond the veil. An oak wood as old as this would be home to fairy creatures and probably spirits even more ancient.

It was easier to keep out of sight in this denser wood. Light had dappled the ground around the apple trees, but here only an occasional bright beam penetrated the canopy. After a few minutes of walking, patches of low fog began to drift among the trees, making the forest feel even more close and secretive. Through a small opening in the foliage, I saw that dense clouds had replaced blue sky. If the fog continued to thicken, I might have difficulty finding my way back to the house.

To my relief, after a few more minutes Mr. Rochester slowed, and I saw a church rising from the mist in a clearing ahead of us. The structure looked roughly the same age as the cottage. It was small, square, and mostly intact, but as we drew closer, I saw the bell tower had partially collapsed, and the great rusty bell lay on its side in the weeds.

My employer bypassed the church and continued toward the grounds in back. With my heart racing, I hurried into the cover of the small porch. When I dared to peek out, I saw he'd gone into the graveyard—ragged rows of lichen-covered headstones overgrown with meadow flowers and grasses. He followed a faint path toward the back of the yard, where a great yew tree held court. I dared not follow him at this point, as there was no place for me to hide.

I shuddered to think what Mr. B would have to say if he could see me now.

On entering the porch, I'd noticed the top hinge of the church's door had given way, and it sagged partway open. Now I turned and looked inside—room enough for about forty people to attend service, though the pews were falling to ruin, and there was a hole in the roof. Moreover, an *apple tree* had taken root among the broken flagstones right in front of the pulpit, and a blue tit chirped in the branches. I smiled despite my self-inflicted peril; it was a half-wild, magical place.

This was likely an ancestral church and burial ground; I envied Mr. Rochester this connection to his past and his people.

I turned again to gaze out of the porch. My employer was standing at the far side of the graveyard with his back to me. Hands folded behind him, he intently stared at something—a grave marker, I presumed, most likely his wife's. If I hadn't felt the rudeness of my curiosity before, I certainly did now. Who was I to intrude on such a moment?

*The person hired to discover the cause of an apparent haunting.*

Maybe I was justified, but it didn't ease my guilt.

As I considered again whether it wouldn't be best to show myself and beg forgiveness, he slowly turned in my direction and began retracing his steps. Sucking in a breath, I pressed against the wall of the porch. A drop of sweat slipped down between my shoulder blades. I could imagine nothing worse than for him to find me here spying on him. The shame of it. The consequences for Lowood. Every extreme outcome flashed before my mind's eye.

Then he passed without slowing. The sound of his footsteps faded into the forest, and I let out a sigh.

Looking out again to make sure he'd truly gone, I left the safety of the porch and took his path to the back of the graveyard. Witnessing him paying respect to the lady who'd briefly been his wife was important in its own right, but now that I was here, it would be foolish to go without seeing her grave.

Passing the old headstones, I found a row of newer ones in the back. It was easy to see where Mr. Rochester had stood by the depressions in the damp grass. Placing my feet in the same spot, I read the inscription on the stone before me—and found I was not as clever as I thought. Marion Fairfax Rochester, 1788–1823. By the name and birth year, very likely his mother. Only thirty-five years old when she died.

To the right of her stone stood one for Cora Grace Rochester, 1810–1812. Mr. Rochester's sister? Had she lived, she would now be thirty-seven years old. And that wasn't all. Next to Cora was a stone for Evelyn Anne Rochester, 1823–1823. The fact Evelyn had been born and died the same year her mother passed suggested they both died during the birth. On the other side of Marion was Osborne Edward

Rochester, likely her husband, who died less than a decade after his wife and youngest daughter, at the age of fifty-one.

This was a story of heartache. Everyone in Mr. Rochester's family had died before their time, especially the females. Then his wife had done the same.

I glanced around, looking for her stone. A light-colored monument caught my eye, rising against the dark-red yew columns at the back of the yard. I made my way toward it. The small mausoleum, gothic in style but clearly quite new, stood out starkly and struck me as unlike Mr. Rochester. Drawing closer, I saw the marker—Antoinette Mason Rochester, 1828–1846. Had he attempted to make up to his wife for her tragically short life by commissioning it? Or maybe it had been her family's idea. I wondered whether Mr. Rochester intended to be buried with her or with the other members of his family. Perhaps he might marry again.

*Would I, with his history?*

Keenly feeling the weight of this sorrow, I let out a sigh and looked past the grave to the great yew. Its long roots curled along the ground like tentacles, reaching toward the monument. Yews, long associated with death and rebirth, were often found in churchyards. This one gave me a shiver, and I couldn't bring myself to raise my hagstone for a better look. The tree's spirit would be ancient and venerable, and it probably wouldn't take kindly to me nosing about.

I was turning to go when something caught my eye. A few feet away from the mausoleum, a penknife lay on the ground, pearl handle bright against the dry yew needles. A good-quality knife, probably Mr. Rochester's. I moved closer and knelt for a better look. The knife was open, and red-brown rust marred the blade. If he'd dropped it, it hadn't been today. I reached to pick it up, but a hard chill ran up my arm to the back of my neck and I jerked my hand away.

My sudden aversion to touching it made me wonder whether it had been left intentionally, perhaps as an offering. To interfere with such things was to invite trouble. A knife seemed an unusual item to leave for a woman, and I would expect to find it closer to the monument. But I could think of no other explanation for my reaction.

I noticed a sudden heaviness to the atmosphere, and I stood up and looked around. Dark clouds crowded the sky, and all sound and movement had ceased. Small birds harvesting seeds among the grasses had flown, as if sensing a coming storm. The gravestones began to feel like figures gathering around me in the mist, bearing witness to my intrusion. The shadow beneath the yew deepened, and it tugged at me, as if beckoning me to another world.

*The melancholy of the place is getting to me.*

I turned my back on the tree and the monument and started toward the church. Quick steps carried me past the porch where I'd hidden, and by the time I reached the forest path, I was almost running.

As I put distance between myself and the churchyard, my sense of dread gradually eased. I slowed my pace so I wouldn't overtake Mr. Rochester. The atmosphere remained unusually still, though. No breeze stirred the dry leaves, and no crows or squirrels harassed me. Nothing but the sound of my own boots crunching acorns.

Nearing the orchard, I paused for a moment to listen to the silence. Instead, I heard an echo of the same crunching sound that my feet had been making.

Mr. Rochester up ahead? No, the sound was coming from behind me.

I turned to look, and the crunching *stopped*. Heart thumping, I scanned the path and the trees to either side. But the mist had thickened in my wake.

"Who's there?" I called faintly.

A slight sound came through the dead silence. A bare whisper—or more of a rustle. *The swish of a woman's skirt.*

Dread seized me. Lifting the hem of my dress, I murmured a protective spell and I *ran*.

I'd run halfway through the orchard before reason overtook me—mightn't I be running from the very thing I was hoping to find?

Forcing myself to stop, I turned and raised the hagstone. I almost called out again but remembered Mr. Rochester might be close.

No one appeared, corporeal or otherwise. It was impossible not to feel relief. I may have missed an opportunity, but if the footsteps behind me *had* belonged to a spirit, confronting her while alone and so far from the manor was not a thing I would advise anyone else to do. I could easily imagine what Maria—or Mr. Rochester—would have to say.

As I drew closer to the arch between the orchard and garden, my panic further receded. The mist was already clearing, and the clouds looked like they might break. Changeable weather was one of my favorite things about this time of year, yet the events of the last quarter hour had a supernatural feel, and they had shaken me. I was relieved to be almost back to the cottage.

*A strong cup of tea is in order.*

My thoughts returned to the family graves, and my heart went out to the master of Thornfield. I often pitied myself for my lack of relations. How painful must it be to have and then lose them all? I wondered what had made him want to visit them today. At least I now knew the full cause of his melancholy.

Safely back on the grounds, I immediately began to question what I thought I had heard in the woods. The simplest explanations were usually the right ones, and there was no reason to assume the steps had belonged to a ghost rather than another person—one of the staff or possibly a tenant. (*Would* a ghost in fact crunch acorns?) Likely I had been affected by the stories I'd heard from the servants today.

On the stoop of the cottage, I checked my pocket watch—still nearly an hour until I must return to the house. That gave me time to write out my account of the day so far. Or, probably, to visit the hawthorn wood. Feeling foolish for letting my imagination run away with me (quite literally), I thought I could safely visit the place on my own, just to get a sense of it. Like fairies and other elemental creatures, I had always been drawn to hawthorns, and in observing the wood from the drive I'd guessed it to be very old.

As I hesitated, the sun did finally burn a hole through the clouds, brightening the day again. That decided me—a quick visit, and then after I'd spoken with Agnes again, Mr. Rochester and I could return there together. I stepped into the cottage for my staff—no reason to go unprepared—and started back toward the front of the house.

# *Interlude*

## *(Rochester)*

Slipping a hand into my jacket pocket, I drew out the stone.

*I hoped you might carry it for protection.*

An ordinary river stone, yet it rested perfectly in the palm of my hand and had a pleasing smoothness and weight. Did the stone and the woman share some connection? Maybe it had drawn her to me as I'd left the grounds.

*I have an inquiring and independent nature.*

I smiled.

She'd hardly made a sound, but somehow I'd felt her there. And I should have said something, of course. I put her in a very awkward position, knowing she ought to reveal herself, probably arguing with herself the whole way. But if I'd spoken to her . . . I could imagine her cringing, apologizing, and returning to the house, ashamed of that native (and rather endearing) curiosity.

*I want no more of that.*

In truth, I'd been glad of the company. I'd liked showing her, if only indirectly, the oak forest and the picturesque ruin of the church where my ancestors lay, with its melancholy beauty. Earlier that day, I'd glimpsed her from a window as she studied the house from the drive, and I thought I saw in her face an appreciation for the old place.

If we'd truly walked together, there were stories I could have told her. Less grim stories than the ones the gravestones told. Like how the old church bell had been rung for every birth at Thornfield, and how people had continued to hear it ring even after the tower fell.

Foolhardy to regret something I could never have permitted myself to do—escorting her alone into the woods, regaling her with family lore. If only I had met her under any other circumstances than as a paid employee of my estate.

*To what purpose, Rochester?*

To what purpose, indeed. It was the reason I'd gone to the graveyard in the first place—to root out any nonsensical ideas that had seeded in my brain the night I met her on the road. Because I was certain now that the estate was under some kind of curse—and *had* been, long before the death of Antoinette. No female of my family had survived, and I wasn't about to let my thoughts wander in any direction that might result in the installation of another one on the estate.

No matter how intriguing.

No matter how kind.

No matter how lovely.

There came a tap on the door of the study.

"Come."

Mrs. Fairfax stepped in. "Pardon the interruption, sir. You haven't seen Miss Aire, have you?"

My breath caught at the worry in her face. Miss Aire was safely back, wasn't she? I'd waited near the garden until I'd seen her return.

"No more than half an hour ago," I said. "Why, is she overdue?"

"Not exactly. But Agnes has told me she saw her go into the hawthorn wood alone, and it seemed to trouble her. I don't exactly like the idea myself, what with all the . . . goings-on."

Out the window, I could see the threatening clouds had withdrawn, and the day was once again golden and fine—hardly the kind of day for giving in to morbid presentiments. Yet I couldn't help feeling the danger around my witch was growing.

I rose from the desk. "Quite right. I shall find her."

# “My Own Wee Thing”

The hawthorn wood was everything I had expected as I’d viewed it from the drive that morning. Some of the trees had trunks wider than a carriage wheel—no doubt the reason the estate had been called Thornfield. I had seen ancient hawthorns before, but never a whole forest of them. I moved carefully among the trunks, avoiding shrubby branches with their long thorns. Some folk referred to thorns as witch trees; their twisting trunks and branches made them resemble crooked crones.

There were mossy boulders scattered about, and under the largest of the trees, I found a flat-topped stone that would make an excellent sit spot. Raising my hagstone, I first checked the area for otherworldly inhabitants. Though I couldn’t see any, I made a small offering—a couple of stanzas of a poem Maria and I required first-year students to memorize.

“Ancient oak, ash, and thorn,
Out of these was magic born.
Rowan, elder, apple too,
Hazel, birch, and also yew.

“’Tis the thorn tree folk most fear;
You see her when a sprite is near.
Blossom sweet and berry sour,
These will feed a witch’s power.”

I sat down on the stone and closed my eyes. I could feel the hum of magic—in my mind, but also in small vibrations that traveled from the tip of my staff to my hands. I listened to the birds hunting the bright-red berries among the yellow foliage—the papery movement of dry leaves. The birds and I were not alone. Such an ancient glade would be peopled with fairies, especially at twilight. Did a ghost wander here as well?

*Why would Agnes come here?*

Why indeed. If she had business at the lodge, she would walk down the drive. She might be able to pass from the lodge to the orchard through this wood—a path I'd crossed in the orchard had led off in this direction—and it was conceivable her duties might send her there. But alone, at night?

Maybe she wasn't alone.

What if Agnes had glimpsed a figure like Mrs. Rochester slipping into the trees? Would she have followed?

Something small struck the top of my head—a hawthorn berry, likely disturbed by a bird in the thicket of branches above me. They littered the ground all around. But then I heard . . .

*Meow.*

Looking up, I smiled. "How long have *you* been up there?" Sybil was moving stealthily among the leaves. Another berry plunked down, this one landing in my lap.

She made her way down to a V in the trunk and crouched there, staring at me, tail twitching. Her green eyes were bright like lanterns.

"What is it?"

Her tail continued to twitch, and I worried we weren't alone. I stood up and looked again through the hagstone at the trees around us but could see nothing unusual.

Until my gaze came back to Sybil. Through the hagstone, suddenly there was no cat. A *fairy* crouched in the V above me—*the fairy woman from my dreams.*

Gasping, I stepped back, and I lost my grip on the hagstone. As it slipped from my eye, the fairy vanished and Sybil reappeared.

*Sybil* is *the fairy.*

A strong sense of unreality flooded me. I looked again through the stone. Like the dryad of the previous morning, this fairy had pale-green skin with leaflike veins running beneath. Her hair was a vivid red, like the fruit of the hawthorn tree, hanging loose in waves and adorned with coils of threaded dried hawthorn berry, much darker in color. She wore a diaphanous white-and-gold gown that, when I looked closer, I discovered was made of blossoms. She had thin limbs and pointy features—nose, chin, elbows, fingers. *Thorny.* Her ears curved up and out of her hair.

Clear, detailed, and not at all dreamlike.

What did this mean?

The creature stared at me, unmoving, from her perch. Having no idea of the proper way to address a dryad who had been visiting my dreams and masquerading as a witch's familiar, I curtsied and said, "Thank you for your protection, lady."

The sound of her voice, when it came, was a stream of light, staccato sounds that made me think of spring rain on green leaves. "Something unnatural walks this ground."

My breath caught. "You have seen this unnatural thing, lady?" As Sybil, she had certainly sensed things that I hadn't as she followed me on the grounds. Now I had a wholly unexpected opportunity to ask her about them.

The dryad gazed up into her tree, head nodding atop the long, slender neck.

"Do you know what it is?"

Her eyes—the same color as the cat's, the light, bright green of new leaves—came back to my face. "A thing that should not be."

Fairies were notoriously difficult to understand. The fact that this one was also a cat—well, that only complicated matters. I wondered whether I'd get any clear answers from her.

"Is anyone in danger?" I asked.

She blinked at me. "Is anyone not?"

*I suppose that's clear enough.*

What I most wanted to know was whether this "thing" was the ghost of Antoinette Rochester, but my hunch was that such a question would get me nowhere and might be a waste of a limited opportunity.

"The unnatural thing," I began carefully, "is it somehow related to what happened to the blackthorn tree and its dryad?"

The lady brushed a fingertip against a bright berry on a branch above her. "A fairy spoils a bucket. A devil spoils the cow."

This I had to think about. I supposed she meant that a fairy might spoil a bucket of milk, while a devil could lame or sicken the cow. Which, during the burning times, was a crime that those accused of witchcraft were often charged with.

Could she be trying to warn me that the unnatural thing was more dire than an offended fairy? A thing that was spoiling *Thornfield*?

"Thank you, lady," I replied earnestly. "Is there anything else you can tell me?"

She eyed me through half-lowered lids, like Sybil when she was napping. "I have made thee."

I stared. I had been too broad in my question, and we seemed to have left the topic of Thornfield's ghost.

"I'm sorry—I don't understand."

"Child of thorn," she continued, gently plucking a yellow leaf from the tree. "Conceived beside the first flame of summer."

Was it a story of some kind? Perhaps *her* story—"child of thorn" could be a poetic way of referring to herself. "The first flame of summer" was vague enough, but it might be a reference to bonfire night—May Day, an old rite of the first day of summer. Beltane was the Celtic version of the celebration that, like Maria Temple, had drifted into Lancashire from Scotland. Maria and I and my students observed it quietly, forbidden from any official celebration.

"Do you mean to say you were conceived on bonfire night, lady?" It was an odd personal detail to share. But again, *fairy*.

The lady's lips curved down in a frown. She raised a thin red eyebrow. "*I* have made *thee*."

She seemed to mean *me*—which made no sense. Was it some kind of trick?

"You don't mean to say that *I* was conceived at Beltane? You don't mean to say that you're . . ." I could hardly bring myself to say it. "That you're my *mother*?"

She smiled.

My head spun, and I leaned on my staff. Beltane celebrated the fertile season, and children were not an uncommon result of the revels around the bonfire. It was also a time when the veil thinned—when mortals and fairies might intermingle.

*And I am an orphan of unknown origin.*

Yet the child of a *fairy*?

The dryad climbed gracefully down from the tree and sank onto the stone, where I'd sat earlier. Her body was never truly still. Her fingers moved against surfaces, or her eyes followed birds in the branches.

I opened my mouth, but what question could I possibly ask that might result in clarity? She seemed only able to communicate with me in a roundabout way.

"My own wee thing," she said in the rain-shower voice. "Tried and tried, but it refused to be content. Refused!" Resentment flashed in her eyes. "No berry, no nectar could stop the wailing." She squeezed her eyes closed and put her hands over her ears.

I could do nothing but stare at her, jaw slack. Her eyes opened again and moved over me. "Too much like *he*. Salt and clay. I could not keep thee."

"He?" I tried to swallow, but my mouth felt full of dry leaves. "Do you mean my father?"

She frowned. "Brown."

"Is—is that his name?"

She took hold of a lock of her hair, then closed one eye and widened the other, giving me a look of extreme annoyance. "Dirt. Brown."

Brown hair, brown eyes. *Like mine.*

My pulse pounded in my ears. "Where is he?" I asked faintly.

She stood up and climbed back into the tree.

"In the place where he abides. In the place where my sisters left thee."

*Where my sisters left thee.* Lowood? I had indeed been left there, by a person no one had seen. There were only two men at Lowood who had been there since I was a babe—our ancient driver and . . .

Mr. Brocklehurst, who had brown hair and brown eyes. Mr. Brocklehurst, who grew up near Thornfield.

*It cannot be.*

My vision swam, and I dropped the hagstone. My body felt light and heavy at the same time.

And then I felt nothing.

# *Protective Impulses*

"Miss Aire!" The voice revived me. A familiar scent filled my nostrils. *Rosemary, lavender, leather.*

"Miss Aire, can you hear me?"

"Yes, sir."

I was awake and clearheaded now—possibly more than I ever had been. My head and shoulders were cradled in Mr. Rochester's arms. He bent over me, his gaze close and anxious.

Light, staccato laughter sounded nearby, then moved away through the trees.

Mr. Rochester glanced up and called out, "Who's there?"

"You hear her too?"

His eyes came back to my face; his expression was bleak. "Who is it?" he asked in a low voice.

*Not a dream, then. But is it* real*? Is it* true*?*

"Miss Aire, please tell me."

I pulled myself back to the moment and my employer's grave countenance.

"It was no ghost, sir," I assured him. "Help me stand, and I'll try to explain."

His hand gently squeezed my arm, causing my breath to catch. "You've fainted. Just rest a moment."

I was mortally ashamed of the swoon, yet the position I now found myself in—well, I wasn't overeager to leave it. The nearness of him flooded my senses. His smell, his voice, his arms around me. The *warmth* of him. I felt as if my insides had all gone to honey.

"I've never fainted before," I forced out at last, "and I assure you it won't happen again. I've just had a shock."

He studied my face, then supported me in sitting up. "How is that?"

I nodded, but my vision went splotchy, and I placed my hands next to me on the ground.

"There's no hurry," he said. "Try to take some deep breaths."

I did, and it helped. But it also brought back every detail of my conversation with the dryad, and soon I was trembling.

He took off his jacket and helped me put it on. *Wearing* his warmth and his scent now, it almost felt like an embrace.

"Something has clearly frightened you," he said.

"No, sir, not exactly. Just something—something altogether unexpected has happened. I haven't quite taken it in."

Accepting this for the moment, he said, "Do you feel ready to stand?"

"I think so."

He stood up first, then bent to take my hands, pulling me to my feet. He kept hold of me, watching me closely. "All right?"

"Indeed, I am well. I'm so sorry for the trouble."

He released my hands. "What you *should* be apologizing for is defying my orders," he said in his brusquer, more usual tone. "But we'll leave that for later. I'll walk with you back to the cottage, and maybe by the time we get there, you'll be ready to talk to me."

"Yes, sir."

But *how*? How was I to speak to him of this? It was extraordinary and strange and also very personal. I still had many questions and no one to ask. If what I'd been told was true—and I began to feel it might be—I was no orphan, not in any sense of the word. I needed more time to take it in and to decide what, if anything, I was to do with this information.

Could the moralizing Mr. Brocklehurst really have *produced a child* with a fairy? Why had he never told me he was my father? Why had he in fact *lied* to me about who I was?

*Maybe he didn't know.*

Mr. Rochester started toward the drive, and I said, "Might we walk through the woods, sir?" I wasn't ready to face Mrs. Fairfax, nor anyone else at the house.

He opened his mouth, probably to deny me, but hesitated. At last he said, "If you wish. But the path is rough. Take my arm."

Bending first to pick up my staff, I took his arm with the other hand. He pressed his hand over mine to steady me as we made our way. These protective impulses—they were perhaps common among gentlemen, yet wholly outside my experience. They made me feel that I was in his care. I was surprised to find that not only did this feeling not annoy me, I *liked* it. Would his manner toward me change if I were to tell him all?

*Not an orphan but illegitimate, and not even wholly human.*

Again I shivered, drawing his eyes back to my face.

"How did you come to find me, sir?" I asked, hoping to delay his questions.

We stepped over a fallen limb and then bent away from a low branch. A few leaves fluttered down around us. He reached and removed one from my hair.

"Mrs. Fairfax was worried about you," he said. "You had been seen going alone into the woods."

"It was kind of her to worry, and of *you* to come."

"It *was* kind of me, considering you were specifically asked not to venture out onto the grounds on your own."

"Respectfully, sir, what you asked me to do was come to you if I intended to embark on any 'dangerous adventures.'"

His keen eyes fixed on me. "Did you happen to notice the size of the stone you would have struck your head upon had I not arrived in time to break your fall?"

I composed my face into what I hoped was an expression of contrition. "Your point is taken, sir, and I thank you again."

The thorn wood path did indeed lead to an orchard entrance. As we passed through, a crow cawed overhead, gliding toward the rookery. It startled a mouse, sending it skittering through the dry leaves.

I'd almost forgotten that no more than an hour ago, I had skulked after Mr. Rochester here; I felt a stab of guilt.

"Can you now tell me what you saw in the woods, Miss Aire?"

I took a deep breath and met his gaze. "I met a dryad—a living one. We spoke at some length."

Surprise replaced anxiety in his expression. Though he said, "I almost hate to ask what she told you that caused you to faint."

I shifted my eyes to the path. What was I to say to him? I didn't think I could bring myself to tell him the truth. At least not while I was still reeling from it. Maybe not ever. I tried to think what counsel Maria would give.

*Tell him as much of the truth as you can.*

"The dryad did tell me something about Thornfield, but that wasn't what gave me the shock. *That* was of a very personal nature. I know as my employer, and as the master of this estate, you are within your rights to ask me, but I hope that you won't. At least not until I've had time to try to understand it myself."

We reached the herb garden, and Mr. Rochester guided me toward the well, where there was an old stone bench, cushioned by moss and bookended by elder bushes. A few clusters of shiny black berries remained. We sat down, startling a thrush from its meal. The sun was still shining, making it a lovely and warm spot to linger. But I was uneasy about the conversation to come.

Finally Mr. Rochester said, "I must say you've made me very curious, but of course I'd not want to intrude on your personal business." Then came another pang about my clandestine visit to the graveyard. "May I know why you went to the wood and what you heard about Thornfield?"

"Yes, of course." Though I didn't exactly have good news to deliver, it was at least progress. "This morning, one of the maids told me that on a recent evening, she heard someone singing in the hawthorn wood and it frightened her."

He raised an eyebrow. "So, naturally, your first thought was to go into the woods looking for this spectral singer."

I flushed. "Not exactly, sir, I . . ." *Actually, yes exactly.*

"Quite. Did the maid have an idea of who the singer might be?"

"She said not, but . . ."

"You think it was Antoinette."

"I have reason to believe so, yes." Then rather timidly, I asked, "*Did* Mrs. Rochester sing?"

His head turned, gaze drifting toward the well. "She did."

"The maid said the voice was the sweetest she'd ever heard. Would you say your wife's voice was sweet?"

He gave a single nod. "As an angel's."

Something tightened in my chest. Again I found myself trying to see behind a carefully controlled expression.

"As evidence goes," I said, "I know it's by no means conclusive. But when I entered the wood and encountered the dryad, she warned me that something dangerous—something *unnatural*—was wandering on the estate."

"And did *she* say it was the ghost of my wife?"

"No, sir. But fairies speak in riddles, and for the most part, they don't take an interest in mortals. My attempts to clarify her revelations were not very fruitful." *To put it mildly.*

I followed his gaze to the well and noticed a large snail making a slow, precarious journey across the pole suspended over the hole.

"Let us say for the sake of argument it *was* Antoinette," he said finally. "I simply cannot understand why her spirit would be a danger to anyone at Thornfield."

How I wanted to tell him all I knew—about my conversations with Dr. Poole and with Agnes, and about my theories. Yet I felt it would be wrong to call the physician's actions into question at this stage or to reveal a possible attachment between Poole and Antoinette. It would only cause pain, and possibly conflict.

"I think I mentioned last night that a spirit who continues to walk the earth after death can become corrupt," I said. "That's especially true if the person believed they were wronged in some way in life. They may become angry, even vengeful."

"Wronged in *what* way? She was given everything she needed or desired. Everyone was kind to her—doted on her, in fact. I cannot think of a single person who did not love her."

"A person can wrong another without intending to," I said quietly. "Please forgive me, sir, but I dare not say more until I *know* more."

He looked at me. "What you mean is you *will* not. I have come to know you, Miss Aire, and I know that you're hiding some theory."

"I must beg your patience. I need to feel that I can consider all possibilities without seeming to accuse anyone."

*"Accuse?"* He looked truly shocked, and I regretted my word choice. "You can't possibly suspect her death might not have been a natural one. I assure you it came as no surprise to anyone. We all knew she was very ill."

"I know that, sir. Understand—I don't suggest that her life was *put* to an end."

"I should hope not!"

"With that said, I haven't ruled out some accident or mistake in her care that could have precipitated her death." I let out a sigh. "Now I've said more than I'd like to, having had so little time for investigation."

Slowly, he filled his chest with air, and as he exhaled, the lines of his face began to soften into weariness.

"What will you do next?"

Some of the tension seeped out of me, too, and I unclenched my hands. "I will return to the thorn wood to search for the singer. Tonight, if possible."

"And if you find her?"

"I'll speak to her. Try to find out what happened."

He nodded. "I shall go with you, of course."

I had suspected he would insist on going. I was glad, though he might end up hearing things he wouldn't like. It would be reckless to go alone, and I knew of no one else. Agnes wasn't up to it, and though Mrs. Fairfax was hale enough, I feared that dealing with an embittered, ghostly version of the late mistress of Thornfield might be too much even for her.

But if he was to accompany me, it must be on my terms. "Very well, sir. On one condition."

"Condition!" He glowered.

"If we find her, you must let me do my work. You are there to observe, not to interfere or to protect. And you must do whatever I say."

My heart fell out of rhythm while he continued to glower at me, but then I caught glints of amusement in his eyes. "That is *two* conditions, but I submit. When do we go?"

"Midnight will be best. Spirits are freer to roam in the between times."

"You are terrifying, Mistress Jane—do you know that?"

# *Intertwined*

*Mistress Jane?* The sudden familiar address—I might truthfully say *fond* address—charged the air between us and knocked my poor heart out of rhythm again.

"Terrifying?"

His gray eyes were now bright with mischief. "Wholly. Are your pupils frightened of you?"

Even I, inexperienced at this sort of banter, knew he was playing with me. Yet not unkindly. I straightened and replied, "Only when I want them to be, sir."

His easy laughter transformed his face, softening the lines, drawing color into his pale skin, and making his eyes dance. At some point I would leave Thornfield, and when I looked back, I knew this was how I'd remember him. Not as the thorny gentleman in black. It surprised me how this weighed on my heart.

*Heaven help me, he's becoming dear to me.*

As the thought presented itself, our eyes met. His mirth faded, but his smile remained. Our gazes held, and I felt like a teakettle at the simmer.

"Miss Aire—"

"Miss Aire?"

It had seemed we were the only two people in the world, and I jumped at the sound of another voice. Mrs. Fairfax was approaching, an anxious expression on her face. Mr. Rochester rose from the bench, and I did too.

I had been expected back at the house and had forgotten all about it. First the revelation in the thorn wood and then . . . What exactly had happened between Mr. Rochester and me?

*He has been charming me.*

Indeed. But not intentionally, surely.

What had he been about to say? I wasn't to know.

"Here you are," said the housekeeper, a little out of breath. "I'm so glad."

"Mrs. Fairfax, forgive me," I replied. "The time got away from me. I'll come back to the house at once."

She eyed me curiously, and suddenly I was conscious of Mr. Rochester's jacket.

"If Miss Aire has neglected some duty," said Mr. Rochester, "it is entirely my fault. I hunted her down and have been holding her prisoner."

I shrugged out of the jacket and handed it to him, heat stinging my cheeks.

Mrs. Fairfax's gaze moved between us. I was sure she hadn't missed my blush. What would she make of it?

"There's no harm done," she said. "I'm glad to find her safe. I hope there's been no trouble."

"No trouble," I assured her, wondering how much I would tell her about my day. "Is it too late for me to continue with the interviews?"

She shook her head. "I'll need to reschedule Cook, but we can—"

Mr. Rochester muttered under his breath, and both of us looked at him. "Mrs. Fairfax, I've completely forgotten—I happened to meet with Lady Ingram in Hay upon my return. She intends to call with her daughter today. No doubt they'll expect to be given tea."

A shade of panic colored her features. "Indeed?"

"Yes, I'm afraid so. Come, I'll walk back to the house with you and take the blame."

Mrs. Fairfax shot me an apologetic glance. "We'll have to postpone the rest of the interviews until tomorrow, if that's all right, Miss Aire."

"Of course."

They were going, but Mr. Rochester stopped and turned. "Why don't you join us for tea, Miss Aire?"

"Me, sir?" Though I couldn't help feeling pleased he had thought to include me, tea with Mr. Rochester's society neighbors was exactly the sort of engagement I avoided when I could.

"Yes," he replied. Decisively.

"Very well." I felt a knot forming in my stomach. "What time are your guests expected?"

He took his watch from his waistcoat pocket. "Four. I'll see you then."

I returned to the cottage, but before I had even a moment to reflect on the day's events or to fret about what I had suitable to wear to tea with a *Lady Ingram*, there came a timid knock on my door.

I found Agnes on the stoop. Sybil darted around her skirt and into the cottage.

"Could I come in, miss?"

As Agnes moved into the room, I glanced at Sybil, who was curling up for a nap. Everything and nothing had changed between us. I regarded her with the same grateful respect, the same humble awe, that she would choose to be my ally. And yet . . . My whole life I had keenly felt the lack of a mother. Both Mrs. Shaw and Maria Temple had been something *like* a mother to me, and I loved them for it. But finding a true mother, even after nearly three decades, felt like *everything*.

"I'm sorry to bother you, miss," said Agnes. "There's something I must tell you."

I turned my back for the moment on my past and future, and I studied the young maid. Something in her demeanor had changed.

*She looks determined.*

"Please sit down," I said. "I'm glad you've come."

Her eyes flitted to the table. "I don't think I will, miss, if that's all right."

"Of course," I said, folding my arms. "However you're most comfortable."

She nodded, and she squared her shoulders. I waited and let her work up to it, though I was painfully curious. Was some kind of confession coming? I could feel Sybil watching us even with my back turned.

"The voice that sang—the one in the thorns . . ."

"Yes, I remember."

Her eyes fixed on me. "She was my mistress."

*Here, at last.* "You mean the voice you heard was that of Mrs. Rochester?"

"Yes, miss." She hugged her arms over her chest and looked away. "I should have said so before. It's only that . . ."

I waited. But she didn't go on.

"Agnes?" Her eyes came back; she looked frightened. "I'm here to solve a mystery and to help restore the peace at Thornfield if I can. Some things I am bound to share with Mr. Rochester, but I would never share anything of a highly personal nature."

Color came into her cheeks. "It wasn't just her voice, like I said at first. I *saw* her go into the thorns, and I followed." She knotted her hands in her apron. "'Course I knew she had died. There was the funeral and all, and her father went back to Thrush Hall. But I'd know her anywhere, miss. I thought there might have been some mistake or some trick."

I held my breath in anticipation. This would be the first real breakthrough since my arrival. Gently, I said, "Go on."

She moved toward the hearth, and I could see her shaking. "When I caught up to her in the wood, she smiled and came toward me. It was *horrible*. I could still see my mistress, but . . ." She shook her head.

"It's all right, Agnes. Tell me what happened."

She turned back to me, and I saw the tears shining on her cheeks. She reached for the charm in her bodice. "Her face was—it was all wrong, like she was up from her grave. She opened her mouth and started to sing the old song she used to, when I would brush her hair in the evenings before bed. 'The trees they grow high, the leaves they do grow green . . .'"

Agnes's voice was faint and soon faded completely.

"What happened then?"

She closed her eyes, and another tear slipped down. "Her song turned cruel. Her *face* . . . When she came closer, I could see the bones behind it, and her eyes—they had gone all hollow and dark."

At last, she sank into a chair at the table. I went and sat in the other. "Thank you, Agnes. Thank you for telling me this."

She looked at me with desperation. "It couldn't really have been her, could it? My mistress never spoke like that to me, nor anyone. She was never once cross with me, even though I could see how much she suffered."

"She is no longer your mistress. Something has kept her spirit here on Earth. The natural course of things has been prevented, and it has changed her."

"*What* kept her here, miss?"

"That is the mystery we must solve. It could be that she felt she had been wronged in some way. Or there was something or someone she felt she couldn't leave behind. Do *you* have any idea why she might be lingering? Was there anyone she was particularly attached to?"

A shadow fell over her features, and she looked down. "*He* loved her. It was easy enough to see. She was always good to everyone, but she never *loved* him. I'd swear to it."

"Mr. Rochester?"

She shook her head.

"Do you mean . . . Dr. Poole?"

A nod now. Agnes looked up. "You don't think she meant it, do you? She said that I had cared for her . . . *unnaturally*. She said that God would punish me for it. That I'd never—"

"Agnes," I said firmly, "I don't want you to think of this spirit as your mistress. She is a kind of likeness of her, trapped here for reasons we don't yet understand. Imagine a child who has missed his afternoon nap. By evening, he is bound to be ill-tempered, but we know that he is not to blame. And come morning, the good child will have returned. The best thing we can do for your mistress is help her to her rest."

Again she nodded, and she sat up straighter. "How do we do that, miss?"

"Trust that to me. It will be much easier now that you've told me everything."

I was by no means so confident, but for Agnes's sake, I pretended. She rose from the table, brushing tears from her face with the backs of her hands. "I should go back before I'm missed. Mrs. Fairfax said guests are expected."

"Ah yes, Lady Ingram," I said with a sigh. "Mr. Rochester has asked me to join them. What do you think of her?"

I caught Agnes's look of sympathy. "Her ladyship is very . . . refined."

I laughed. "Perhaps I'll get on with the daughter."

Agnes's brows lifted. "As it's only tea, they an't likely to stay long." She tried to smile, curtsied, and left me.

"It's only tea," I echoed.

Thinking I might change my dress, I went to the wardrobe. Because of the morning interviews, I had already put on the neatest of the dresses I wore for teaching, and I really had nothing more suitable.

Thankfully, the garment hadn't been much soiled when I'd fallen in the forest.

*He caught me in his arms.*

Heat crept across my skin and down into my belly. I closed my eyes and took a breath. How this surge of feeling frightened me! *I mustn't think of him this way, for one hundred reasons.* Foremost among them, he certainly would not be thinking of *me* this way. Even if he was, no good could come of it. He would never think to *marry* someone like me—a witch, half-human, of illegitimate birth, over and above the fact I was without fortune or rank.

*Meow.*

Opening my eyes, I saw Sybil was awake and watching me. On impulse, I looked through the hagstone. This time it showed me nothing that wasn't already there—a petite cream cat curled on a patchwork quilt. Could I only see her in the thorn wood? *Have I dreamed the whole thing?*

All that was real and certain in this moment was the job I had to do. I sat down and got started recording the day's events. I made notes about my morning's interviews, the visit to the estate's old church, and everything that had happened since then. My own story had become intertwined with that of Thornfield. If this strange dream *was* real, I was *part of* Thornfield, and had always been, even before I knew of its existence. I liked the idea. I liked the old estate.

*I like its master.*

*Mistress Jane.*

I dropped my pen on the table and got up, attempting to flee my own thoughts by pacing.

No sooner had I shut out Mr. Rochester than I let in Mr. Brocklehurst. I wondered, again, did he know? How could he face me every day, watch me being raised by the staff, and never say a word? Even if he didn't know, how could a morally superior man like him do such a thing and then remain oblivious to the potential consequences? I supposed I was naive.

And as for my mother . . . She had visited my dreams at least a dozen times over the course of my life. Why had she waited so long to tell me? Could she have somehow known she'd see me here one day?

When my pacing carried me back to the table, I took up my pocket watch and gasped. I had lost track of time, and there remained less than a quarter hour until I was expected at the house. I hurried to the dresser.

After washing my face and tidying my hair, I removed the hagstone and clasped Helen's brooch at the neckline of my simple cotton day dress. The fabric was light in color, and I noticed I'd dripped tea on my cuff. Hopefully the flower pattern would hide it from the casual observer. Though I had a feeling there wouldn't be anything casual about Lady Ingram.

I arrived at the manor's entrance the same moment the carriage did. Hanging back to watch the guests alight, I discovered Lady Ingram was refined indeed—and her daughter was a very beautiful young woman. Her burnished-rose dress, expensive and fashionable, complemented her healthful complexion, and fine flaxen ringlets peeked out of her matching bonnet.

Mr. Rochester came out to meet them.

"It's wonderful to see you, Lady Ingram, Miss Ingram."

"Pish-posh," said Miss Ingram, smiling archly. "You never think it's wonderful to see anyone. But you see, Mama and I don't care about that."

Mr. Rochester bowed his head. "Yes, I do see."

Miss Ingram laughed, a musical, ladylike sound. Clearly my employer was on friendly and even somewhat intimate terms with these ladies.

Mr. Rochester offered his arm to Lady Ingram, who was also richly dressed and an older, slightly stouter version of her daughter. She was probably not much older than Mr. Rochester.

As they turned toward the house, he noticed me standing to the side.

"Miss Aire," he said, "there you are. These are my nearest neighbors, the baroness and her daughter, Lady and Miss Ingram. Lady and Miss Ingram, Miss Aire of Lowood School."

Miss Ingram's eyes were bright, her amused smile displaying all of her very even, very white teeth. "How good of you to join us, Miss Aire! As soon as we heard Thornfield was to host a Lowood witch, I began pestering Mr. Rochester for a look at you." Despite my employer's desire for privacy, it seemed his troubles were fairly common knowledge. Miss Ingram turned her pretty smile on him. "You like to think you're an old crosspatch, but you're always so good to me."

"I knew you'd never leave me alone otherwise," he replied dryly, and both ladies laughed.

He gave me a significant look—meant to be conspiratorial, I think—but my heart dropped like a stone. Had he invited me to tea for the purpose of amusing his guests?

My feet heavy, I followed them into the house.

*I can endure this.* It wouldn't be much different from dinners with potential patrons that Lowood teachers were sometimes made to attend. Conversing with wealthy strangers about our teaching methods, sharing anecdotes about our more successful graduates, and praising our superintendent's frugal management.

Yet somehow it felt very different.

*This is what comes of forgetting my place.*

After the shedding of wraps and bonnets, he led us to a drawing room I had not yet seen, at the farthest end of the south wing, facing onto a grassy lawn. At the back was a small wilderness of wildflowers—a few Michaelmas daisies still bloomed there—and an assortment of statues and fountains. This side of the grounds was lighter and more open. I could envision the lawn being used for pall-mall or outdoor fetes in the summer, had Mrs. Rochester lived long enough to entertain.

The room itself was prettily furnished. Cheery and bright, with paper and upholstery in shades of green and rose. I tried to take a seat slightly away from the others, but Mr. Rochester insisted on seating us as he liked. I found myself with the ladies on my right hand, on a moss-green damask sofa, and Mr. Rochester on my left, in a comfortably padded rose velvet chair that was the twin to my own. The table before us was covered with sandwiches, scones, tea cakes, and fruit. A footman appeared and poured the tea.

"Did you know, Miss Aire," began Miss Ingram, stirring a lump of sugar into her cup, "Mr. Rochester despises afternoon tea and never takes it?" I wondered whether I was ever to hear her mother speak.

"I did not," I replied, feeling I was left out of some joke as she directed a wicked yet charming smile at him.

"Obviously untrue," he said, though it was clear he was playing along with her game. "I reserve afternoon tea for the occasions when I find myself in fine company."

Again the ladies laughed, and Miss Ingram said, "He flatters us, Mama."

"No indeed," said Mr. Rochester, sipping his tea.

"Tell us, Miss Aire," continued Miss Ingram, turning to me, "has Mr. Rochester changed his habits?"

I recognized that the young lady was using me as a foil for her flirtation with my employer. I also saw that there was a cleverness to her question. She seemed to flatter me by implying I would know something of Mr. Rochester's habits, while in fact she was calling attention to the fact I was not one of *them*. That I would not be enjoying tea with Mr. Rochester if it weren't for the ladies' visit.

"I'm sure I couldn't say, Miss Ingram," I replied politely, "having only been at Thornfield two days."

"How diplomatic!" cried the lady. "Bravo, Miss Aire."

She helped herself to a frosted tea cake, giving her mama an opening.

"You found everything well on your return from London, I hope?" asked the matron, appearing genuinely concerned. "We're always worried about you, living so isolated here."

"You are very kind, Lady Ingram. We're managing well enough." Mr. Rochester directed a faint smile at me, and I wished that he hadn't.

Mercifully, Miss Ingram didn't snap up the bait he had perhaps unintentionally left dangling. I was sure she hadn't missed the glance, nor any other move he had made since the ladies arrived.

"Have you considered a medium, Mr. Rochester?" asked the young lady. "Amy Eshton and I attended a séance when we were in London for the Season, and I think it might be just the thing."

"Oh, Blanche," said Lady Ingram, rolling her eyes to the ceiling. "Spare us, please."

"*What*, Mama? You weren't even there."

"And I thank heaven for it."

"Miss Aire," said Miss Ingram, fixing her animated gaze on me, "tell them."

I glanced at Mr. Rochester to see how he was taking this suggestion of consulting someone who specialized in *contacting the dead*, but his expression was one of mild amusement.

"I'm sorry, Miss Ingram," I said, "what shall I tell them?"

"That it is *real*, of course. That there are people who can talk to the dead."

"I do believe there are those who can talk to the dead," I replied. Maria had a student who went on to be a medium. Sadly, most of those who advertised themselves as such were no more than opportunists hoping to separate the bereaved from their money.

"And don't you think a medium might be able to help Mr. Rochester?"

Again I glanced at my employer. His smile was still placid.

"Blanche, *please*," persisted Lady Ingram.

But Miss Ingram would not be dissuaded from making a flirtation of Mr. Rochester's troubles. Apparently the thoughtless girl had made no connection between whatever she had learned about Thornfield and Mrs. Rochester's death a year ago. I was so uncomfortable for him that I didn't even feel the slight that was implied—that *I* might not be up to the job I'd been hired to do.

"I have no need of a medium," he said finally. "I have Miss Aire."

My stomach lurched as everyone's attention fixed on me.

"Are *you* a medium?" the younger lady asked, apparently rapt.

"That has not been my course of study."

"And what has been your course of study?" she asked lightly, but I could see the challenge in her bright gaze.

"I believe you have heard that I am a witch."

"What does that entail, dear?" asked the mother. "Being a witch." Lady Ingram was clearly a skeptic, but at least she didn't appear to have complicated motives for asking.

"It's not as interesting as it sounds, I'm afraid. Most of my time is spent harvesting herbs, which I use to prepare cures for various ills."

"Like an apothecary?" asked Lady Ingram.

"Something like that, yes."

"And have you found a cure for Thornfield?" asked Miss Ingram.

"Not as of yet."

"She's been here but two days," Mr. Rochester gently reminded her. "But I must say, I find her mere presence a balm."

I froze, strongly fighting an urge to look at him. Instead I watched Miss Ingram's face try not to fall. It resulted in a smile you might find on an automaton.

"In any case, miracle workers don't come cheaply," he said in a firmer tone. "I can afford but one."

There was a heavy lull. I sipped my tea, studying the leading actors in this strange little drama.

"Come now, Mr. Rochester," said Miss Ingram. "We all know that's not true. You could hire ten witches if it suited you."

"Thankfully, it doesn't suit me, because I assure you I could not."

Miss Ingram laughed, but she wasn't sure whether she was supposed to, and it was awkward. She and her mama exchanged the briefest of glances, and I saw that his reply had unsettled them both.

Based on my interviews with Mr. Rochester and his housekeeper—not to mention the nature of his agreement with Mr. Brocklehurst—I believed him in possession of both wealth and considerable property. Had he some reason for wanting the ladies to think otherwise?

There was only one I could think of—to encourage Miss Ingram to direct her flirtation elsewhere. Yet the lady was beautiful *and* the daughter of a baron. I thought many men would also find her charming.

Perhaps my employer was not one of them.

To my immense relief, the conversation now moved on to the parties' plans for the winter festivities, which didn't involve me and allowed me to fade into the background. The ladies pressed Mr. Rochester to join them at their estate for Christmas, rather than "sit home alone like Ebenezer Scrooge," and he tormented them by refusing to commit.

I confess my attention had drifted by the time I was spoken to again.

"I beg your pardon, Miss Ingram?"

"I believe your witch finds us dull, sir," chided the lady, smiling. Always smiling.

"I'm certain she finds *me* so," he replied, "but no one could find you dull, Miss Ingram."

She was gratified by the compliment and emboldened to continue.

"I'm curious, Miss Aire, how does one become a witch? Was your mother one too?"

My heart faltered. "It is often passed down from mother to daughter, but that was not the case with me."

"Your father, then?" She nibbled innocently at a scone.

My fingers trembled as I set my teacup on the table. "I learned my craft at school, like my pupils."

"Mm. And what made your parents send you there? Had you exhibited an aptitude?" She cast a sly look at Mr. Rochester. "Had you transformed your brother into a toad?"

Suddenly I had my fill of being toyed with. Smiling tepidly, I replied, "Lowood is a school for orphans, Miss Ingram."

Lady Ingram murmured something like "oh."

"I beg your pardon, Miss Aire," said the younger lady. "I didn't realize."

Before she lowered her gaze, I saw something very different from contrition in her eyes: *triumph.* She had set out to humiliate me before Mr. Rochester, and she had done so. Not only was I a witch and the only person in the room without wealth or rank, no one knew who my parents were (and of course revelation of *those* details would have only made her triumph more complete).

The visit must be almost at an end by now. But meekness was not one of my virtues, and I wasn't sure what I might say if I was forced to endure another slight. Worse than that, *tears* were threatening. I stood up, drawing everyone's attention.

Avoiding Mr. Rochester's eye, I cleared my throat and said, "Please excuse me, ladies. I've enjoyed meeting you both, but I find I'm feeling unwell."

At least my voice had not betrayed my emotions. No one would believe my excuse, but escape had become more important than keeping up appearances.

"I'm very sorry to hear it, dear," said Lady Ingram, though without much feeling.

As for Miss Ingram, she was getting just what she wanted and offered no more than a polite nod. I was only too happy to yield her the field.

And Mr. Rochester? He said nothing, and I couldn't help glancing in his direction as I turned to go. He rose politely from his chair, but an expression of distaste sat upon his lips—like he'd taken a bite of rotten fruit. My stomach twisted into multiple knots.

*Bravo, Miss Ingram.*

# *Interlude*

## (Rochester)

One of the two ladies had just spoken to me, but I had no idea which or what she'd said.

"I'm sorry?"

Lady Ingram cleared her throat delicately. "I said thank you so much for your hospitality. We really should be going."

"It was delightful to see you," added the younger lady warmly, offering up her sweetest pink-cheeked smile. Behind it, I could see her uncertainty. "You really were a dear to humor me and let me get a look at your witch."

My witch was never going to forgive me for this. Nor should she. I'd played her a cruel trick.

The ladies raised themselves from their seats.

"Jonathon," I called to the footman. "Please escort Lady Ingram and Miss Ingram to their carriage. I've something to attend to."

"Yes, sir."

The mama looked bewildered, the daughter anxious. I bowed my head to each. "Good day to you both," I said and left the room.

I reached the hall and left the house ahead of them, and I was making for the cottage when my rational mind asserted itself.

What had happened—it was for the best, and I should know it. When we'd all sat down to tea, I'd taken in the two younger ladies at one glance—finery and bright smiles on the one, modest dress and demeanor on the other. There was no comparing them. My thoughts were full of the one and oblivious to the other. So much so that I hadn't seen what was happening in time to prevent it.

But yes, it had been for the best. Because now she would hate me, and that would be her armor until she was safely back where she belonged.

When I reached the break in the wall that led to the herb garden, I walked on to the greenhouse at the back of the house. Passing through the gabled entry, I was greeted by humid, earthy warmth and the scent of roses.

Jane always smelled like herbs and roses.

*Blast.*

# Another Knock

Hot tears ran down my face as I made my way back to the cottage. Almost more than Miss Ingram and her pettiness, I was angry with Mr. Rochester for setting me up to be sneered at by her. Yet his expression as I left . . . Even angry with him, I couldn't help worrying he had thought my abrupt departure rude to his guests. It *had* been a weakness, hadn't it? Mr. Brocklehurst would undoubtably say so. I could hear him now: *Was it worth it, losing the position over foolish pride?* Allowing myself to be wounded by Miss Ingram, worrying she might have diminished me in Mr. Rochester's eyes . . . So long as Mr. Rochester was happy with my work, what did it matter? What would it have cost me to endure their slights for a few minutes more?

*Too much.*

When I reached the cottage door, Sybil ran out. I wished she hadn't. If ever I had needed a mother—even such a mother as she was—it was now.

I sat down at the table and dried my tears with my handkerchief. Then I folded my arms and rested my forehead on them, listening to the sound of my own breathing and the crackling of the fire, which Agnes had attended to in my absence.

*Steady, Jane.*

As the cascade of emotions subsided, I realized only one option was open to me: I must apologize at the first opportunity. Mr. Rochester had a quick temper, but he was not unreasonable. Everything else I was feeling—it must be forgotten. I would take the evening to clear my head and start fresh in the morning.

I got up and went to my herb jars—chamomile and rose to calm, borage for courage. I boiled water for the infusion and then sat and drank it, building a mental wall between the green-and-rose drawing room and me.

Then I remembered the planned trip to the hawthorn wood. Mr. Rochester was to go with me. Not only that, *I was expected at dinner*. I groaned and felt my spirits sinking.

Still, having given illness as an excuse at tea, it should be easy enough to beg off the evening meal. With luck, Mr. Rochester would assume that the visit to the wood would be postponed, and instead I would go alone. If all went well, I would be able to provide him with new information along with my apology. While I didn't relish going without him, I had many protective tools at my disposal, and I hoped to have my mother's company.

Having settled on a course of action, I breathed easier. Then came a knock on the door, and my heart jumped into my throat.

My hand shook as I opened the door—but it was only Agnes.

"Mrs. Fairfax sent me to ask if you need anything. She heard you were poorly."

Kindly Mrs. Fairfax. "I'm well, Agnes. It's only a headache."

"I'm sorry to hear it, miss. Can I bring you anything?"

"There's nothing I need, but could you let them know at the house that I won't come for dinner? I'd like to rest this evening."

"Yes, miss. I can bring your dinner here if you like."

The change in her manner toward me lifted my spirits. "I would be grateful for that."

Thinking of my return trip to the thorn wood, I said, "There *is* one thing I need, actually, if you can get it. Might there be any small item left at Thornfield that belonged to Mrs. Rochester? Anything will do, even a button or ribbon. And I will return it."

She hesitated, thinking. "Mr. Mason took all her things away with him, but . . ." After another pause, she continued. "She had a fine brush with a bone handle that I used on her hair at night. Mr. Mason gave it to me when she died."

A brush! "A strand of your mistress's hair would be the perfect thing. Do you think there are any still in the brush?"

She nodded. "I keep it in a drawer. I've never cleaned it."

This was more than I could have hoped for. "If you are willing, it will help me in my work."

"You're going looking for the spirit, miss?" Her brow furrowed.

"I am. I promise you that I'll do all I can to help her."

"I'll fetch it for you."

When she'd gone, I collected more jars from my shelves and made a charm, similar to the one I'd made for her. There were several plants with protective properties that would also bolster Sight—thyme, mugwort, lavender, and yarrow.

By the time I finished, Agnes had returned with a handkerchief folded over several strands of hair. I carried it to my worktable and sat staring at them. They were black, or nearly so, like Mr. Rochester's. I recalled that he and Antoinette were distantly related. Had they been intimate enough that he had touched her hair? Picturing the tender gesture threatened to unsettle me again.

Picking up the strands, I coiled them carefully around a finger. Then I secured them with thread and tucked them into the charm bag. I laid the bag on the table and lit a candle to charge the charm. While the flame guttered and danced, I chanted, *"Restless spirit, come to me. I call you forth. So mote it be."*

I blew out the candle and watched the tendril of smoke curl into fanciful shapes as it rose toward the rafters. I breathed lightly into the smoke, and a spiral twisted in on itself to form a hollow-eyed visage. A chill ran through me, and the scent of moldy earth hung in the air.

This was the first charm I'd made for such a purpose, but by these signs, I deemed it ready.

Setting the charm aside, I began a letter to Maria, asking her to send books on spirits and hauntings. I was sorely tempted to pour out my heart to her. But I couldn't bring myself to tell her about my mother in a letter, and the idea of committing a description of my confusion about Mr. Rochester to paper . . . It made me feel schoolgirlish.

I folded, sealed, and addressed the letter, leaving it on the table. I'd ask Agnes to add it to tomorrow's post. I wondered how quickly the books could be sent. Though I hoped tonight's meeting with the spirit—if it happened—would be illuminating, I didn't dare hope the issue could be so quickly resolved.

As I got up to add peats to the fire, there came another knock at the door. Again my heart leaped, but it was only Mrs. Fairfax, come to personally deliver my dinner tray.

"How are you, Miss Aire?" Setting the tray on the table, she turned to study me.

"I am well, Mrs. Fairfax. Only a headache, and I'm feeling better now."

"I'm glad to hear it. Mr. Rochester was afraid you'd found his guests' company tedious."

My cheeks burned. "I hope he wasn't displeased that I excused myself before they'd gone. I felt I couldn't stay."

"Well, you know how he is. It's impossible to ever tell if he's truly displeased."

I had observed that Mrs. Fairfax struggled at times to read her employer. But this implied that he *appeared* displeased, and was not exactly comforting.

"Thank you for delivering my meal," I said. "I'm sorry you had to go to the trouble."

"No trouble at all, dear. Agnes told me you were feeling better, but Mr. Rochester insisted that I inspect you myself. I shall reassure him."

Mr. Rochester missed little, and he very likely knew that my illness was feigned.

"I expect a night's rest will do wonders," I said. "I would like to continue with the interviews in the morning, if it's convenient."

"I'll arrange it." Wiping her hands on her apron, she straightened. "I'll send Agnes around for the tray and to see that you have everything you need for the night."

"Please don't bother her, Mrs. Fairfax. I want nothing else, and she can collect the tray in the morning."

"If you like. Good evening, Miss Aire."

When the door closed behind her, I removed the tray's cover. Though the feast was as kingly as the night I'd dined with Mr. Rochester, the thing that first caught my eye lay alongside the plate—a perfectly formed rose, the same color as the glass of wine that rested on the tray. I lifted it to my nose and inhaled. Whose idea had it been to place it there?

*Mrs. Fairfax, most likely, so eat your dinner and have done with this.*

There were slices of venison in sauce, roasted apples with mace, fresh bread, and three kinds of cheese. Also a large slice of cake. I'd been too nervous to eat at tea and was only too happy to make up for that now.

When I finished, I carried the tray to the table by the door and tidied my work things. Then I retrieved a novel from my bag and sat down by the fire to read until it was time to return to the thorn wood. But I soon set it aside. I was restless, and the cottage felt close. Maybe a turn around the garden under the stars would settle me.

I took my cape from the peg and put it on. As I reached for the door handle, there came yet another knock. Agnes must have come for the tray anyway. I pulled open the door, and my breath caught—Mr. Rochester stood on the stoop.

"Sir," I said, the tremor in my voice betraying my emotion.

"Miss Aire." He cast a critical eye over me. "Going out, were you? You must be feeling better."

"I was." I drew myself up. "And I *am*, as I'm sure Mrs. Fairfax has told you."

His eyes widened. "And saucy too."

So much for apologizing at the first opportunity.

He held out his arm. "I shall accompany you."

"I . . ." My thoughts were swirling again; I hardly knew what to say.

His brows lifted. "Yes?"

I took a deep breath and tucked my hand into the crook of his arm.

Lifting the lamp from the post outside the door, he asked, "Where is it we're off to in the middle of the night? For I'm certain you weren't returning to the thorn wood without me."

He stared down at me, and I cleared my throat. "Outside for some air. Now that you've come, we might go to the apothecary garden, as I'm forbidden from going there alone." *Petty, Jane.*

Mr. Rochester stared straight ahead, refusing the bait. "Perhaps you can give me a tour."

We circled round to the back of the cottage in piqued silence. The evening was clear, moon a crisp crescent and stars bright and sharp like diamonds.

"You had some work in gaining entry," he observed as he opened the old wooden door.

"I did. I'm sorry about the roses."

He laughed. "The *roses*."

Inside the garden, I stopped and turned to him. "I also want to apologize for walking out on your guests. I confess there was no headache. It was rude, and while there can be no justification for it, Miss Ingram . . ."

He was shaking his head, and I fell silent. Who was *I* to fault Miss Ingram?

"While I derive far too much enjoyment from needling you to be expected to stop, it is for *me* to apologize. And to confess. For I set it up."

I stared at him. His eyes were soft, his expression contrite. My voice wavered as I replied, "It was unkind of you, sir, summoning me before my betters to be gawked at like some exotic creature."

"Indeed it was, Miss Aire. Though 'exotic creature' you certainly are, that was not at all my intention. And Blanche Ingram is in no way your *better*."

My heart lifted. Began to dance, even. My mind urged caution. "Then what *was* your intention?"

He eyed me speculatively. "I will tell you, but on one condition."

"Yes?"

"I very much wish to know what caused you to faint this afternoon. You're far too rational a person to do such a thing, and I cannot stop thinking about it."

My heart now stopped, its elation replaced by a cold dread. "That—that is hardly fair, sir. I told you it was personal."

"Agreed, yet it is my stipulation. I never claimed to be fair. Nor reasonable."

How I had wished for someone to confide in. There was a part of me that longed to tell him, both for the relief of saying it out loud and to hear his clear and level thoughts on the matter. But most of me worried about how it would change things between us. What he would think of me for believing such a thing. What he would think of me if *he* believed it. *Exotic creature, indeed.*

Before I could reply, he said, "Come, let us sit down."

Raising the lamp, he led me toward the south wall of the garden. The silver moon hung in the sky above the manor, beyond the bramble-covered stones. There was a bench here, out of the reach of the elm tree. Mist rose from the ground, pooling like milk around our ankles, and the night blossoms of poisonous thornapple perfumed the air with honey. I sat down, and he beside me, the lamp occupying the spot on his other side. This squeezed us close enough for me to feel the warmth that came from him.

*Go on, then. Tell him, and let that be the end of romantic fantasies.*

Without preamble, I said, "The hawthorn dryad told me that she was my mother."

He stared, as well he might.

"She said I was a child of bonfire night and that she had given me up because she didn't know how to care for me."

He wore an expression of frank disbelief. "I don't . . ."

"I know. It's outlandish. In so many ways."

"Yet you're in earnest."

"I am."

He shook his head. "Why would she say such a thing? I mean, you don't actually believe it?"

I sighed. "I didn't at first. But she knew I was an orphan and that I had been left at Lowood as an infant. Other details as well. I know you'll think me foolish."

His gaze drifted outward, into the garden. I could see him struggling to keep an open mind, and my heart filled with gratitude. "If she lives here," he said, "on the estate, how, then, did you end up at Lowood?"

"She said I was taken there by her 'sisters.' I'm not sure what that means. Dryads are elementals, tied to place. It could be she needed help to deliver me there."

"But why Lowood? I mean, I know it's a school for orphans, but how would she know of it?"

"Perhaps because, according to her, my father is there."

His eyes came back to my face. "And whom does she say is your father?"

I wasn't ready to tell him what I suspected. The idea of a tryst between Mr. Brocklehurst and a dryad at Beltane—I still struggled to take it in. I might have misunderstood, and it would be wrong to mar his character in the eyes of a patron.

"She was unclear on that point."

No more than the truth, but I saw that he knew I was holding something back.

"This is extraordinary," he said. "You really don't doubt her story?"

"I do, of course. It's not a thing that could ever be proven. But when I first saw her in the wood . . ." I unfolded and refolded my hands in my lap. The movement drew his eye. "She's been visiting me in dreams for years. And I'm not sure what the point would be of telling me such a story."

"Fairies aren't exactly known for their honesty." There was a kindly concern in his eyes.

"No indeed. But I do have a reason to trust this one. You remember Sybil?"

"Your feline protector."

I nodded. "The dryad—she *is* Sybil. Her physical form in our world is that of a cat." I tugged my hagstone free. "I wouldn't have seen the dryad had I not been looking at Sybil through *this*."

His gaze moved between the talisman and me. "Extraordinary," he repeated. "It's some kind of stone?"

"Yes, given to me by my mentor at Lowood. I wear it for protection and for seeing into the spirit world."

His gaze drifted again into the garden. I turned the hagstone in my fingers, wishing it could open a window into his thoughts.

"Do you know, Miss Aire," he said finally, "I once attended bonfire night when I was a child."

"Did you?"

He nodded. "Growing up, I spent a great deal of time in the oak forest."

Those magical eyes of his glinted in the starlight, and for a moment I was certain that he knew I had followed him this morning.

But he went on. "Though the wood is part of the estate, the majority of it is still quite wild. There are some enormous trees, at least a century old. The largest ones form a circle around the clearing where the May Day bonfire was lit. I think I was eight the year my mother and father argued about the revels. He thought they were immoral and blasphemous and wanted to put a stop to them. My mother worried this would antagonize the tenants and servants and offend the fairies." He gave me a sly look. "Your people, you know."

I laughed. "It sounds like she won the argument."

He shook his head. "My father forbade it, and she went around behind his back and told them all to ignore him. That was my mother in a nutshell. You remind me of her."

I stared, startled by the intimacy of this statement. "I'm flattered, I think?"

"No indeed. She was obstinate as the day is long." Yet a fond smile rested on his lips. Warmth bubbled in my chest.

"You attended the celebration with her, then?"

"Oh, she would never have defied him so openly. The moment I was put to bed, I snuck off. Stole a lantern from the stables and walked the whole way. Climbed up into a big tree and watched the festivities from there. I was afraid to be seen, lest they report me to my mother. Truth be told, my crow's nest was so comfortable, I fell asleep before things really got going."

*Before everyone became drunk enough on mead and the promise of long summer days that no one would notice a pious young man and a hawthorn dryad slipping off to find a bed of moss.*

Considering Mr. Rochester's age, and the fact Mr. B had grown up near here, it wasn't outside the realm of possibility that it happened right there, that very night. The idea that Mr. Rochester could have been nearby on the night I was conceived . . . it was somehow both intriguing and mortifying.

"Miss Aire," he continued, fixing his eyes on me, "I must confess it hardly surprises me that you're not only a witch but a fairy—"

"Half fairy."

"Quite right, and I expect we'll next discover your father was a centaur, but that's beside the point. This of course came as quite a shock to you, as evidenced by the swoon, and I can't help asking, as your employer, whether you intend to stay on here?"

I studied him. Was this a kind way of suggesting it might be best for me to go?

"What I mean to say," he continued, "is that I suppose you'll want time to recover from the shock and maybe delve further into the particulars. I have mentally connected a few pieces of information and, joking aside, I think I have a fair idea who your father might be—as I'm sure you do too. I would understand if our troubles at Thornfield are an unwelcome distraction right now."

It sounded like Mr. Rochester had arrived at the same conclusion I had about my father. That being the case, he could be thinking that if a scandal attached itself to Mr. B and myself, it might touch him as well. I could hardly blame him for that.

"I would choose to stay on and complete my task first," I replied frankly, "unless you have a reason for feeling it's better that I go." I hesitated, then added, "If you do, I will certainly understand." *Miss Blanche shall clap her hands in delight.*

I couldn't read his face, yet I sensed he was struggling with some emotion. After a few moments, he seemed to relax and even smiled. "If you consider it no hardship, I would much rather you stay on."

Relief washed over me. But that obstacle overcome, I recalled we had some other business to settle between us. "First you must keep your promise, sir."

He glanced up.

"Your reason for insisting I take tea with the Ingrams. I have told you my secret, and now you must tell me yours."

"Ah." He looked down. "Indeed, and I must also say that I'm honored you trusted me enough to tell me your story. Had I better understood the nature of the revelation, I'd not have pressed you about it."

He cleared his throat and sat up straighter. "I've no intention of wriggling out of our agreement. I will begin by saying that Lady Ingram wishes me to marry her daughter."

# *Pretty Words*

This unsurprising revelation caused a prickling pain in my chest. "She is an eligible young lady."

He inclined his head in agreement. "Quite a desirable match."

The prickling pain deepened. "From what I saw, Miss Ingram has the same idea as her mama. It would seem you're well on your way."

"Oh, undoubtedly."

I couldn't imagine why he was telling me this or what I was expected to say.

"I have entertained two suspicions about the eligible Miss Ingram," he continued. "Shall I tell you what they are?"

His eyes had a conspiratorial gleam. I was baffled by his manner, but I said, "If you like."

"The first is that Lady and Miss Ingram are more interested in my fortune than they are in anything else about me."

I recalled the remark about the cost of ten witches and the ladies' looks of concern.

"No pity, please, Mistress Jane," he said, noticing my frown. "This is not fatal to their ambitions. I know that I am pleasing in neither looks nor manner."

A number of competing impulses and emotions bloomed in my heart. Firstly, I very much wanted to protest that his self-assessment was inaccurate, though of course I could not. Another thing I could not say was that if I felt pity, it was only because I did not like to see him hurt. Thirdly, my sinking heart was buoyed by the possibility he had not been taken in by the Ingrams. Finally, and most dizzying of all: he had once again called me "Mistress Jane."

"But my second suspicion . . . ," he continued, unaware of my mental disarray, "*that* was the one that caused me the most concern."

"What was it, sir?"

His eyes met mine. "That behind frills, lace, and full-lipped smiles hides a hard-hearted and selfish woman. At tea today, I had the proof of it in the monstrous way she treated you. Though I promise you, that is not the reason I brought the two of you together, and had I known it would play out that way, I never would have instigated it."

My heart strained against my chest. "Why, then?"

"I confess that I wished to contrast your characters because it pleased me. It was selfish, and I am heartily sorry. Their opinions and approbation mean nothing to me, and it never occurred to me that you might be hurt by them."

I stared at him. "Do I not *feel*, sir?" Tears stung my eyes, and I looked away.

"More deeply than most, I suspect," he said gently. "A trait we perhaps share. But I also underestimated *her* capacity for cruelty. Can you forgive me?"

His features were soft now, entreating. My heart swelled and pulsed.

I took a breath and drew back my shoulders. "I can, and I will. But again I must say, sir . . ."

"Go ahead—let me have it."

"It was unkind of you to use me that way and no better than how *she* tried to use me. As one of your servants, I was put in an impossible position. I had to smile at my tormentor and then humiliate myself by claiming to be ill when I knew no one would believe it. And all for what? Your own amusement? Do your inferiors mean so little to you?"

His expression darkened. "First, I'll not hear you referred to as my, or anyone else's, 'inferior' again. Second, 'amusement' had no part in it."

I sat in confusion, unable to order my thoughts enough to speak.

"I simply took pleasure in reinforcing another belief of mine about Miss Ingram. That with all her skin-deep charms, she cannot hold a candle to *you*, Jane, with your quick mind and honest goodness."

His words carried me headlong into a rushing river. I struggled to right myself in the current.

*"Pretty words, dark-hearted deeds. Men's tongues will run like bedeviled steeds."*

We started to our feet at the unexpected voice. "Who's there?" called Mr. Rochester.

A gust of wind extinguished the lamp. Great billowing clouds rolled from the west like storm-driven ships; soon the starlight would be gone as well. I looked for the source of the high, singsong voice. Finding nothing, I peered through the hagstone. Only shadows shifting in the changing light.

"Call to her," I said softly.

He looked at me through widened eyes. "What?"

"Your wife," I said. "Call to her."

"*That* can't be my wife."

I laid my hand on his arm. "I hope you're right. But if it is, we must try."

He looked at the elm tree—the direction the voice had come from—and then he took a couple of slow steps toward it. Mist swirled around its base. "Antoinette?"

The clouds blotted out the sky, and he gave a quiet gasp. Dry leaves scraped across the brick path as I circled my palm with my finger, raising the cool flame of my spirit-light and drawing his eye.

As I stepped closer to him, I noticed movement beneath the tree. "Mrs. Rochester?" I called.

A shadow organized itself into the shape of a woman. She drew closer, her full skirt swaying from side to side like a bell. *The swish of a woman's skirt.*

"Antoinette," said Mr. Rochester in a soft tone of shock.

My spirit-light was feeble under the dome of October clouds, but as the specter drew closer, I could see that her fashionable gown hung in tatters over her hoop, while her hair hung in loose, mussed waves over her shoulders. Where her eyes should have been, there were only recesses. Like her gown, her *flesh* was torn in places. The rents were dark, contrasting with exposed bones in her hands and face. *Like she was up from her grave,* Agnes had rightly said.

This spirit was vastly different from the one I'd seen at Lowood—Helen, whole and at peace, as she crossed from the earthly realm to the afterworld. Antoinette's spirit was much like the specter of the blackthorn dryad. Maybe the dryad had meant to warn me about *her*. Could Antoinette have even had a hand in the tree's destruction?

"What has happened to you, Mrs. Rochester?" I took a step toward her. Mr. Rochester's hand came to my arm—*close enough*. "What keeps you from your rest?"

She stopped four or five feet away from us, her ragged lips contorting into a smile. A frigid dread crept over me.

"Has my husband been wooing you?" Her tone was light and mocking. "You're a pretty maid. I think more to his taste, judging by the sheer number of words he's directed at you."

This settled like a great stone in my belly, casting a pall of doubt over all that had just passed between Mr. Rochester and me.

The specter watched me, the horrible broken smile fixed on her face, and I recalled how she had toyed cruelly with Agnes.

"Antoinette," Mr. Rochester repeated mournfully.

Her head moved strangely, like there was something wrong with her neck, as her attention shifted to him. I thought my blood would freeze in my veins. "You've got it all now, haven't you, Edward dear? My dowry. My father's estate when he dies—my *home*. How many times did you darken the door of Thrush Hall?"

I looked at him. His expression was wretched.

"Ah," she continued, "just the one time. When you asked me to marry you." She stepped closer, and together we took a step back. "Remember how you and Papa arranged it all between you? And once it was done, no reason for poor Antoinette to linger. The sooner, in fact, the better."

"You're not her," said Mr. Rochester, his voice raw with pain. "You're not like her at all."

I didn't know what to make of the things she was saying. Did her corrupted spirit have a need to see others suffer? Or was she actually trying to tell us how she had been wronged? It hurt me to see his pain, but I couldn't allow myself to interfere while she might reveal more.

Slowly her head turned back to me. "Dear Edward. As if you hadn't profited *enough* from my death."

A feline yowl tore at the night, and another fierce wind blasted through the garden. Then came a loud crack, and I was shoved to one side.

I stumbled and fell onto the path, bruising my knees. My spirit-light went out, and at first I couldn't make sense of what happened. I conjured the light again, though it was a finite resource and wouldn't last without time to renew. I found Sybil crouching beside me.

"Mr. Rochester!" I called, holding out the light. Another branch had fallen from the elm. I'd thought us a safe distance from the tree, but the wind had been strong, and there the branch lay, right where I'd been standing a moment ago.

*He is under it!*

I let out a cry and hurried to his side. I tried shifting the branch, but it was too heavy and awkward; I worried I'd make things worse. My light was gone again, but I couldn't see his face anyway through all the leaves and twigs.

"Sir, can you speak to me?"

No answer came. I shouted for help, hoping a servant on the grounds would hear me. But the wind swallowed my voice.

I jumped up, panicked and unsure. I must go for help, yet I couldn't leave him alone and unprotected. *If he survived.* My eyes stung, and my throat ached. I let out a sob as my mind flailed for a spell.

Something brushed at my skirts, and I flinched away. The wind suddenly broke the clouds apart, sending down welcome starlight. I saw it was only Sybil standing beside me. She sat down next to the fallen branch, looked up at me, and mewed.

Praying the faint light would last until I could reach the path to the house, I turned and ran.

Mr. Rochester was carried away unconscious, and I stumbled along behind in the cold rain that had started to fall. Mrs. Fairfax offered me her sitting room while Dr. Poole was fetched. She made me take her chair—and tea with milk and sugar—and I dried myself before the blessedly warm fire while listening to muffled voices and rapid footfalls along the corridors above. I thought the waiting would kill me.

Over and over, my mind returned to the last scene between us and the astonishing words he had spoken.

*With all her skin-deep charms, she cannot hold a candle to* you, *Jane, with your quick mind and honest goodness.*

*Jane.*

My thoughts flitted about like feathers in a storm—the wonder of Mr. Rochester's words, worry over his injury, dismay over the bitter accusations uttered by his wife's spirit. We'd had no opportunity to discuss it, yet I couldn't believe him capable of behaving dishonorably toward her.

And what of the tree branch? It could hardly have been a coincidence. Antoinette had gone so far as accusing her husband of wanting her dead. Might the falling branch have been an attempt on his life?

Footsteps sounded in the corridor outside the room, and I held my breath. The door opened, admitting Mrs. Fairfax.

"I thought you might not have gone to bed yet," she said.

I stood. "No, ma'am. I'm eager to hear how he is."

She folded her hands in front of her. "Dr. Poole has seen him. Mr. Rochester's head is concussed."

Though that could be serious, the news might have been much worse considering the size of the branch. "Is he awake?"

"He did wake and is resting now. He has asked about you."

A flame kindled in my chest. "You told him I am well?"

"I did. He asked to speak to you, but Dr. Poole forbade it until morning. The physician wants him to remain calm." Her expression turned questioning. "I got the sense from Mr. Rochester that something troubling happened in the apothecary garden? Beyond the accident, I mean."

I nodded. "I believe we are much closer to understanding what is amiss at Thornfield."

Her brows lifted. "Indeed?"

"We saw—and spoke to—the spirit of Mrs. Rochester."

The good woman gasped. "Heaven help us. It pains me to hear it, Miss Aire. You'll forgive me for hoping that particular theory would prove false."

"We shared that hope, ma'am."

"What will you do now?"

I had given little thought since the accident to how I would proceed with my investigation, but something came to me now. "It would be very helpful if I could speak to Dr. Poole before he goes. I'd like to ask a question or two about Mrs. Rochester's state of mind before she died."

Worry had settled on the housekeeper's forehead. "Cook made him a bite to eat, and he's alone in the dining room. He'll stay the night at Thornfield so that he may monitor Mr. Rochester. I can take you in to him now if you like."

"Yes, ma'am, thank you."

*This time, you'll not be able to hurry away.*

# *Interlude*

## *(Rochester)*

I knew I was dreaming by the color of the meadow grass. As a boy, I'd spent many summer days playing among the vivid green stalks, their blushing seed heads tickling my nose.

I knew I was dreaming because I reclined on one elbow beside a picnic basket, gazing down into the face of a beautiful woman. A bit of cake frosting smeared over her bottom lip, tempting me closer. Her brown eyes smiled in a way that both teased and caressed. She had just said something, but try as I might, I couldn't remember what. I only knew it filled my heart with joy.

I reached to touch her cheek, and the dream shattered. Now, instead of summer meadow grass, I lay on a hard wood floor. Something sharp dug into my hip, and I saw there were pieces of broken crockery and bottles all around. The woman beside me—her eyes were wide with fear, and she was saying something urgently. My ears buzzed, and I strained to hear.

*Be ready. Be ready, Edward.*

Be ready for *what*?

I reached for her, but her body was broken somehow, and she cried out at my touch. Then blood began to stream from a gash across her pale throat.

*No!*

Laughter filled the room. Unwholesome laughter. Laughter that brought the bile to my throat.

The door to the cottage flew open, and a figure stepped inside. A woman, silhouetted by bright light streaming through the door. She carried a knife. She turned it so it flashed in the light, and I saw blood staining the blade.

"Jane!" I cried. "We must go!"

I bent over the woman on the floor, but she was no longer Jane. She was Antoinette, hollow-eyed and rotting. She reached for me, covering my lips with hers.

I woke with a shout.

# Secrets

I followed Mrs. Fairfax to the dining room. She knocked lightly and opened the door. The room was dark, with only the fire and two tapers lit.

Glancing up from his meal, the physician quickly stood.

"Please sit, Dr. Poole," I said. "I'm sorry to disturb you." I gestured to the chair across from him. "May I join you for a moment?"

Still chewing a bite of his supper, he sat back down and waved at the chair.

"I'll leave the two of you," said Mrs. Fairfax. "If you need anything, just ring the bell."

When the door had closed behind her, I said, "I wanted to talk over the accident with you, if that's all right. I was with Mr. Rochester when it happened."

"An elm branch, was it?" said Dr. Poole. "There's a big elm at Thrush Hall that often drops branches at the end of a dry summer. Quite a gusty night too." He took another bite and sipped from a glass of brandy.

"How is your patient?" I couldn't prevent the slight tremor in my voice.

He frowned. "Far too agitated. He's sustained a concussion. He's strong and healthy and should recover, but only if he keeps quiet and rests."

I knew my employer well enough to understand how challenging this might prove to be.

"I'm relieved to hear it. I feared worse. Has he talked to you at all about what happened?"

"Only the essentials. Is there more to it?"

"I'm afraid there is. Mr. Rochester and I were talking in the apothecary garden, and right before the accident, we saw Antoinette Rochester."

His glass plunked down, brandy sloshing onto the table, and he began to cough.

"Are you all right, sir?" I rose from my chair, but he waved me back.

"Fine," he managed between coughs.

When the spasm settled, he wiped his mouth with a napkin and drank from a teacup. "Pardon me, Miss Aire. I thought I heard you say that you *saw* Antoinette Rochester."

Nodding slowly, I replied, "Saw and spoke to her."

I studied him closely. Shocked and distressed, exactly as I would expect.

"That's impossible."

"It's not *common*. In the course of my investigations at Thornfield, I have come to believe that its afflictions are a result of Antoinette Rochester having failed to move on after her death. I'm even more convinced of that now. What I'm trying to understand is *why*."

How he stared at me. "Why would you think I'd know anything about it?"

This *wasn't* exactly what I'd expected. Knowing him to have been very fond of Antoinette—even in love with her—wouldn't he want to know more about the encounter, even if he was skeptical?

"I was hoping you could give me an idea of her state of mind near her time of death," I replied. "Was anything distressing her besides her illness? With regard to her husband, her father, or anyone else? It could help me understand why her spirit may be lingering."

Again he wiped his mouth, and I noted a slight trembling of his fingers. "She was frail and confined to her bed. When she was awake, she was calm and composed. She was doted on by her father, and I know that she was devastated to be leaving him." His stare hardened. "She was an angel, Miss Aire. She'd never harm anyone at Thornfield, in life or in death. Certainly not her husband, if that's what you're getting at."

Something in his manner—a movement of his eyes at the end of this declaration—left me feeling he might not fully believe all he was saying. "Sometimes spirits who linger are changed," I said. "Especially if something about their death felt wrong or unfair to them."

He studied his empty brandy glass. "She was eighteen. Everything about it was unfair."

"Indeed."

Then his gaze lifted, and I saw something new. The shadows beneath his eyes had deepened, and weariness rested on his brow. *He looks haunted.*

"What did she say?" he asked.

I smoothed the table linen under my fingers, watching him closely. "Nothing that I feel at liberty to share, I'm afraid, as it was said to her husband. But I will tell you that there was nothing angelic about it. If you can think of *anything* that might have disturbed her thoughts at the time of her death—or even after—it could be a great help."

He took a deep breath, and I hoped for a revelation. But he simply shook his head. "You might do better to ask her husband." He stood up. "If you don't mind, Miss Aire, I'd like to rest for an hour or so. It will be a long night."

"Of course. Thank you for your time, Dr. Poole."

When he'd gone, I sat thinking. The more I went over our conversation in my mind, the more convinced I became that he was hiding something. I was about to follow him out and go to bed myself when my gaze fell on the teacup beside his plate. I reached out and tipped it, peeking inside. A little of the red-brown liquid sloshed in the bottom of the cup, and the mote spoon beside it held a pile of soggy leaves.

Glancing first at the door the footmen used, I picked up the spoon and dumped the strained leaves back into the cup, stirring them clockwise a few times.

*"Leaves of tea, reveal to me, whatever I most need to see."*

I covered the cup with the saucer and flipped it over. Then I righted the cup, studying the leaves that had stuck inside.

The first thing I noticed was the letter *A*, clear as day, though upside down. Beside it was a crescent moon—*which indicated a secret or trick.*

I heard the door between the blue drawing room and hall open. Setting the cup down in the pool of tea, I hurried to the dining room door, arriving just as Mrs. Fairfax was opening it.

"Oh!" she said, startled to find me so close. "I've come to tell you that I had a room made up for you here in the house. I thought you might like to remain here, after all that's happened."

"How kind of you, Mrs. Fairfax." For once I had been dreading returning to the cottage, where I might not receive updates about Mr. Rochester.

"Let me know what things you need, and I'll send Agnes with a footman to collect them."

She took me to a bedchamber near her sitting room. It was light and pretty, with floral-patterned paper and furnishings and paintings of the house and gardens adorning the walls. Over the fireplace hung a lovely landscape of the heath and the village beyond, heather in full bloom and hills dark purple against an evening sky. It was well executed but, to my untrained eye, looked unfinished; the hills on one edge of the picture had not been filled in. I moved to take a closer look and found the letters *AMR* in the bottom-right corner.

*Antoinette Mason Rochester.*

Beautiful *and* accomplished. I was glad she hadn't spent all her time at Thornfield abed. Having signed it unfinished, she must have known the end was near. Or perhaps had simply lacked the strength to finish it. It made her more real to me than all the descriptions of her I had heard at Thornfield, and I felt a pang over her too-brief life.

I wondered at the painting being hung in an unused bedchamber, out of the flow of traffic of the house. Because it was unfinished? Or had Mr. Rochester found it painful to look at?

*Maybe it's painful to look at because it's unfinished.*

It was nearly midnight by the time I went to bed. If not for Blanche Ingram, Mr. Rochester and I would be setting out just now for the hawthorn wood. It was tempting to blame her for his injury, but if we'd succeeded in finding Antoinette, it might have happened anyway. And I might not have the memory of the things he'd said in comparing me to Miss Ingram.

When I thought back over everything that had happened that day, I felt like I hadn't slept for a week. Yet sleep would not come. If I wasn't thinking about Mr. Rochester, I was thinking about my mother. If I wasn't thinking about her, I was thinking about Antoinette and Poole. I supposed there'd been a kind of warning about all this in that confounding tea leaf reading Maria had done for me before I left Lowood. How I missed her counsel!

As I was finally dropping off to sleep, a sudden knock on the door snatched me awake again.

"Miss Aire?" Mrs. Fairfax, her voice creaky with fatigue. "I'm so sorry to wake you, but Mr. Rochester is calling for you, and I fear will not be still until you appear. He has threatened to come down if I don't fetch you."

I sat up and swung my legs down, heart pounding. "Of course," I called to her. "I'm coming."

"If I may come in, I've brought a lamp."

"Please do."

"Where is Dr. Poole?" I asked when she had joined me.

"He is with Mr. Rochester and has sanctioned your visit, I think in hopes his patient will rest easier afterward."

I didn't take the time to dress or pin up my hair, but Mrs. Fairfax helped me put on my dressing gown, and then together we went out to the great hall and made our way up the dark staircase. The house was silent, with all the other servants abed at this hour. The fire in the hall had burned down to glowing coals, and upstairs, the lamp outside Mr. Rochester's bedroom was the only one still lit. As we made our way toward it through the gallery, Mrs. Fairfax's lamp illuminated the family portraits one by one. I glimpsed a modern one of a raven-haired young lady in a forget-me-not-blue dress that I thought was likely Mrs. Rochester. Her beauty had not been exaggerated.

We reached Mr. Rochester's room, and Mrs. Fairfax knocked once and pushed the door open.

"Miss Aire, come in," Mr. Rochester called shortly. "Mrs. Fairfax, leave us."

Relief flooded me to see him alert and sitting up. There was no sign of the physician, and I was grateful to have at least a moment alone with him. Yet my employer's expression was dour. Mrs. Fairfax shot me a look of sympathy and went out.

I moved closer to his bedside. "How are you, sir?"

He was pale, with depressions under his eyes. A bandage covered the wound on his forehead; a few splotches of bright blood had seeped through. He wore a nightshirt and sat against the headboard, the coverlet pulled to his waist. Scratches marked his hands and exposed wrists.

"I've been better," he said, "but I will live. I must speak with you."

He frowned and stared blankly at the foot of the bed. I didn't like this return of coldness in his manner.

"Miss Aire," he said at last, looking at me, "you must go."

The floor dropped from under me. "Sir?"

"You heard me. You must go at once. At first light."

I stared, my thoughts a dizzying whirl.

"I'm not displeased with you," he continued, though still without warmth. "On the contrary, you've done exactly what you were brought here to do."

"But I've done nothing as of yet," I countered. "I spoke earlier with Dr. Poole, and I feel I'm getting closer to—"

"Enough, Miss Aire. I'm afraid you need look no further than *me* for the reason behind Thornfield's troubles."

I flinched at the sharpness in his tone. My voice wavered as I said, "What can you mean, sir?"

"You were there. You heard my wife."

My heart began to thump, and I stepped closer to his bedside. "Yes, but you must not take that to heart. She was equally awful to her maid. She's not herself."

"Yet all of it was true."

I shook my head, unwilling to believe. "You contradicted her yourself, remember?"

His frown deepened. "I've kept something from you, Miss Aire. I was selfish. I didn't want you thinking ill of me."

Dread knotted my insides. What was he about to confess?

"I *knew* that she would die."

I frowned. "I—I know you did, sir. As did her physicians and her family."

He set his eyes hard on mine. "You don't understand. Before we married, I knew that she would die."

# "Many Shadows"

The room felt close, without enough air. Was he trying to tell me he'd had a hand in his wife's death?

"How could you have known?" I asked faintly.

He turned to look at the window, though the curtains had been drawn. "Her father told me. Her cough had been diagnosed some time ago. Charles Mason is a widower with no other children. He had made Antoinette his heir. If she had died unmarried, the estate would have eventually passed to a dissolute rascal of a nephew. Now the estate remains in the family without the risk of ruin." His eyes came back to my face. "So you see, we 'arranged it all' between us, just as Antoinette said. And I married her knowing I, too, would be a widower."

It took a few moments of silent contemplation, but finally the cloud of uncertainty began to lift. While it was hard to hear this—it wasn't romantic; it was even a touch mercenary—nothing he'd said was particularly shocking.

"Neither of you could have known for certain," I said. "But even if her death was probable, many families would do the same under those circumstances."

There was no expression in his gray eyes. "Would they?"

I had no doubt there was a precedent for this sort of thing. Old families behaved in such ways over property and status. But the events in the garden had taken his mind to a dark place. I would have to help him out of it.

"Did Antoinette know why the marriage had been arranged?"

His lips formed a small, wretched smile that made me shiver. "I don't know. I wanted to tell her, but her father insisted that I leave it to him."

If she was maneuvered into the marriage without knowing the real reason, that could certainly have bred the resentment we'd witnessed in the garden. Yet I couldn't help but feel this was more a case of a corrupted spirit lashing out at the living. In accusing her husband of something he already felt he was guilty of, she had simply used his own integrity against him to make him suffer. Just as she'd used Agnes's love for her mistress to make *her* suffer.

"I must again urge you not to take the spirit's words to heart," I said. "She also accused you of being eager for her to die, and you and I both know that to be untrue."

"Perhaps, but tell me—what does it say about me that if I'd not known she was dying, I would not have married her?"

On the surface, it was troubling. He had married his wife for personal gain, knowing she would die. He would not have married her otherwise. But I had learned early on that you could not judge Mr. Rochester by the surface.

"The very fact that you wouldn't have married her is the one that proves you were blameless. You wouldn't have married her because you were not *in love* with her, and you had no designs on her inheritance. You made a choice to save her father's estate, and along with it all the livelihoods that depend upon it. You did what you thought best for everyone involved."

The smile that answered me was weak and resigned. "And now I must do so again. In trying to save her estate, I have doomed my own. She was my wife, and it is my burden."

I shook my head in exasperation. In *desperation*. "What is best *now* is that this shadow be lifted from Thornfield. For the sake of everyone here, you must not turn me out yet."

"Miss Aire," he said, warmth creeping into his tone at last, "I am your employer." With these four words, he reestablished the boundary between us. "*As* your employer, I'm telling you, as I will soon tell the others, that your services are no longer required. Everyone here has been endangered by my choices, but no longer. From now on, it will be only me."

I stared at him in horror. "You don't mean to stay here *alone*?"

"Dr. Poole has offered to stay with me, at least until I've fully recovered."

"Dr. Poole!"

"He was Antoinette's physician, and he knew her well. We will face this together."

*Poole* had endorsed this scheme? Or was it worse than that?

"Was it Poole who suggested this?" I demanded. "Think, sir, what might be his motive?"

"I am aware that you are suspicious of Dr. Poole, though you have never quite said so. But you are mistaken, and I won't hear you speak against him."

One by one, doors slammed closed on my arguments. I trusted Poole even less than before, but what evidence could I give against him beyond shapes read in tea leaves?

"I beg you," I said, "consider again in the morning, when you've rested. What is to be gained by such haste?"

His gaze locked with mine. "Did you not follow me to the estate churchyard?"

My face flushed hot with shame, and my heart sank. "Forgive me, sir, I—"

"No doubt you found the graves of my family. You are quicker than most to add two and two together. I should have thought the reason for my haste would be obvious."

Helplessly, I shook my head.

"Jane, I am not about to sit idly by while your life is cut short."

*My life.* At last I understood. "I know you lost your mother and sisters before their time. But there is no reason to think that will happen to me."

Fire flashed in his eyes. "No *reason*? Not the blackthorn creature that threatened you? Not the falling branches in the apothecary garden? You were brought here to interfere, and *she* is trying to stop you."

I recalled the shove I'd felt in the apothecary garden. Had Mr. Rochester taken an injury that was meant for *me*? How had this not occurred to me?

"And that's not all, Jane. This very night I dreamed your end."

"Dreamed, sir?"

"I watched it happening. There was nothing I could do to stop it." Closing his eyes, he took a breath. "I've always resisted the visions that come to me. My mother had them, and they frightened me. I didn't want to believe in events that were fated to happen. But I thank God for them now."

Shaken and desperate, I closed the small distance between him and me. "Even if it was the Sight, events seen in dreams are often warnings, and therefore may be avoided."

He looked at me. "And that's exactly what I'm doing."

Well, I had walked neatly into that.

"You must understand," he said, "there has always been a curse on this estate. You know I'm a skeptic, but you have opened my eyes to many possibilities, and I've come to believe that no woman who holds a place in my heart can survive here."

*A place in my heart.*

Trembling, I replied, "You have a witch now, sir. You must trust her to help you."

The sudden tenderness in his gaze brought an ache to my chest. His eyes moved over me—my loose, mussed hair and bedroom attire—like he was only just now really seeing me.

Then he turned his head. "You are dismissed, Miss Aire. Have no fear of Mr. Brocklehurst. I will tell him that you've been very helpful in uncovering the cause of our troubles, which is no more than the truth. Lowood will receive the second half of the agreed-upon fee, and I'm including something more for *you*—enough for you to leave Lowood, should you wish to establish yourself independently. An endowment of sorts, in appreciation of your services and recognition of your potential. I had no right to say to you the things I did yesterday. I suppose I was swept up in feeling. I hope that you'll for—"

Forgive? Forget? I don't know which he intended, because I interrupted with, "I don't want it! I'll not accept money from you for such a reason."

I felt like a vase smashed to pieces on the floor. He'd given me something wondrously sweet and then taken it back in the very next breath.

*Yet what did you expect, Jane?* Suppose I had stayed on. Suppose I managed to lift Thornfield's curse. It would not have changed what he and I could and could not be to each other. Men like Mr. Rochester did not marry women like me. He, too, would have remembered that before the end.

Mr. Rochester's gaze turned cold again. He repeated brusquely, "Pack your things. Mrs. Fairfax will arrange your journey."

I went back to bed, thinking I would rest and let my head clear, hoping that by morning Mr. Rochester would change his mind—or that I would think of some way of changing it. Whatever feeling or regret between the two of us, I couldn't bear the idea of him remaining alone at Thornfield with Poole and the angry ghost of his dead wife.

I tried not to dwell on the things he'd said that had caused my heart to race, except to consider whether I had imagined them. *I suppose I was swept up in feeling.* My time at Thornfield was beginning to feel like a fevered dream.

A great clock in some part of the house chimed four in the morning. I hadn't slept, nor had I come up with any new arguments to use on Mr. Rochester. So I got up and dressed and went back to the cottage to pack my things, as I had been ordered. I didn't wake Mrs. Fairfax, as I was sure she would seek me out in a few hours.

When I arrived at the cottage, I found Sybil waiting for me at the door, mewing and pacing on the stoop. I let her in and, using a taper I'd brought from the house, lit the candles. The hearth was cold.

Sybil hopped up and curled on the bed as usual, watching as I numbly packed. When I finished, I stopped and looked at her. She slowly blinked at me, and my throat tightened.

"I wish we had more time."

She raised her head from her paws. *Meow.*

A tear slipped down my cheek.

There was a knock at the door. I wiped my face and went to open it—Agnes with a breakfast tray.

"Is it true, miss?" she asked, eyes wide, as I took the tray from her.

"Is what true, Agnes?" My voice was rough with grief and fatigue. I set the tray on the table.

"That you're leaving today. That *all* of us are to be sent away!"

"I wish it weren't."

She sighed, and as tears pooled in her eyes, a heavy stone of guilt settled in my chest. To think I had dreamed of opening a school! My very first assignment outside Lowood had resulted in injury to my employer—not once but twice—and with the loss of employment for everyone on the estate. Mr. Rochester would waste away here, alone with his ghost. Might the consequences of my failure even extend to Thornfield's tenants?

*One thing is certain: I leave the place far worse than I found it.*

Trembling, I moved closer to Agnes and reached for her hand. "Do you have someplace to go?"

Nodding, she said, "Mr. Rochester asked Mrs. Fairfax to write to Mr. Mason."

"Good." I bent over the table and uncorked the ink bottle. Then I scribbled Lowood's postal address on a scrap of paper. Handing it to her, I asked gently, "Do you read and write?"

Pink rose to her cheeks. "A little."

"Write to me at Lowood so I'll know you're settled. A few words will suffice, or perhaps someone at Thrush Hall will be willing to help you with a longer note. Can you do that?"

Taking the paper, she said, "Yes, miss."

"All will be well, Agnes."

*I wish I believed it.*

"Miss?" She eyed me sheepishly.

"Yes?"

"I want to say that I'm sorry for . . . for at first. I never knew a witch before. When I was a girl I heard stories, and I was frightened of you."

"But no more?"

"You're kind, miss. Far kinder than some who an't witches."

Moisture pooled in my own eyes as I clasped her hand between mine. She managed a smile, another tear slipping down her cheek. I assured her again that all would be well, and she took her leave.

Mrs. Fairfax came directly after.

"Mr. Rochester's carriage will take you to Leeds within the hour," she said, eyeing me sadly. "From there, the coach will take you on. With luck and fair weather, you'll sleep in your own bed tonight."

"Thank you, ma'am."

"I hate this, Miss Aire; I don't mind saying so." The fatigue of the long night was written on her face. "I can't help wondering if Mr. Rochester is all right in his mind after his injury."

"Nor can I," I admitted. "I'm even more worried that Dr. Poole seems to have been an influence on him. What can he mean by stranding Mr. Rochester here with no one to help look after him?"

Her frown deepened. "You still suspect Dr. Poole?"

"More than ever. He's hiding something to do with Mrs. Rochester; I'd bet my life on it. But Mr. Rochester won't hear a word against him."

"If only he'd given you more time," she replied, shaking her head. "Why must he take this on himself?"

If only I'd made better *use* of my time, instead of dwelling on things that could never be.

"He feels responsible," I said. "He doesn't want harm to come to anyone else on the estate."

"I don't know *why* he should feel responsible. I wish I could do something. He is kin and has always been kind to me. But I'm still only a servant. Not even that now. He respects you, Miss Aire, that's plain to see. If you couldn't get through to him, I never shall."

My heart gave a mournful throb, and I fought not to choke on my reply. "I'm so sorry, Mrs. Fairfax. Will you be all right?"

"Oh yes. I'll go to my daughter in Hay. She and her husband have a public house, and she has asked me many times to go and work for her. There'll be a baby soon, so I suppose it's time I did."

This gave me some relief. "That sounds like a happy arrangement. And I'm glad you'll be close. In case he needs you."

She eyed me speculatively. "I know you've only been here a few days, but I must say—I did begin to think Mr. Rochester had grown fond of you." My cheeks flamed, and so did hers. "It worried me a little, but Mr. Rochester has never been anything other than honorable."

This was more than I could take, and a tear finally slipped onto my cheek. I quickly wiped it away. "Rest assured his treatment of me was never less than gentlemanly."

We embraced, and I already felt the loss of the good-hearted woman. As she said, my time here had been short, but I hadn't known so much kindness and acceptance in my life that I had learned to take it for granted.

When she'd gone, I determined that I must make one final effort. Picking up the charm I'd made the day before, I set out for the apothecary garden. I wouldn't have long, but if I could speak to Antoinette again, perhaps she would reveal something about Poole that might persuade Mr. Rochester not to remain here alone with him. That might even persuade him to give me more time.

*And if Mr. Rochester was right that she meant to harm me?*

I was willing to take the risk.

Sybil followed me as far as the gate and sat down to wait. The servants had already shifted the fallen elm branch off the path, and my breath caught when I noticed drops of blood on the old blond brick.

"Restless spirit, come to me.
I call you forth.
So mote it be."

The day was gray and uneasy, with wind tossing the treetops and a cold rain occasionally spitting forth. I kept a weather eye on the old elm, ready to quickly cede ground if necessary.

After a minute or two with no result from my spell, I chanted again. Then I made a circuit of the garden, peering into every damp and weedy corner. Though I felt the whole time like someone was watching me, I saw nothing.

Discouraged and dispirited, I was returning to the cottage when Sybil stepped onto the path in front of me. She obviously didn't like this garden and had only entered previously when I was in danger. Before I could turn to check behind me, she *rose on her hind legs like a dog*.

The legs on the ground began to elongate, and her shoulders shifted backward until her front legs hung at her sides. Her fur smoothed and began to recede, revealing greenish flesh beneath. From her head sprouted red hair that rapidly grew, thick and gleaming, until long waves rippled like a banner in the wind.

The transformation had taken only a few seconds, but it was something I would never forget. And I'd seen all of it without using the hagstone.

She had crossed the veil to reveal herself to me.

I stared in wonder, waiting for her to speak. The wind gentled around us, and the rain slowed to a cold sprinkle.

"No place for thee," she said at last. Her gaze shifted to the elm tree, and she narrowed her eyes. "Many shadows."

"Yes. I'm going today."

Now she frowned. "Back to *he*."

"Back to the school," I said. "Not by choice. I'm no longer employed here. But I intend someday to return. To . . . to visit you here." *Surely he won't deny me that.* Tears started down my face again, and my voice broke as I continued. "I want to thank you for your help and protection. And for telling me my story. I have so often wondered."

I could only hope she'd understood at least some of what I'd said. How cruel it seemed to find her after nearly thirty years, only to lose her a day later.

"Do you have a name?" I asked.

She opened her mouth, and what came out was not a word but a sound, like the wind in the autumn leaves. She laughed at my perplexed expression. Then she shrugged and said, "Sybil."

"Do . . ." I swallowed. "Do *I* have a name?"

She sobered, and this time she made a sound like a fish swishing and splashing upstream. I easily recognized it because the stream near Lowood was choked with salmon this time of year.

She moved closer. The almond-spice fragrance of hawthorn blossoms drifted from her. She bent and pressed her lips to my cheek. There came a pinprick of pain, and I jumped, reaching to touch the back of my scalp. She laughed and moved away, holding up a few strands of my hair. Then I watched her fade into the mist at the back of the garden.

*"Miss Aire?"*

Someone at the cottage was calling for me. The carriage must be ready.

Mrs. Fairfax had prophesied true: I would sleep in my own bed this night. It was a relief not to have to stop on the road, my mind and heart being so weighted down by my last day at Thornfield. I needed familiar things around me.

The carriage hired for the last short stage of the journey deposited me at Lowood after nine that evening. I disturbed no one except Mr. Carey, our groom, who kindly transported my trunks to the apothecary. There would be time enough for my interview with Mr. Brocklehurst in the morning.

Everything in my little dwelling was just as I'd left it. Stacks of books and diaries that I'd straightened but had no time to return to the bookshelf. My cures cabinets, with gaps like missing teeth where I'd packed herbs for the journey. The rosemary I'd hung to dry strongly scenting the room. I longed for Sybil's comforting presence.

I had been cold since leaving Thornfield. The memories and deep shadows of the apothecary garden still held me in their embrace. I considered piling quilts onto my bed and leaving everything for the morning. Exhausted from the sleepless night, ill from the long journey, heartsick from . . . from *everything*, I craved both rest and forgetfulness.

But I knew my mind was too disarranged for sleep. In particular, my thoughts kept returning to the softest and kindest of the words Mr. Rochester had said to me last evening. I couldn't help grieving for what might have been.

*What, Jane? What might have been?*

Even had there not been many obstacles—even had he declared himself in love and asked me to be his wife—would I really be content to leave Lowood for a future without my students or my craft?

*But there are, and he hasn't, so let that be an end to it.*

Woodenly, I moved to my stove and lit it. Water still sloshed in the kettle, and I put it on to boil for an infusion.

*Lavender, motherwort, rose petals. Hawthorn flowers for healing the heart—and to remind me I have a mother who hasn't forgotten me.*

I filled a cup and sat down in my well-worn armchair to sip.

Recalling the scene of farewell with my mother, I reached a finger to my scalp where she'd plucked out my hair. Strangely, I had been touched by the gesture. She'd wanted to keep something of me with her.

I continued sipping the infusion, allowing my busy thoughts to settle. Then I got up to dress for bed. Soothed by my potion and the soft popping of the coal fire, I crawled under the quilts and dropped off to sleep before more tears could come.

I woke with the remnants of a painful dream ribboning through my thoughts—painful because it broke my heart afresh. Mr. Rochester and I *married.* The ceremony was conducted in the church on the estate, which had been made whole again for the specific purpose of the ceremony. My students attended, and Maria Temple. And Mr. Brocklehurst of all people. I wore a lilac dress with cream lace and carried butter-yellow primroses. My mother came, too, in the form of Sybil, sunning herself on the threshold of the church while we exchanged our vows.

It all felt so real. The way he smiled at me as he spoke. His hands holding mine and, at the end, my lips against his. How it wrenched me to force these happy images from my mind.

I rose and dressed, preparing myself to face the dining hall. I thought about the questions that were sure to come from my curious students. There were few details I could share, and I doubted my ability to talk about it *at all* without them seeing my distress. I would simply have to tell them I was obligated to keep my employer's secrets. It wouldn't satisfy them, but that couldn't be helped. At least today was Saturday, which was reserved for chores and catching up on studies. I wouldn't face them in class.

Anticipating the inevitable interview with Mr. B, I pocketed the sealed letter for him from Mr. Rochester, which one of Thornfield's maids had brought me as I was climbing into the carriage yesterday morning. I had held it against my chest most of the way to Leeds.

Cold October rain drummed my bonnet as I walked through the garden and up the drive toward the school. The reality of its humble and familiar lines on this dreary autumn morning reinforced the notion that the last few days had been but a dream. Yet somehow *this* began to feel like the dream. Nothing familiar was really the same anymore, not even my beloved apothecary. A tiny, cold distance had inserted itself between me and all the things that had made up my world for so long. Nothing had changed but me.

I had almost reached the entrance when a maid intercepted me.

"Welcome back, miss." She was one of the younger maids, brought on earlier this year. She, too, had once been afraid of me.

"Thank you, Carrie. Is everyone well?"

She nodded. "I was just coming to find you. Mr. Brocklehurst has asked to see you in his study before breakfast."

Knowing this moment would come had done nothing to lessen my dread of it.

# *Pert Thing*

I took a deep breath and altered course, once again making my way up the tree-lined walk that led around to the back of the school. The wind gusted suddenly, releasing a flurry of fan-shaped gold linden leaves.

My stomach was busily tying itself in knots. Mr. B would demand answers that were unlikely to be in the letter, and I doubted I would get away with citing confidentiality as a justification for refusing *him*. I could only hope that the payment in full of the agreed-upon fee would soften him toward me.

But of course there were new reasons for awkwardness between us. Would I find the courage to confront him? Would he finally tell me the truth? Hard as it would be to learn I'd been lied to my whole life, a part of me acknowledged that revealing the truth would have come with risk. Were it to become public, Lowood's board would very likely strip him of his position. Though I had always detested him, I understood now that Lowood was everything to him, as it had been to me. He had devoted his life to it, much as a clergyman to the church. Currying favor with patrons and frugal management of resources had been a necessary evil, even if he did have a tendency to carry it to extremes. On his watch, the school would never be closed.

I reached the cottage, and the maid led me to Mr. B in his dark-paneled office. His chair was angled toward the window, and he gazed out at the rainy garden over the tops of his pressed-together fingers. I thought he might be praying.

I cleared my throat quietly, and he turned his chair toward the desk. A characteristic frown rested on his lips.

Before he could start in, I took Mr. Rochester's letter from my pocket. "This is for you, sir."

It took supreme effort to appear to wait patiently as he broke the seal and read the letter, which consisted of several sheets. In fact, he read it several times, maintaining the same furrowed-brow concentration throughout.

Finally, he set it aside and looked at me. "I confess I'm hardly surprised to see you back here so soon. Though I *am* surprised that payment in full of Mr. Rochester's fee has arrived along with you."

Which should be interpreted as Mr. B having assumed that I'd be dismissed for any one of my numerous faults and that all fees would be forfeit.

"Indeed, sir?" It was the kind of answer he hated. But I'd resolved to give as little information as possible—especially nothing that might hint at my unhappiness with the situation.

He studied me across the desk, and I couldn't help trying to imagine him as a young man. One who would attend a May Day celebration. One who could give in to his passions. My imagination failed me. Could I have gotten it wrong? Now that I was away from Thornfield, it was hard not to start questioning the astonishing things that had happened there.

Lifting an eyebrow, he said, "You have nothing else to say about it?"

"I'm not sure I understand what else you *wish* me to say, sir."

He made an exasperated noise. "Don't be coy, Aire. Have you truly completed the work, or has Mr. Rochester sent you home for some reason you'd rather not tell me?"

I folded my hands in my lap, holding them still. "Mr. Rochester said that I had performed my duties satisfactorily."

"He has told me as much, you pert thing. There's something amiss here; I'm sure of it." His eyes narrowed. "As your employer—as overseer of this institution—I need to understand why he has included an additional, *substantial* sum for your own personal use. Whatever would motivate him to do such a thing?"

I cringed inwardly. Heat crept up my neck and into my face. "I assure you that I discouraged him from doing this."

His coffee-dark eyes bored into me. "That is not an answer to my question."

What now? The truth was thorny. Mr. Rochester had given me the money out of feelings of guilt. For summarily dismissing me but also for having said too much in the apothecary garden. I couldn't tell this to Mr. B, yet I dare not lie. I had no idea how much Mr. Rochester might have said, and I might be caught—which would reinforce any suspicion that this gift of money was in some way compromising.

*Redirect, Jane.*

"I don't feel at liberty to tell you all, sir, it being the personal business of Mr. Rochester. He is a very private person." No lie thus far. "But I will say as much as I can."

Mr. B pursed his lips together and waited.

I told him about my discoveries at Thornfield—the ghost of Antoinette Rochester and how I believed that something about her death was the reason for the trouble on the estate. I could see his shock at the strange nature of the story.

"All this was disclosed to Mr. Rochester?"

"Yes, sir."

"And he believed it?" Clearly Mr. B was struggling to.

"He saw the spirit himself, sir."

"What was his reaction?"

"For reasons I cannot go into, he concluded that he was to blame for the haunting of Thornfield, and he dismissed me, along with the rest of his servants."

Mr. B stared, flattening his hands on the desktop. "Why on earth would he do that?"

"To protect us from the ghost, as I understand it." A fresh wave of regret threatened to overwhelm me, and I worried the sharp-eyed trustee would see it. But he was deep in astonishment.

"Has the man broken the law in some way? Did he . . . ?"

*Did he have something to do with his wife's death?*

"Mr. Rochester felt that he had wronged his wife, owing to some private circumstances regarding their marriage, but I discovered no evidence of any real wrongdoing." I thought about Poole, and my stomach churned.

"Good heavens." Mr. B sat back in his chair, taking it all in. After a moment, his sharp eyes came back to my face. "This still doesn't explain the money."

My fingers knit tightly in my lap. "All I can do is relay to you what he said to me. He said that he believed I had potential, and he wanted to make it possible for me to establish myself independently."

I well understood that when Mr. Rochester had dismissed me, he was in the process of burying himself in guilt about many things. But a new thought came to me now. What if he'd actually meant what he said? That he believed in me, and he was giving me the money because it would free me from Lowood if I wished it. Not out of guilt but because he *wanted me to be happy*?

My eyes stung, and my mind buzzed. I avoided Mr. B's gaze. I needed to get away from him and think.

"This is a considerable sum," he said, lifting one of the sheets of the letter. "The idea that he would give it to you for such a reason, especially after such a short period of time—frankly, it's impossible to believe. What else has passed between you and this gentleman?"

I raised my eyes to his face, and my blood began to boil. There was no stopping what came next.

"*Frankly*, Mr. Brocklehurst, I don't care what you believe." His eyes opened wide. "Moreover, I am uninterested in continuing this discussion while you insinuate something improper occurred at Thornfield. I tell you plainly that no such thing has happened, and if you accuse me of lying, then you must accept my resignation."

He stared, and my heart pounded. I found I had no regrets. I felt nothing but exhilaration. I had never so forcefully or fully spoken my mind to him. Here was a man whom I believed had lied to me my whole life. Why should I continue to submit to living within the narrow confines he had set for me? I had Mr. Rochester to thank for helping me to look beyond them—and for preparing me to meet whatever consequences might follow from my rebellion.

When Mr. Brocklehurst found his voice, he muttered, "Is *that* how it is now?"

I took a full, slow breath, letting my passion subside. While I wouldn't take any of it back, there was no point in making an enemy of him if I could help it.

In a milder tone, I said, "How it *is* is that Mr. Rochester's gift means I need not sacrifice self-respect to remain employed. I ask that you treat me as I deserve to be treated—as I have *earned the right* to be treated. You may not like witches, but having chosen to employ one—one whose talents have helped to support the institution we both love—I expect you to at least be civil to me. I am a grown woman who has worked hard to raise herself up from a pauper in a basket, and I will not be treated like a wayward child."

His expression shifted, anger replaced by . . . I couldn't interpret the emotion. It wasn't one I'd ever seen cross his face. *He looks haunted, like Poole. A man with a secret.*

Then I realized what I'd said—*a pauper in a basket, a wayward child.*

He collected the papers and moved them to one side of his desk. "You may go, Miss Aire."

"I have one question for *you*, sir." Mr. B raised his eyes again to my face, trying to silence me with a look.

I fidgeted in my chair, but I forged on. "Did you never learn anything about who might have left me at Lowood?"

He went still, the expression of disapproval frozen on his face. "As you know, inquiries were made at the time. No one came forward."

I nodded as if accepting his answer. Then I said, "You grew up near Thornfield, did you not, sir?"

His gaze dropped to the desktop. "You may *go*, Miss Aire."

The interview had shaken me, and I no longer had the spirit to appear in the dining hall. I had already missed breakfast anyway. Instead I stopped by the kitchen, where Mrs. Shaw was sure to give me something, despite it being against the rules.

Cook's domain (and Cook herself) was steamy and fragrant from the daily baking. Hands deep in dough, she directed one of her helpers to pour me a cup of tea and spread jam over a thick slice of bread.

As I sat at the servants' table and ate my late breakfast, it occurred to me I *was* somewhat spoiled. The staff having raised me, I enjoyed privileges other teachers and students didn't. I'd always assumed Cook's displays of favoritism had gone unnoticed, but Mr. B had been known to count *potatoes*. Might it have been an intentional oversight? Secret indulgences from a father who wished to remain unknown? And his harsh treatment of me—even that, in this light, looked different. I thought it was because I was a witch, and a painfully headstrong one; to some extent it probably was. But mightn't a father be more critical of faults in his child than in another?

It didn't exactly engender warm feelings in me, but it seemed that by degrees, I was coming to understand him better. I also began to see all the ways he was desperately afraid. Afraid someone would discover that parts of his life had been a lie. Afraid he would lose Lowood, the only thing that gave his life meaning. Perhaps even afraid I would take my endowment and go—so much so that he lashed out with a shameful accusation.

Along with all this, another truth began to rise to the surface. How his view of me had shaped my view of myself. Willful. Ungrateful. Self-destructive. Not good enough to succeed at Thornfield. Not good enough, full stop.

I returned my tray to the kitchen and dashed off to find Maria. I needed her clear mind to help me sort it all. I was almost to the house she shared with Madame Allard, in a small hazel wood to the back of the property, when I encountered her on the path.

"Here you are," she said brightly. "You failed to appear at breakfast, so I was going to search you out. Are you well after your journey?"

"I can't say that I am," I admitted, smiling bleakly. "But I'm glad to see you."

"Let's go to the apothecary," she said, hooking her arm through mine. "Sabine is *à la maison*."

As soon as we'd reached the apothecary, she made a single inquiry, "Tell me everything," and I melted, giving way to the tears I'd been damming up all morning. She lit the stove and steeped herbs, their fragrance wafting soothingly through the room, and when the drink had calmed me, she inquired again.

"So much has happened," I said. "I can't even think where to start."

"Why don't you tell me about your employer?"

Maria always let her instincts guide her, and she always cut to the heart of things.

"He is the biggest tangle, I'm afraid."

"Then simply start at the beginning."

I set down my cup with a sigh. "I met Mr. Rochester for the first time on the road to Thornfield, after having ridiculously insisted on walking the last two miles."

Her eyes went wide. "You didn't!"

"Have you ever ridden all day in a coach? It's truly awful."

"How did he react?"

"Well, after I startled his horse—which reared and threw him into the heather—he was inclined to be prickly. But he turned out to be rather prickly in general."

Maria's eyes danced, and she laughed. "I'm so sorry, but *Jane*! Did you manage to patch it up between you?"

I couldn't help but smile at her amusement. "We did, and gradually I came to understand him better."

She gave me a knowing look. "And to *like* him better."

"Indeed, he is kind and good but also deeply sorrowful. Everyone he's loved has died before their time. It has cast a deep shadow over him and his estate."

"Which is why he wanted a Lowood witch."

"But I couldn't help him, Maria. We discovered the restless spirit of his dead wife is haunting the place, but before I could do anything about it, he sent me away. Now things are worse."

She studied me closely, and I knew she was "listening" to everything—my words, my gestures and glances, my *heart*. "Why did he do that?"

A lump formed in my throat. I picked up the teapot and refilled my cup. "He blames himself for her discontent. He thinks it's his responsibility. And he's worried that I'll be hurt by Thornfield's curse. The night he ordered me to go, he dreamed his wife's spirit . . ." I looked at her. "He dreamed she caused me harm."

"But if it was only a dream . . . ?"

"Mr. Rochester has the Sight."

She shook her head in wonder. "How fascinating, Jane. And do *you* believe you were in danger?"

"I don't know, but *he* most certainly is. I feel it, Maria. I should never have left him."

A small smile rested on her lips, which seemed odd, but Maria *was* odd. "Why did you?"

"He ordered me to go, quite forcefully. I was his employee. I felt I had no choice."

Her eyebrows slowly lifted. "That doesn't sound much like the Jane *I* know."

It came to me then, like a blow to the stomach. "Oh, Maria." I folded my arms over my middle. "I think part of me was *relieved*. I think I was afraid I wasn't good enough to finish the job."

Her eyes narrowed. "And what has changed now?"

I looked out the east-facing window. The rain had stopped, and a streamer of sunlight fell through a break in the clouds. An unexpected calm came over me.

"He's in danger. I'm meant to help him. There's no question of doing anything else."

# "Love has Come to Mean Death"

Just saying the words released something that had been holding tight inside me.

Maria, still eyeing me keenly, nodded.

"It means defying him," I said.

Her eyes rolled skyward. "So the man has decided to be a martyr—that need not deter you. He's in love with you, and you're in love with him, even if you haven't realized it yet. The rules between you have changed. It puts you on equal footing."

My heart stumbled and fell. Some part of me had dared to hope—to believe it might be so—and yet to hear it stated outright . . . It was absurd, wasn't it?

"You can't know he loves me, Maria."

"Jane! Have you even been listening to yourself? Everything we saw in your teacup makes sense now. *Of course* he loves you. But in his world, love has come to mean death."

*No woman who holds a place in my heart can survive here.*

I stared at her, reeling from a fact that deep in my own heart I already knew. *He's in love with me.*

*And I'm in love with him.*

I sat still another moment, letting the soft warmth of these thoughts flow over me. Could it really be as simple as that?

Though I hadn't voiced the question out loud, Maria said, "Don't think too much about what it means for now, Jane. You're returning to Thornfield to save the man you love. You must prepare yourself."

"Mr. Brocklehurst will never agree to it. But I suppose that no longer matters." I told her about Mr. Rochester's endowment.

"Good heavens, Jane! What else haven't you told me?"

"There is indeed a great *deal* more," I said, laughing wearily.

Maria stood up suddenly. "It must wait awhile. I shall see to your travel arrangements. Tomorrow is Sunday, and there will be fewer options, but I fear we can't afford to delay. A few extra coins here and there may ease the way."

"I don't yet have access to the funds from Mr. Rochester, but you may have all my savings." Lowood teachers received room and board, so I had spent little of my small salary in my decade of employment, mostly using it to replace clothing as it wore out.

Maria nodded. "And mine will be added to it if needed. I'll put Mrs. Phillips on the case. If anyone can manage it, she can. After I see her, I'll inform Mr. Brocklehurst of your decision. Then I shall return to you, and we'll put our heads together about facing this spirit."

Though buoyed by her support and resolve, as soon as she'd left me, my courage, if not my determination, flagged. What reason could I give for disregarding Mr. Rochester's dismissal and showing up at Thornfield again?

I might not *have* to give a reason. He had dismissed the entire staff, and I might find no one there to stand in my way. No one but Poole, and if he attempted to stop me . . . I would simply refuse to leave without seeing Mr. Rochester.

*You'll not insert yourself between us again.*

I set about preparing for the journey. There was no need to pack, as I'd yet to *un*pack. I dashed off a note to my top pupil, Alice, apologizing for leaving without seeing her and asking her to reassure the others. I'd felt like I was abandoning them the *first* time I left for Thornfield. But

I knew Maria would make sure they kept up with their studies and do her best to shield them from the unpredictable weather that was Mr. Brocklehurst.

Now that I'd decided on a course of action, I was impatient to be gone. I could almost *feel* the danger growing around Mr. Rochester. I even resorted to peering at the soggy herbs in the bottom of my teacup. All of it looked sinister, and I knew I was far too close to the question for divination to help me.

In checking again that I had everything I needed for the return journey, I came across the charm I'd made to summon Antoinette's spirit. It hadn't worked in the garden yesterday morning. Maybe because I hadn't made a charm for such a purpose before. I was grateful I'd have Maria's help before I returned.

Too agitated to wait idly, I got out my sewing basket and sat down next to the stove. I opened the linen pouch I'd used to make the charm and took out its contents. Rummaging three black glass buttons from my basket, I sewed them onto the bag, for eyes and nose, and used thread to stitch a mouth. Then I put the herbs and strands of hair back inside and also added some wool batting to fill it out. When I had a rounded shape, I sewed the bag closed, and I knotted and sewed long black yarn to the top of it for hair. Finally I took some faded scraps I'd saved from old clothing and sewed them around the bottom, forming a crude dress.

The poppet, though limbless, was a fair enough representation of a woman. The real hair inside would create a sympathy between Antoinette and the doll—or at least it would have if she'd been alive. I taught poppet making to my students, to use in healing spells. Particularly when self-healing was needed, whether physical or mental, it could be easier to focus a spell on something outside of oneself. Poppets could also be used for baneful magic, such as cursing or injuring enemies. It wasn't something I practiced, however sorely I might have been tempted by Mr. Brocklehurst on occasion. I wasn't sure why

I'd made the doll; Antoinette was a spirit and couldn't likely be either healed or cursed with it. Maybe it would be more effective in a summoning spell than the charm had been.

As I was tucking the poppet into one of my trunks, Maria returned with news that the trip to Thornfield was in Mrs. Phillips's capable hands, and I should expect to leave in the morning.

"And Mr. B?"

"I've left him in a foul temper. But I made it clear Mr. Rochester's life is in danger, and as you are now an independent woman, there was little he could say."

I breathed relief. "Thank you, Maria. For everything."

She smiled, dipping her head. "Now we have work to do, my dear. Let us start with all you have yet to tell me."

I gave her my Thornfield journal to read while I brewed a pot of strong tea for us, and this was how she learned about my mother. I knew exactly when she reached that page by her sharp intake of breath.

"Jane! What a secret to hold on to!"

I placed the teapot and cups on a tray and joined her at my apothecary table. "I tried to write you about it, but it didn't feel right. Then suddenly I was back here again and there was *so* much to tell. I guess, too, I've worried what you'd think of me, believing such a story."

"But whyever would I doubt you?"

I laughed. "Because it's preposterous?"

She frowned down at the page. "You've been quite thorough in your reasoning. There are pertinent details here. But really all I care about is what you *feel*."

I lifted the pot and poured our tea. "There's no resemblance between us whatsoever. It sounds just like a story a fairy might tell for some kind of gain or even just to make mischief. Yet I do believe her. Besides the dreams, and the things she knew about me, she looked out for me the whole time I was at Thornfield."

"And thank goodness for that. I'll feel much better about your going back there, knowing you'll have her." She sipped her tea. "As for Mr. B, I suppose this does help explain why he's always been so hard on you."

"Well, I wasn't the most obedient child," I admitted. "And that didn't exactly improve as I grew up."

She pursed her lips in a fond smile. "Do you intend to confront him?"

I sighed and picked up my cup. "I don't know. I would far prefer he tell me. I gave him an opening in his study this morning."

"And he didn't take it."

"His lack of response was a kind of answer. Honestly, I can't imagine him *ever* telling me."

"It would be awkward, to say the least. Potentially ruinous, were it generally known."

Maria opened a tin of biscuits, and the buttery aroma transported me back to my earliest years as her pupil. Though old enough to be my mother, she had never quite been motherly. With her dedication to the enrichment of young minds, she'd been more like a benevolent governess. As a child, I'd both loved and slightly feared her.

"Let us not spend valuable time trying to puzzle out Mr. B," she said, offering the tin to me. "Tell me about Mrs. Rochester."

Taking a biscuit, I said, "She was the only child of Charles Mason, a distant relative of Mr. Rochester on his father's side. Mr. Rochester married her when she was eighteen to save her family estate, and she died of consumption shortly after. She was mourned by her husband, but he didn't love her. Her physician did and also her lady's maid."

"Yet she herself was in love with no one."

"Based on what Agnes has told me."

"Not an unbiased source, nor always forthcoming."

"True."

"And you have a theory about the physician . . ."

"That he may have accidentally poisoned his patient."

"Or intentionally."

I raised my eyebrows.

"To abbreviate her suffering."

"That hadn't occurred to me, but yes. Either way, it would mean Antoinette's death wasn't natural, even if inevitable, and could provide an explanation for her disturbed rest." I nibbled the biscuit, thinking. "What could be his reason for siding with Mr. Rochester about sending everyone away?"

"Ah, that *is* interesting." She folded her arms, leaning on the table. "You tell me."

I plucked another biscuit from the tin and broke it in half. "He's desperate to see and speak to Antoinette, and he'd prefer to do it alone. A servant might discover his secret."

"And *you*, my dear, might banish her."

"Right. In truth, I think he may have been looking for Antoinette for some time. May even have had some contact with her already."

"Like the day in the apothecary garden, when you heard the voices?"

I nodded. "Yet it's odd, isn't it? He's a medical man; he deals with life and death as a natural course of his practice. What might have made him think to go looking for a ghost?"

Maria's gaze clouded. "Desperation again? Or . . . suppose his love *was* requited. Might they have had some agreement? Maybe she told him she would try to return."

"Maybe." But I wasn't satisfied. I could feel it like a glove that stuck because one finger was inside out.

"The important thing," said Maria, "is that you remember to think of him as your adversary. He may not be in his right mind. He may not *want* the lady returned to her rest. That could make him a danger to you and Mr. Rochester."

"I still hope that I'll be able to reason with him," I said. "I keep trying to cast him as the villain in this story, yet it's likely he's no more than a man who fell in love with the wrong woman and let it cloud his judgment."

Maria reached for my hand. "I hope you're right, but take care, Jane. Don't stay with them in the house. Return to your cottage, and ward it well. Accept your mother's help."

"I will," I promised.

The dinner hour came and went, as did two more pots of tea. We sat up poring over Maria's collection of grimoires, which, along with the texts on herbs and remedies, were the foundation of witch education at Lowood. We refreshed my memory on banishing spells for foes, sprites, and spirits. Everything we could think of that might help.

We also read through a fascinating and strange little volume called *Book of Highland Hauntings*, written in a spidery hand by a seeress who called herself the Lady of Loch Tay. Not only had the author collected the stories, she had spoken to some of the spirits herself. One spirit she was even able to persuade to move on, and another she swept out using a besom made of stiff green twigs from the broom shrub, known by northern witches for its protective and cleansing properties. I had seen broom growing just outside Thornfield's gate.

Finally, we were too tired to focus our eyes anymore, and Maria bid me a restful night and safe journey. We embraced, and she touched my hagstone talisman, closing her eyes and chanting, "*Witch's stone, protect your own.*"

Then she smiled and said, "Follow your heart, Jane. All will be well."

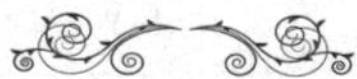

That night in my sleep, I approached the great hawthorn. The one that had always haunted my dreams, which I now recognized as my mother's tree. Night had fallen, and I found my way by my spirit-light. I discovered the tree charred, like the blackthorn, and no sign of my mother. Upon the flat stone beneath, a figure was curled—*Mr. Rochester*. I reached out to shake him awake. His body, clothed only in a blood-stained nightshirt, had gone cold and stiff.

With a cry of terror, I sat up in bed, heart pounding and sweat dampening my nightdress.

Whether it had been prophecy or simply a product of my anxious imagination, I was even more eager to leave Lowood. I rose and quickly dressed.

A kitchen maid arrived with a tray from Mrs. Shaw, but I had no appetite. I drank my coffee and wrapped bread and bacon in a napkin, tucking them into my carpetbag. I noticed Maria had left the biscuit tin, and I added that to the bag as well. Eating a bite on the road seemed to help with the nausea.

Then I left the apothecary to meet our driver. The fog was so thick this morning that I might have lost my way had I not known the grounds so well. But before I reached the gate, I met a shadowy form.

Mr. Brocklehurst waited on the drive between me and my carriage.

He looked like a parson in his black capelet and squared hat. I met his gaze, expecting dark looks and threats. Instead, he seemed uncertain.

"Miss Aire," he uttered.

Imagining that he'd come to prevent me from leaving, I set my jaw. "I'm returning to Thornfield, sir. I believe Mr. Rochester is in danger."

He frowned. "So Miss Temple has told me."

Heart racing, I moved to pass him. "If you'll excuse me, then."

"One moment."

I stopped abruptly, silently vowing I'd not let him cow me.

He drew something from his pocket and held it out to me. "This was found in your basket when you were left here as an infant. I thought you should have it."

It was a plait of shining red hair, about the thickness of a finger, tied at both ends with a silky cord. Slowly I reached out and took it from him.

"My mother," I murmured, brushing my thumb over the plait. I looked at him in astonishment. "I met her while I was at Thornfield."

Red stained his cheeks. A few moments of brittle silence passed, and I felt needles of anticipation. Would he tell me? In a way, it didn't matter. After all these years of wondering who my parents were, and why they had abandoned me, the greatest treasure I'd carry away with me was the realization that I could be whole without them.

"I should have given it to you long ago," he said.

I curled my fingers around the plait, finding I didn't have it in me to be angry with him. He might have tossed it into the fire that very day or any day since then. I could only imagine how hard it had been for him to come to me with it after all these years.

"Thank you for saving it for me."

He folded his hands behind his back, gaze dropping to the gravel at our feet. "Keeping it from you is hardly the only mistake I've ever made," he said. Tiny beads of moisture collected on the brim of his hat. "Sometimes we may start down a path thinking we're doing what's best for everyone. We can get so far down that path, it feels impossible to turn back."

His head came up, and his eyes fixed on mine. I held my breath.

"I hope you've never wanted for anything at Lowood. Had I . . . had I lost my position here, things would have been much harder for you. For us both."

There it was—the closest thing to a confession I was likely to get. I found it was enough. The circle was closed. *Motherless and fatherless no longer.*

"Yes," I said faintly. "I can imagine that."

He gazed off into the fog to one side of the drive. "I don't like this, Jane. I hope you'll take proper care."

My breath caught. He'd never once called me Jane, and he certainly never told me to take care unless I was trying his patience.

"I will, sir."

He looked down toward the gate. "Your trunks are ready?"

"They—they are. Mr. Carey took them down for me."

Mr. B nodded, and he took a step back. "You'll not want to keep Mr. Whitcomb waiting."

"No, sir."

I started toward the carriage, but he called after me, "We'll see you again at Lowood?"

My heart softened toward him as his grim countenance revealed a tinge of sadness.

Though Mr. Rochester had made it possible for me to permanently take my leave of this place, I found it hard to imagine. Lowood had always been my family and was even more so now. I would be back, even if not forever.

"I should think so," I said, "if I would be welcomed."

He hesitated, then uttered, "Indeed, you would be."

I continued toward the coach, choking back tears.

Gone were the golden autumn days; I had fog, rain, and wind for traveling companions. Just in changing from carriage to coach, I was soaked and chilled to the bone. At least the provisions I'd brought, and light naps along the journey, kept the travel sickness at bay.

My clothes were still wet when we reached a roadside inn outside the industrial town of Bradford, where I would await the hired carriage to take me the final leg to Hay, and Thornfield beyond. I found a table next to the fire and dined on bread, sausage, and cider.

The closer I got to Thornfield, the more I worried over what I would find there. I told myself that by now, Mr. Rochester would likely have somewhat recovered from his injury and might be easier to reason with. I tried not to think about the dark dream.

Feeble daylight had given way to dismal twilight by the time we reached Hay. This time, the driver was issued no strange order to let out his passenger and carry only her trunks to the manor. I couldn't get there fast enough.

Our approach failed to lift my spirits. The grounds were silent and still, a single lamp burning near the entrance. When the driver pulled up and stopped the carriage, he opened my door and asked, "You're expected, miss?" I could see the concern in his eyes.

"Not to worry," I said with false brightness.

He put down the box and unloaded my trunks.

"Could I ask a favor, sir?" I said. "I'm staying in a guest cottage here, and I know the servants are away. Would you mind carrying my trunks a short distance?"

His gaze shifted to one and then the other end of the manor. The place was not particularly inviting at present, and it was almost dark. I held out sixpence—the last I had, but I was here now—and he grunted assent.

I carried my bag and staff, and he also handed me one of the carriage lanterns. Then he followed me around the house to the herb garden. When we reached the cottage, I found the box of matches on the mantel and lit a candle. He set down the trunks, took the lantern, and tipped his hat to me with a murmured "good evening" before hurrying back out into the night.

There were still peats in the basket beside the hearth, and I soon had a comfortable blaze going. As I warmed my hands and dried my skirts before the fire, there came a scratch at the door.

# *Elixir*

Before panic could set in, the scratching was followed by a meow. I hurried to the door and opened it. Sybil ran past me and hopped onto the bed. She found her usual spot and sat down, mewing again.

I laughed. "I'm very glad to see you."

She watched me light more candles and then move around the cottage casting salt and warding spells. When I'd made the place as secure as I knew how to, I said, "I'm going to the house. Wish me luck."

*Meow.*

Sybil's appearance had boosted my courage. Not knowing what I would find at the house, I opened a trunk and picked out a few jars of herbs along with a bottle of my best healing syrup—endive, plantain, violet, Saint-John's-wort, and gillyflower—and put them in a basket.

When I opened the cottage door, Sybil dashed back out into the night. I tucked my staff under one arm and conjured my spirit-light.

The rain had picked up again, along with a punishing wind, and by the time I made it to the front of the house, my cape was soaked. Reaching the dimly lit entrance, I let the spirit-light go as I raised my fist and pounded, hoping to be heard. After a few moments with no answer, I called out loudly.

"Mr. Rochester? Dr. Poole?"

I pounded again. This time when no one came, I tried the handle and found the door unbolted. I slipped inside and looked around; a single candlestand had been lit in the hall, and there was a lamp at the foot of the stairs, below the unsettling portrait of the Montagu woman. The great fireplace was dark. I closed the door quietly and started toward the stairs.

A soft, melodic voice drifted from the south wing, and I froze. It barely rose above the racket of wind and rain lashing the manor. Someone was singing a sad old ballad. *Antoinette?*

I wasn't ready to face her. I must find Mr. Rochester first.

A quiet mewing sound drew my gaze down. Sybil must have slipped in behind me as I'd entered the hall. She walked a short distance into the corridor that led to the south wing, tail held stiff like a bottle brush. She stopped there, looking back at me.

"Thank you," I murmured.

I went to the staircase, lifting the lamp from the table while avoiding the gaze of the Elizabethan lady. As I stepped onto the stairs, a sudden flash at the windows, followed by a loud clap of thunder, made me jump, and I bit back a cry of fright.

Securing my hold on my staff and basket, I raised the lantern and began climbing, wet skirts dragging at my every step, dread gnawing at my heart.

*Please let him be alive.*

When I reached the upper floor, I paused and looked around. The corridor on my right was clear, as was the gallery above the hall. I crossed the gallery to the opposite corridor, then stopped outside Mr. Rochester's door and knocked lightly.

No one responded, and I slowly pushed open the door. The room wasn't much lighter than the corridor, with only the stub of a single candle burning. I could make out the lines of a body in the bed.

I rested my staff against the wall and set the basket beside it. "Mr. Rochester?"

No reply, no answering movement. Dread seeped into my blood and bones. Fear and despair plucked away at my courage.

Holding my breath, I carried the lamp to his bedside table. I gasped as I looked into his face. His eyes were sunken and deeply rimmed by shadow. The bandage had slipped from his head, and his wound was swollen and angry.

*Heaven help me, I'm too late.*

Tears flooded my vision, and my fingers trembled as I reached toward his cheek—*not* cold with death but hot with fever! I laid a hand on his chest and leaned close, my ear to his lips. Air drafted faintly against my skin.

A sob escaped my lips as my head fell onto his chest.

I allowed myself to rest there, relief flooding through me, for only a moment before I stood up and retrieved my basket. Taking out a jar of dried rosemary, I uncorked it and held it under his nose.

He flinched, then sucked in a ragged breath. "I have died and gone to heaven."

The relief in his eyes and his broken voice threatened to undo me. I tried to smile. "You have not, sir."

"Jane. My Jane. It can't be true, for I'm sure I ordered her away."

I stifled another sob and reached for his hand. His fingers weakly squeezed mine. "I'm afraid your Jane is rather obstinate. But you may scold her later. Answer me quickly—where is Dr. Poole?"

His smile faded. "With *her*, I believe. I haven't seen him, not since the servants left. But I can sometimes hear them."

I stared at him in shock. "But who is caring for you?"

"I should have listened to you, Jane."

"Heaven above!" I looked around for meal trays, medicine, evidence of wound care—there was *nothing*. Only a pitcher on a distant table. I hurried over to investigate and found the pitcher empty, next to it a glass with a small amount of water. I sniffed it, took a tiny sip, then carried it to the bed. Taking the healing syrup from my bag, I poured a healthy dose into the water and sloshed it around. Then I slipped my hand behind his head and gently lifted. He groaned.

"I'm sorry," I said. "But you must drink this."

The water reached his lips, and he drank eagerly.

What now? His wound had festered. He needed more water, medicine, food. But I wasn't about to leave him here with "them," even just to gather supplies. It appeared they'd done nothing worse than neglect him, but that might change once they realized I'd returned.

"I'm going to take care of you," I said. "But I have to get you out of here."

His eyes rested on my face. "*How*, Jane?"

"You're going to walk. I'm going to help you."

He looked dubious, but he also already looked more awake and alert.

"Come," I ordered, rising from the bed.

Shaking, he dug an elbow into the mattress and levered himself partway up. I moved behind him and used my weight to shoulder him into a seated position. Then I got up and tossed the bedcover away from his legs.

"I hate for you to see me like this," he muttered as I slipped my arm under one shoulder, supporting him so he could stand. He wore a long, rumpled nightshirt.

"Put that out of your mind," I said. "Now, on the count of three . . ."

I counted, and he made an effort to stand. I got my weight under his shoulder and pushed.

"It's no use," he said, sinking back down. "I'm too weak."

"I don't believe it," I replied, determined enough for both of us. "Again, on three."

He gave another good effort, and this time he made it to his feet.

"That's it, sir," I said with relief, though bowed under his weight.

"For the love of god," he said with a hoarse laugh, "can you not call me Edward?"

My heart managed a happy bounce despite the circumstances. "Let us strike a deal. You make it to the cottage, and I will call you whatever you like."

He laughed again as we stumbled toward the door. I picked up my staff and put it in the hand of his free arm. His boots were also resting next to the door, and as he leaned on the staff, I bent and helped him put them on.

Rising, I scanned the room until I spied the clothes he'd been wearing two days ago, folded across a chair by the desk. I made sure he was steady and hurried to grab them, rolling them and stuffing them into my basket. As I did so, I noticed something hard in a pocket—the stone I'd given him, I thought. I also noticed a roll of clean bandages on the desk. I added the roll to the basket and returned to him.

Hanging the basket over my arm and picking up the lamp, I pressed close to him, supporting one side of his body while my staff supported the other. We began a slow, precarious progression through the gallery toward the stairway.

We made it to the top of the stairs and stopped to rest. Breathless and red-faced, he gave me another dubious look.

"We can make it," I said, desperate for him not to give up. "Catch your breath, and we'll keep going slowly."

"Do you have any idea where they are?" he asked in a low voice.

"I heard Antoinette in the rose drawing room. Sybil is watching the corridor. My staff and talisman are well warded. We'll be safe. Let's concentrate on the stairs."

I gave thanks for the rain and wind buffeting the manor, covering the sounds we were making. Covering any sounds *they* might be making; it was not a distraction we needed right now.

At first our progress was frightfully slow, as we stopped to rest and regain balance after every step. By the halfway point, he seemed to regain some of his strength, my staff helping him carry more of his own weight.

We were nearing the bottom when her voice reached me again, closer than before. Mr. Rochester and I exchanged an anxious glance but kept going. I watched the landing and the corridor as it came into view. Sybil was still stationed there, and low growls vibrated out of her. Just a few more steps.

*"Ed-ward . . ."* The singsong voice of the spirit echoed sweetly down the corridor. "Where are you *going*?"

Sybil yowled, and the spirit's responding shriek was a harrowing contrast to the ladylike tones. The sweat that had soaked my dress on the stairs suddenly went icy as chills ran all over my body. Foul air wafted from the corridor—death and decay.

"Kill that *beast*, George!" cried the spirit shrilly. "It's surely rabid."

We reached the bottom, and I steered him to the right, whispering urgently, "Don't look at her. Keep moving toward the entrance."

But we'd made it only a couple of strides when we heard rapid footfalls along the carpeted corridor. I stopped and turned as Sybil yowled again, darting past us toward the entrance, the physician in pursuit.

"Dr. Poole!" I shouted. He flew past, too, almost knocking me down.

The wind suddenly blasted the door open, snuffing out the candles. Rain pelted across the entryway flagstones. Sybil fled into the night with Poole racing after her.

I hazarded a glance in the opposite direction. Antoinette's gruesome figure moved into the pool of yellow light cast by our lamp.

"You are in no condition for visitors, Edward." Her voice had hardened like mortar. "Your foolhardy act of heroism has left you gravely ill."

He was right about the falling branch; it *had* been meant for me.

I slipped out from under his arm and placed his hand against the wall. Then I set down the lamp and basket and took my staff from him.

"Jane," he said urgently, "let us go."

I turned from him to the spirit, and a ghastly smile spread over her ruined face. "Little witch fell in a ditch. Water covered her, black as pitch. The townsfolk danced to see her drown, not a soul was seen to fr—"

*"By ageless ash, I banish thee! This is my will, so mote it be!"*

I cast my staff at her, and to my surprise, it struck her square in the chest, knocking her backward into a wall before falling away. She let out a cry of rage as her legs buckled beneath her. I had expected the staff to pass right through her, hopefully dragging her in its wake to the world beyond. I realized with horror that I had misunderstood what we were up against.

"Quickly!" I reached out to Mr. Rochester, and he took my hand. I grabbed the basket with his clothing and medicines but left the lamp. Together we staggered toward the entrance, the door still open to the autumnal tempest.

As we crossed the threshold, Antoinette shouted in a voice breathy and coarse from the blow, "You silly fools!"

I reached for the door and slammed it closed, and we stumbled onto the drive. With the basket on my arm, I conjured my spirit-light and slipped under Mr. Rochester's shoulder, wrapping my other arm around his waist.

"Let us go on to the cottage."

"Jane, we should get away from here."

I looked at him, his features washed in pale spirit-light and the cold, driving rain. I could feel him shivering. "I'd like nothing better. But which of us will hitch the horses to the carriage? Or did you think we would mount Phoebus and ride to Hay in the wind and rain?"

His jaw clenched. "Worse, there *are* no horses. With no one here to care for them, I ordered my groom to stable all but the good doctor's mount in the village. I suppose it will be useless for me to suggest that you take Poole's horse and ride for help."

"It will, insomuch as I have never in my life saddled or bridled a horse, nor have I traveled cross-country three times in less than a week just to leave you to—"

"I withdraw the suggestion."

As we made our way, I couldn't help looking behind us every minute or two to see if we were followed. The blow seemed to have set her back, and Poole was presumably still chasing Sybil. Likely he would have to abandon the chase once she reached her woods. If we could but get to the cottage, my protections should at least buy us some time.

*Should.* I thought over the things I'd learned in the last few minutes: Antoinette *had* tried to kill me, not her husband. And she was no ghost; my staff had struck flesh and bone. So what *was* she?

Mr. Rochester's strength was failing, and our slow, unsteady march to the cottage felt like a nightmare that would never end. But at last we did reach it. I helped him to a chair, fed the fire until it was bright and hot, then pulled a quilt from the bed.

"We must warm you," I said, giving him the quilt. "Take off your nightshirt and wrap up in this."

He gripped the quilt but then sank against the chair back and closed his eyes. "I must rest, Jane."

I bent over him, worry sharpening my tone. "Yes, but once you're dry. If you won't undress yourself, I will have to do it for you."

His eyes opened, and he forced himself upright, muttering, "Terrifying indeed."

*You are terrifying, Mistress Jane—do you know that?* It wrung my heart, remembering how he'd teased me by the well, and how I'd glimpsed a happier version of him.

When I saw that he was following my instruction, I stepped out to the stoop for the bucket. There'd been water in it when I left Thornfield, and in the time since then, it had been filled to overflowing by the rain. I tipped some out and brought it in slowly, trying not to slosh, then filled the kettle and hung it over the fire.

I kept my back to him as best I could while I worked, giving him privacy. When the small noises he was making ceased, I went to him and took hold of his arm. "Let's get you into bed."

I thought he would collapse as we crossed the room. Though he was shivering, I could feel his fever through the quilt.

I folded back the bedding, and he sank down. Then I helped him raise his legs and lie back, and I covered him with more quilts. Getting him tucked into bed at last, warm and dry, felt like half the battle. Now at least he could rest comfortably. But in truth, my work had just begun.

His eyes had closed the moment his head touched the pillow, but now he opened them and said, "We had an agreement, did we not? Let me hear it just once. It will do me more good than anything."

I felt the moth wings in my chest as I bent to his ear. "I'm going to heal you, Edward."

"*You* are all the medicine I need."

I straightened and touched his cheek. He smiled before closing his eyes again. His features slackened as he lost consciousness.

Hurrying to the shelves, I fetched the bottle of brandy. It was two-thirds empty, but if I was careful, it would be enough. The ancient Greeks had treated wounds with a mixture of warm water, wine, and vinegar, and I'd found the method so successful that I rarely saw a wound fester. I had no vinegar here, but brandy was stronger than wine, so I hoped it would make up for the deficit.

After pouring brandy and heated water into a small bowl, I cut a strip from the bandage roll and soaked it in the mixture. Then I went to the bed and examined the wound, just under his hairline. It was a hot, inflamed knot. Though the gash at its center wasn't deep, it wept a cloudy fluid. I used the wet bandage as a compress and thoroughly bathed the wound.

Next I got up and filled a teacup with warm water, mixing in more of the healing syrup.

"Edward?" I said, returning to his bedside.

He started, and he took in a quick breath. "Let me rest, Jane."

"For as long as you like, but you must drink this first. It will help your body heal."

He opened his eyes enough to direct a distasteful glance first at the cup, then at me. I lifted his head and held the cup to his lips. A good deal of it dribbled down his chin, but his thirst finally took over, and he gulped the rest.

"Can I bring you more water?"

"You can leave me be."

Going to my trunks, I dug through the contents looking for my favorite poultice herb—marshmallow root—and my jar of wound salve, made from calendula, yarrow, and plantain. The poultice, followed by the salve, would help with the heat and swelling and hopefully draw out whatever impurity was causing the wound to fester.

I mixed the powdered root with a small amount of warm water, then filled another strip of bandage with the paste. He didn't flinch or complain as I applied the poultice. By his ragged breathing, I knew he was again sleeping. It was the best thing for him.

While attending to my patient, I hadn't felt the cold, but now I shivered too. I unbuttoned and peeled off my dress, hanging it over one end of the table. My shift was also damp, and I sank into the chair in front of the fire to let it dry. As I began to warm, fatigue crept over me.

I got up and made a pot of strong tea, adding a few drops of nettle and burdock tonic, and quickly drank two cups.

I wondered how long it had been since Edward ate. Probably at least a day. Could I risk a trip to the kitchen garden for vegetables? Maybe if Sybil had come back, but not alone in the dark without my staff.

Opening my carpetbag, I took out what was left of my provisions—a slice of bread, a few biscuits, and the bacon. Edward would need something easy for his digestion. The bread could be softened by dipping in tea, and I could make broth from the bacon.

I filled the smallest cookpot with water and hung it above the fire, adding the bacon along with rosemary, sage, and thyme—all good, healthful herbs that would also encourage the cantankerous patient to eat.

When the broth was simmering, filling the cottage with a comforting aroma, I picked up a chair and carried it to his bedside. Then I sat down to watch and wait.

A sharp pain in my neck woke me. I had dozed in the chair. Not for long, I thought, as the fire still burned brightly.

My eyes moved to Edward's face—I didn't like what I saw. His cheeks were red as apples, and when I reached out to touch one, my heart jumped. If anything, he was *hotter*. I removed the poultice, and I took the washbasin from the dresser and poured in some cold water, using a handkerchief to bathe his face. When his skin had warmed the cloth, I soaked it again, bathing his neck and chest.

"Edward?" I called softly, a tremor in my voice.

I pressed my ear to his chest. His heartbeat was faint.

I'd never treated such a gravely ill patient on my own. What if it was beyond me?

I cast a frantic glance around the room. What hadn't I tried? He needed to drink, to help cool the fire in his blood, but for that, he must wake. I soaked the handkerchief again and held it to his lips. The water streamed down his chin.

*He's going to die.*

"Edward!" It came out a sob this time. My fingers moved over his face—fevered flesh and beard stubble. I lightly touched his bottom lip with my thumb. It, too, was hot and hard.

His words echoed in my thoughts: "*You* are all the medicine I need." Some small, forgotten thing was trying to work its way out of my memory, like a sliver of wood . . .

Of course! I jumped up and went back to the trunk containing my herbs and remedies. I removed everything left in it, grabbing the small chest at the bottom—the one I'd used to pack tinctures and essences.

Carefully I lifted out each bottle, reading the labels before replacing them, until finally I found it—the unknown tonic I'd made the day after my arrival at Thornfield. My hands trembled as I worked to remove the cork. It was no use; the seal wouldn't break. I carried the bottle to the table and used a knife to cut through the wax. Then I went back to the box for a clean dosage bottle, to which I added water, brandy, and a few drops of the tonic.

Could this work? At the very worst, it would do no harm. It was only herb and flower essence, and I'd collected from no baneful plants. My tinctures and syrups contained much higher concentrations of herbs, but this was something more. Dew from the most betwixt-and-between month of all—the last harvest, right before the witch's new year. Amplified by autumn sunshine and a drop of my own blood. It was medicine *and* magic.

I dosed a bowl of water with the essence and carried it to the bed. Wetting my hands, I bathed his face, making sure to thoroughly cover his wound. With the tip of a finger, I painted it over his lips.

"Open your mouth," I pleaded softly.

He remained still and silent.

I bent over him, laying a hand against his face. "You must live, Edward," I forced past the painful knot in my throat.

I moved closer, and I touched my lips to his. I pressed gently for the space of several heartbeats, praying his lips would wake beneath mine. But they didn't.

When I sat up, I saw that his mouth had opened slightly.

Drawing his chin down farther, I raised the dosage bottle with trembling fingers and carefully dripped a little directly onto his tongue before closing his mouth.

I took off my talisman and placed it in the middle of his chest, covering it with my hand. Then I rested my head below it. My tears seeped down onto his chest as I listened to the faint thrum of his heart.

Voice breaking, I chanted, *"By my blood, my body, and my craft, I would save you. By my love, I would save you. So mote it be."*

His chest rose under my cheek. "I hope you've more of that sweet elixir."

# "So I Know I'm Alive"

I raised my head, letting out a weary, but joyful, half-strangled-sounding laugh. He was *awake*.

His fingers came to my cheek. "Why are you crying?"

I closed my eyes. "I thought you would die."

His thumb brushed my jaw, and I felt like stars were twinkling inside me.

"So did I. But you saved me. Look at me, Jane." Our eyes met. "I could feel myself slipping away. I held on tightly to your voice. To the sound of you moving about the room. To your scent as you bent over me. Roses and herbs. There was nothing else to keep me here—only you. Do you think me a fool?"

"No more so than myself."

He smiled. "Kiss me again. So I know I'm alive."

My heart hammered as he pressed his hands into the bed and slowly sat up. My talisman slid down his chest and abdomen as the quilt pooled around his waist. The sight of his body stopped my breath. No idle country gentleman, he looked strong and fit, the flesh of his arms and chest firm but smoothly rounded. I recalled I was wearing no more than my shift, and my cheeks burned. That fire was matched by one in my belly.

With his hands, he pulled me closer. Then one arm came around my waist, while the other hand reached for my face, gently tilting my head back.

I had never been kissed before. I had imagined a gentle sweetness, mingling with excitement. A feeling like watching the sun sink at the end of the day. But when his lips touched mine, I *burned.* From my lips to the tips of my toes. With a kind of fire I'd never known—a fire that consumed without destroying. As if the sunset had exploded all around me, washing me in flames of orange, red, and pink.

I could feel the strength of him through my shift. The hardness of his body against my own more pliant flesh. My breaths came quicker, and I was losing myself in him . . . when he broke the kiss and held me against his chest.

"I think there is no magic more powerful than this. Would you agree?"

"With all my heart."

His arms tightened around me. "Thank you for coming back to me, Jane. God knows I didn't deserve it."

"You did what you thought best. And so did I."

Laughing, he said, "That's my Jane."

There it was again—*my Jane*. What had caused him to think of me this way? Mr. Brocklehurst had warned me to subdue my willfulness. Threatened dire consequences for Lowood. But to no avail. Looking back over the last several days, had I not defied Edward at almost every opportunity? Ignored his orders, followed him in secret, rejected his dismissal? What did Edward's regard for me say about the constant war I had waged against my own natural impulses?

He gave me a sudden, close squeeze, then released me and sank back against the headboard. "I find I'm still weak."

I stood up, and the room took a slow spin as everything settled back into its place. Except for those things that never would.

"You need sustenance," I said, "and more rest."

"And more such care as you gave me a moment ago."

The fire from our kiss flared anew, threatening to draw me back to him. By his expression of amused concentration, I thought he might very well be casting a spell that would compel me.

Walking on waves, I moved about the room, adding peats to the fire, heating water for tea, and ladling broth into a bowl. There was still a serving tray on the table by the door. I arranged the broth, bread, teapot, and cup on it and carried it to the bed.

"Try the broth first," I said, raising the bowl to his lips. He sipped and then took the bowl from me and drained it. He tore the bread into pieces and ate it with his tea.

"Your appetite's a good sign, s—"

"If you call me 'sir' again, I shall refuse to eat another bite."

I smiled at the flash of temper—another good sign. "It's a habit that may take time to break." Yet to what end? My calling him "Edward"—even my loving him—could do nothing to narrow the chasm between the rich, respected Yorkshire gentleman and the witch of questionable birth whom he had employed. A witch who in fact had no desire to be anything else. I heard Maria's voice in my mind. *Don't think too much about what it means for now, Jane.*

He eyed me over his teacup, like he was trying to read my thoughts. His bewitching eyes were the same silvery gray as my spirit-light. I remembered him on the heath, otherworldly and severe. He seemed a very different creature now. *But there are still depths in him to fathom.*

When he'd drunk the pot of tea, I moved the tray aside.

"There's been no more trouble from *them*?" he asked, glancing at the door.

"My protections seem to be holding, but we won't be able to stay hidden away in here much longer. We've almost exhausted the small supply of food I brought with me."

"We must leave Thornfield, Jane."

I nodded. "In the morning, after you've rested. It will be safer to move about in daylight."

My gaze was drawn to his long fingers resting on the quilt. Then up his wrists and arms to his rounded shoulders, gleaming in the candlelight. Finally his face. He was watching me, wearing an expression of . . . *pleased surprise*.

Heat bloomed in my cheeks, and lower, and he reached for my hand.

*Steady, Jane.*

"There's something I need to tell you," I said.

"Very well." His reply was soft, distracted. He squeezed my hand.

"What's happening at Thornfield—it's not at all what I thought."

His expression became more focused. "What do you mean?"

"There's no ghost. Antoinette, she . . ." I could think of no gentle way to say it. "She has risen, bodily, from the grave."

His face drained of color. "That cannot be, can it?"

"It *shouldn't* be."

"But how is it possible?"

I shook my head. "I'm quite out of my depth. I need to consult my mentor back at Lowood. This may even be beyond *her*."

He looked caught between shock and horror. It had seemed right to tell him, but I regretted not waiting until morning. "Try to put it out of your mind for now. I believe we'll be safe here tonight."

"We're agreed that we go in the morning? No more heroics."

"We're agreed."

Pale and fatigued, he sank back against his pillow. I adjusted the quilt over him, and I bent closer to check his head. He gazed steadily into my face, interfering with my concentration.

His skin was cool now, and his wound was remarkably better. The swelling had gone down, and some of the angry color had drained. I took my salve from the bedside table and applied a thin coating.

"It's healing," I said. "Your recovery is frankly astonishing."

He reached up and shifted a stray lock of hair away from my eyes. "*You* are frankly astonishing." He slipped his hand behind my head and gently pulled me down until our lips met. This kiss was gentle, but my heart galloped on, wanting more.

"Of *this*, there will be more to say." *Of this*—of the two of us. "I sent you away from Thornfield to save you, but I find I'm not strong enough to deny myself. Walking away from this place—something I could not even have imagined a week ago—will be a thousand times easier."

Reeling from this declaration, I put my finger to his lips. "Sleep, Edward."

He smiled to hear me say his name. Then he rolled onto his side and pulled the quilt up to his shoulder.

I went to the chair by the fire and sat down, going back over the last hour in my mind.

*There is no magic more powerful than this.*

*I'm not strong enough to deny myself.*

It was the sweetest bedtime story imaginable, however out of reach it might seem, and I did soon drift off to sleep. But not before making a vow to both him and myself: neither Antoinette, nor Thornfield's mysterious curse, if in fact there was one, would take his ancestral home away from him.

A monstrous clap of thunder woke me. I started up from the chair and looked out the window. Dawn had not yet arrived, but the storm clouds had cleared, and the garden was bathed in the bright light of the ripening moon. Had I dreamed the thunder?

An image coalesced in my mind. My mother stood in a field of lilies. The light was strange, diluted by shadow, turning the flowers a buttery color. Clouds churned overhead—not rain clouds but great billows of smoke. She held out her arms, and I saw that blood stained her luminescent gown.

It was more than a dream; something had happened to her. I knew it with certainty. Otherwise she would have returned by now.

I went to the bed and lightly touched Edward's forehead. Still cool, and he was sleeping soundly. I must let him continue. He would forbid me to go out or insist on going with me.

Then I recalled placing my talisman on his chest—and it slipping onto the bed. Had it gotten tangled in the quilts along with Edward? *If so, I must leave it.* Yet with my staff gone, how could I?

On impulse, I got down on my knees, and there it was, just under the bed. I lifted it back over my head.

I had dropped the basket with his clothes by the door, and I went now and felt for the hard thing I'd noticed when I rolled them up. It was the stone; it gave me a flutter of pleasure to think he had been carrying it with him. His trust in it would have bolstered its power too. I placed it on the chair beside the bed. *Watch over him as I would.*

Next I went to my trunks for a small copper bell. I carried it to the table and pulled a candle close to me, staring into the flickering flame.

*"Be ye fell, then heed this bell."* I rang the bell once and set it beside the candle. *"By this flame, I call thy name. George Poole and Antoinette Rochester. By this spell, I ward him well."* Then I blew out the candle.

Another layer of protection. It wrenched me to leave him in this vulnerable state. But if Antoinette and Poole wanted him dead, they'd had plenty of opportunity before my return from Lowood. And I could not abandon my mother.

I unpacked my pen, ink jar, and a sheet of stationery, writing, "I must find my mother. I won't be long." I set the note on the chair by the bed, anchoring it with the stone.

Finally I went back to my remedies and found my clear-sight tonic. Not Sight, like a prophetic dream, but *vision*, for I couldn't risk lighting my way to the hawthorn wood, not even with my spirit-light, which I must save for protection. An eye wash would be more effective, but there was no time to make one. Instead, I dripped a little of the tonic onto my tongue, whispering, *"Fennel and eyebright shall strengthen my sight."*

I quickly put on my dress, which had dried, and my damp cape.

Without the cloud blanket, the night had turned bitterly cold. My breath formed a vapor before my face, and the season's first frost crunched under my boots. Thin skins of ice had formed over the pud dles left by the rain.

Though I was grateful for the light of the celestial bodies, the wind and rain would have made it easier to avoid notice. I moved quickly to the garden wall, then along it to the orchard entrance.

I tried stepping lightly but couldn't avoid disturbing frosty leaves in the orchard. I scurried from trunk to trunk like a frightened mouse and, every minute or two, stopped and listened for the sounds of someone following.

I managed to cross safely to the arch between the orchard and hawthorn wood. Though I was less exposed among the shrubbier thorn trees, roots along the ground made the footing more treacherous, and my enemies could more easily lurk without my seeing them.

Halfway to my destination, I paused to listen, resting a hand on a nearby trunk. From the direction of the orchard, I heard leaves crunching. Before I could move, intense feelings of sorrow engulfed me, like a river out of its banks. I sank to my knees.

*Danger is coming.* My body resisted my commands to rise, as if I'd sunk into the mud at the bottom of a lake. *Nothing can be done,* this silty sorrow seemed to say. *Just rest.*

Now I heard rustling, very near, and belatedly I thought to concentrate on my hand, on the roughness of the trunk beneath my fingers. With determined focus, I managed to let go of the tree. My mind cleared in an instant.

I got up and tried to run, but my foot hooked a root, and I fell.

"Jane!"

*Edward!*

He appeared on the path, eyes wild with worry. He'd dressed, and he held something in his right hand—a thick thorn tree branch about the length of his arm, two-thirds covered in spiky twigs.

"Are you hurt?" he asked, moving quickly to my side.

My knee throbbed painfully, but it was no more than a hard knock. "I'm fine, but *you*—you shouldn't be here!"

"Neither should you. No more heroics, remember?"

"I had a vision, Edward. She's in danger. I couldn't abandon her."

"Of course not." He stood up and reached out his hand, helping me to my feet. "We'll go together."

I was too relieved to argue.

As we moved quickly through the trees, I wondered about the sudden attack of despair. It had felt like a collective grief. *Like the forest was mourning.*

Fear knotted my belly as we approached the old tree. I saw right away that something was terribly wrong. *Too many stars.*

The thunder that woke me—lightning had split the great hawthorn right down the middle. The two sides had peeled apart and lay smoking on the ground. A few orange flames flickered in the branches on one side.

I let out a cry and fumbled at my neck for the hagstone.

"Good god," said Edward, moving to stamp out the flames.

I searched frantically along the ground, picking my way over twisting branches as twigs and thorns tore at my skirt.

"Sybil!" I choked out.

*She might not have been here when it happened,* said my head. *But the dream,* said my heart.

"Wait," called Edward, holding up a hand.

I stopped rustling the foliage. After a moment, a muffled mewing came, and my breath caught. I moved toward the sound.

She mewed again, louder this time. Edward joined me, and we gently pushed back the leaves. Her white fur caught the moonlight.

She was trapped among the branches. Edward carefully took hold of the thickest branch and bent it upward. She didn't move to escape, so I sank down and gently lifted her, cradling her against my chest. She licked my chin with her rough tongue.

"I've got you," I breathed.

She hadn't died with her tree like the blackthorn dryad. Maybe her tree wasn't dead. The bottommost section of the trunk, though cleaved, had not been burned. Come spring, new growth might emerge. I'd seen it happen with a hawthorn tree at Lowood that Mr. Ross had cut down because it was encroaching on the vegetable garden.

"Is she badly injured?" Edward asked.

"I'm not sure. I need to get her back to the cottage."

He hesitated, and I wondered whether he was thinking the time was right for leaving the estate. But he nodded and said, "Quickly then."

I made my way carefully through the trees, feeling my way, knowing a fall could have more serious consequences now. If we could just make it to the orchard without mishap, it would be easier going. Edward followed behind us, brandishing his hawthorn club.

"I'm sorry I left you," I said in a low voice. "I admit I was afraid you might insist on coming, and I feared you were still too ill. But I can't say I'm sorry you're here."

"Of course I would have insisted. You saved my life, at great risk to your own. That life would be worth little without you."

My heart was too full to reply, and after a few moments, he said, "Do you think this was an accident? I mean—is it even possible it was deliberate?"

"I feel quite sure it was deliberate. Which means we're in grave danger."

"From magic, you mean."

"This would require more power than I knew was possible."

We crossed into the orchard, and he drew up beside me. "I wonder what Poole has had to do with all this. He's always seemed a reasonable and competent fellow, despite having been in love with my wife."

It almost stopped me in my tracks. "You *knew*?"

"It was there to see if one looked closely." His eyes came to my face. "So I suppose it shouldn't surprise me you discovered it too."

"It didn't bother you?"

He shook his head. "He'd known her before I had. And I don't believe he ever acted on his feelings, though now it's hard not to wonder. Antoinette would never have betrayed her vows, though, even had she felt the same—which I don't think she did. Her illness was so piteous, I wouldn't have had the heart to separate her from her physician, regardless."

"You're a rather remarkable man."

A small smile rested on his lips. "And have you known many men, for comparison?"

"I do *read*, Mr. Rochester."

His smile opened wide. "Bravo, *Miss Aire*. You're rather remarkable yourself. I knew it from the moment I met you, of course, though it's taken you an age to come to the same conclusion about me."

"*That* is clearly a falsehood. I made the worst sort of first impression, asserting my independence from modern means of conveyance, terrifying your poor horse, and sending you tumbling and swearing into the heather."

"Oh, I knew that you'd be trouble. And I knew that you'd change everything."

His tone had a somber note by the end, and I looked at him. Then Sybil suddenly stiffened and let out a low growl. We both stopped—and picked up the sound of someone moving through the orchard behind us.

Edward's eyes flashed. "*Run*, Jane."

I couldn't lift my hem or even see the ground well—not to mention the pain in my knee—and I was terrified I'd go down again, but indeed

I *ran*. Puffs of steam escaped my lips, and the cold air burned my lungs. With each pounding step, I worried about the jarring Sybil was taking.

We made it to the herb garden and kept running without looking back until we reached the cottage. Edward flung open the door, slamming and bolting it behind us.

I carried Sybil to the table and set her down. Edward stood before the door like a knight about to defend his castle. I had always trusted in spells and blessings, potions and cures, with good result, yet there were some situations where a man with a club was by far the best remedy. I was grateful he had his strength back.

When a few minutes had passed with no attempts made on the door, I turned my attention to Sybil. She gave a soft grunt as I began to gently probe her for injury. One of her ears was torn and bloodied, and a back leg was bent in a way that made me think it was broken. I had treated beasts in my time at Lowood, including Titan, the old wolfhound the groom kept, and Marigold, the kitchen mouser. I did what I could for Sybil, stitching her torn ear and using a wooden spoon to splint her leg. I'm sure I caused her pain, but she didn't fight or protest. Folding a quilt into a makeshift bed, I moved her to one side of the hearth to keep her warm.

"Will she recover?" Edward asked. He'd relaxed his club arm and had moved to stand by the window.

"I think so. Her leg may not ever be the same, but she should be able to walk on it again. I don't know what will happen to her now, though." I folded my arms and rested against the edge of the table, suddenly bone weary. "I don't know whether she'll survive if the tree doesn't. I don't know whether she'll be able to take her true form again."

"I'm so sorry, Jane."

I looked at him. "She protected us from them."

"I know it."

I took a ragged breath. "I only just met her."

He was coming to me, and how I wanted him. But I put up a hand, and he stopped.

"I can't go away now," I said. "I won't leave her unprotected, and I'm not sure what would happen to her if I tried to carry her away from Thornfield and her wood. But I think *you* should go, as soon as it's light, to the nearest of your tenants. You can send for Maria Temple at Lowood. She—"

*"Jane."* The lines of his face were set. "There is *no possibility* of my leaving you here alone with them. There is nothing you can say to persuade me. We will face this together. I hope it will be the first of many things we face together, and the only one so dire."

Something in my chest melted and pooled like candle wax. They were the loveliest words anyone had ever spoken to me. *I will not abandon you.*

He came close and set his club on the table, then pulled me into his arms. He pressed his lips to my forehead, and I felt his breath in my hair.

"Kiss me, Edward," I whispered.

He drew back, and I saw the happy light in his eyes. He lifted my chin with a finger and touched his lips to mine. I reached up, taking his face in my hands. The taste of him—the taste of us together—was everything. Earth and fire, wind and water—almost more than I could contain. After the first soft and silky caresses, our lips opened, and we moved deeper into each other. I felt the swell and surge of the sea. Tasted its salt and foam. He made a noise that sounded startled—and hungry—and his hands glided down my back.

Suddenly the doorknob rattled.

# *Them*

The rattling was followed by three heavy knocks.

Edward took up his club.

"Miss Aire? Mr. Rochester?"

Poole! Sounding quite desperate. Edward and I exchanged an anxious glance.

"A trick?" he said.

I held up my hand and moved closer to the door. "What do you want, Dr. Poole?"

"Please," he called through the door. "I-I've made a very grave error. All of this is my fault."

Again we looked at each other. *Do we trust him?*

It sounded as if Poole was finally ready to talk, and I was quite anxious to hear what he had to say. But Edward could be right; it might be a trap. Poole had neglected his patient, after all, with nearly fatal results.

*Remember to think of him as your adversary. He may not be in his right mind.*

Yet without him, we had very little to go on.

"We're not sure that we can trust you, Dr. Poole," I said finally.

*"Please,"* he begged. "I've come to confess all to the only person I know who might be able to undo it."

Edward's brow furrowed, lips in a tight line. But he gestured to me. *My decision.*

Finally, I walked back to the hearth, grabbing the broom from the corner, along with my jar of salt from the table. I returned and swept the entry clean, then sprinkled fresh salt in front of the threshold.

*"Those who mean ill, at this line be still."*

I reached for the bolt and glanced at Edward. He nodded and raised his club. I opened the door.

"God bless you!" cried Poole, stumbling across the threshold and the line of protection.

I closed and bolted the door, then poured another line of salt.

Edward turned out a chair at the table, giving the physician a significant look. Poole took his meaning and walked over and sat down. The man looked wrecked. He shivered in his ragged jacket, and his curls hung limply across his forehead. By his sunken and bloodshot eyes, he hadn't slept in some time. There were cuts on his face and hands. *Thorns,* I thought bitterly, remembering his pursuit of Sybil.

A quiet hiss issued from Sybil's makeshift bed, and Poole flinched and turned to look. "It's still alive," he said in disbelief.

"Despite your efforts, you mean?"

His features sagged as his gaze came back at me. "I *had* to go after the creature. I've fallen into the lady's power, you understand, and she was quite insistent. *Hates* the thing." He shook his head. "I can't seem to break free from her."

"And yet here you are," said Edward icily.

He was seething with resentment. I could hardly blame him, but I tried to temper my own anger to keep my head clear and to keep Poole talking. "Do you know what happened to the thorn tree?"

"It was *her,*" he blurted. "I told her the cat had escaped high into the tree, and she dragged me back there and . . . and . . ."

"And?" My heart pounded.

He closed his eyes, cringing. "She called down a bolt of lightning."

"*How*, Dr. Poole? Do you mean she used a spell?"

"I don't know." His shivering had turned to shaking, and he kept nervously glancing at the door and window. "I believe so, yes."

"Where is she now?"

His red-rimmed eyes came back to me. "It weakened her to do it. She said she must rest. But then she'll come. She sent me here to betray you. To help her get in. She can't get past—what did she say?—she can't get past your *wards*. I came to warn you!"

That she could summon lightning was terrifying. That my protective spells could keep her out was *hopeful.*

"You wanted my help undoing something," I said. "What is it?"

The color drained from his face. His hands twitched in his lap. "I must—I must go back to explain." He shifted in his chair. "Please understand . . . my feelings for her, God forgive me, I couldn't overcome them. She was so beautiful. Such an angel to behold. The soul of kindness and goodness."

I glanced at Edward. His barely restrained anger had given way to weary mournfulness.

"You loved Antoinette Rochester," I said.

"From the beginning, when she was still Antoinette Mason. But she didn't . . . I almost told her once, but she anticipated it and stopped me. Even if she had shared my feelings, she was too good to have ever acted on them without her father's approval." He squeezed his hands together. "I didn't mind it. I loved her for her loyalty."

It was easy to see that George Poole had fallen in love with his *ideal* of a woman. A woman who had married a man she didn't love, to please her father . . . it didn't quite match up with my own idea of goodness. But Edward had done the same for the sake of his family. And by society's standards, Antoinette was what every young woman ought to be.

Poole glanced at Edward. "That's not entirely true. Once she was actually married to someone else, I *did* mind it. But in the end, all I cared about was saving her. I had the arrogance to think I could, when none of the London physicians had been able to."

"And you tried some of your own remedies in hopes of easing her pain?" I asked.

He nodded. "After Mrs. Fairfax showed me the apothecary garden. I do think I was able to give her some measure of comfort in her final days. She passed peacefully, with no fits of wheezing or coughing." Tears had started in his eyes.

"There is nothing terrible in any of this," said Edward with a kind of gentle impatience that made him even dearer to me. "What is it that you're not telling us?"

Poole mopped hair back from his forehead. "After she died, I kept coming to Thornfield, using the excuse of checking on the widower."

*He felt it quite keenly, you see.*

"I'm not proud of it. But being here made me feel close to her. I used to visit the apothecary garden, because it reminded me of those final days, when, impossibly, her disposition became even sweeter. She let herself smile on me as she never had, and I did wonder if . . ."

He sat up, clearing his throat. "She'd been gone nearly eight months when I found the book."

Book? I didn't know what I'd expected him to say, but this wasn't it.

"What book?" I asked, feeling a prickling at the back of my neck.

"In the apothecary garden, I had stumbled a few times over some loose bricks under the elm tree. One day, I bent down to see if I could fit them back into place, and when I lifted one, I saw they were resting on a piece of carved wood." The physician's hands began to shake again, and he interlaced his fingers. "I removed more of the bricks and discovered the piece of wood was actually a box lid. I opened the box—I had to use my knife; it was stuck quite tight—and inside found a very old journal filled with recipes. When I examined them more closely, I realized they were spells."

"Continue," I said softly, and Edward looked at me.

"The spells utilized plants from the apothecary garden, though the book called it a poison garden. And indeed there were also recipes for deadly poisons. I was appalled but also fascinated. That's all it was at first—fascination with a ghastly old relic that it had been my good fortune to discover. For a time, it even shifted my thoughts away from Antoinette."

Hugging my arms over my chest, I moved close to Edward. His hand came to the small of my back, and he watched me worriedly.

Poole took a deep breath. Then he said grimly, "There was a spell for awakening the dead."

Edward choked out an oath—he hadn't anticipated it as I had. Still, my blood ran cold.

"I became obsessed by it," he continued. "I carried the book with me everywhere. I read it so many times that it—it rooted into my mind. I dreamed of it. I saw myself *casting* the spell. The book became like a living thing inside me." He shook his head. "I vowed a dozen times to burn it the next day, only to wake and think, *Tomorrow*."

"Do you still have it?"

He glanced up at the abrupt question. Then he patted at the breast of his jacket. He reached in and withdrew a small, dingy journal—cold fear jolted through me. He held it out to me, and Sybil hissed, making him jump.

"Set it on the table," I said.

Doing as I asked, he continued in an unsteady voice. "It clearly stated the dead could be raised within a year of passing. I knew it was wrong—sinful and *unnatural*—but her death . . . it had made my life a misery. I got the idea that having died, she would be free from 'until death us do part.' If she came back, she could freely and honorably be mine."

I moved closer to the table. The cover was plain, the color of tea with milk. Wrinkled and stained, with tears in the vellum. I itched to touch it, but it was clearly dangerous. How much *more* dangerous in the hands of someone with the training to properly use it?

"Don't touch it, Jane," warned Edward, following some similar instinct.

"The spell worked," I said, urging Poole to continue.

He dropped his head into his hands. "It did and it didn't. It took quite a long time to work up my nerve. I made up my mind; I changed it. Finally, just before midnight on the eve of the anniversary of her death, I cast the spell. And I . . . I watched her claw her way out of her grave."

"God in heaven!" cried Edward, sinking down into a chair. "So this creature—it *is* Antoinette?"

"No," I replied. "Go on, Doctor."

He looked at me. "When first she stood before me, my joy overwhelmed the guilt I felt. She was Antoinette, just as I remembered her. For a while she seemed distant and confused—I thought it only natural—yet at the same time, she was happy to see me." A smile twitched on his lips but quickly flattened. "It was not to last. Over the days to come, she began to change—to gradually *decay*. The book had made no mention of it."

"Indeed," I said wryly.

"She was still her sweet self," he continued, voice raw in his grief. "I felt I could adjust to the other changes, so long as she was by my side. Perhaps if I continued to study the book, I could devise a way to stop the physical deterioration." Slowly, he shook his head. "I visited her as much as I could, often in secret, without going to the house. Once, I suggested that the two of us should go away together, so I could spend all my time trying to help her. After that, she changed. She said that she was mistress of Thornfield, and her place was here. She made it clear she intended to drive everyone off the place. Everyone but me offended her, she said. But Mr. Rochester—for some reason, he could not be allowed to leave." Poole folded his arms, trying to control his shaking.

Edward's gaze bored into him, his eyes bright with the profound shock he'd received.

"This is necromancy," I said. "I studied it only lightly, and that was enough to give me nightmares for months. A spirit united with its body is a living person. A spirit can separate from a dying body and remain here on Earth—what we think of as a ghost. A *body* can be raised by necromancy. If you raise a body, you create a vessel that any spirit may inhabit."

"*What* spirit?" demanded Edward. "What spirit is inhabiting her?"

A cold sweat slicked my palms, and I rubbed them on my dress. "A malevolent fairy, perhaps."

He eyed me doubtfully. "Or?"

I arranged the pieces before me, fitting them together in my mind. "We may be dealing with a severed spirit. One that has been watching and waiting for such an opportunity. Possibly even the author of that grimoire, who may have had a long association with Thornfield." I looked at Poole. "Show me the book."

He shrank against his chair.

"You've come for her help," snapped Edward. "Now do as she says."

Reluctantly, Poole scooted the chair closer to the table. Then he reached out and opened the book, paging through slowly, shaking like a leaf in the wind all the while. It was full of spells written in an earlier but decipherable form of English. Each spell included copious detail and very fine illustrations of plants and sometimes animals. I began to sympathize with his fascination with the evil old thing.

*Take care, Jane.*

He stopped on a page titled "For Awakening the Dead."

There was a long list of herbs, including baneful ones from the poison garden. Also required were hair from the deceased person (I could easily imagine Poole having been bold enough to take such a memento), an offering of fire, the sacrifice of a hare, and some of the spell caster's own blood. I recalled the penknife I'd found near Antoinette's grave. The physician might easily have misplaced it in a rush to set the grave to rights after the spell.

"Continue," I said, gesturing to the book.

"That's all of it," he said, turning the blank end page. It was thicker than the others.

This grimoire was a work of art. It was hard to imagine it closing without fanfare.

"Hold the end page up to the candle."

He raised the book in front of the flame, bending back the sections on either side of the page. I could make out faint lines. Poole leaned closer. "Is that writing?" he said.

"Perhaps two pages have stuck together," said Edward.

I nodded. "See if you can separate them without damaging them."

Poole worked his thumbnails against a corner of the page, and I held my breath. After a few tries, the corner separated. I trembled as he carefully peeled the pages apart. "All the times I read this book," he muttered, "I can't believe I never noticed."

"I think perhaps you weren't meant to."

On the final page was a dedication, very faint, as some of the ink had transferred to the other page.

*To the pious little fool Katherine Grace Rochester*
*For thy treachery, I curse thee and thy daughters forever.*
*May all go to early graves, as shall I.*
*E.M.*

"Oh, Edward," I breathed.

He moved close to me, letting out a gasp as he read the words. "Thornfield's curse! In God's name, why? *Who?*"

Initials *E.M.*—they meant something to me, but what? I recalled the line of ancestral portraits in Thornfield's gallery, then the one that *wasn't* in the gallery . . . and suddenly I understood. I fixed my eyes on him.

"The portrait. The suspected murderess. The *witch.*"

He looked confused, but then the light came into his eyes. "Eleanor Montagu! The portrait in the hall. Her ancestors built Thornfield. Why in heaven's name would she curse her own family?"

"I think she has told us why. 'For thy treachery.' Mrs. Fairfax mentioned that Eleanor might have been executed for witchcraft, possibly even murder. Her stepdaughter must have informed on her."

Edward stared at the grimoire in horror. "I thought it was only a family story, told to frighten the children."

"Had I not seen this, I would have thought so too. Witches who use their craft in such ways—curses, necromancy, and other dark magics—they are quite rare. Most of the ones accused in past centuries were innocent victims of their neighbors' fears." I reached for his hand. "I'm so sorry, Edward."

He looked at me, features haggard, the light of the graveyard in his eyes.

"We'll destroy it," I said.

"Yes," he agreed. "Throw it on the fire."

I nodded, glancing at Poole, though I didn't have much hope. The physician rose from his chair and carried the book to the hearth, while keeping his distance from Sybil. He tossed the book in. Sparks flew up the chimney, and flames licked over the cover. I held my breath.

But it was as if the fire didn't know it was there.

"It's not burning," said Poole.

"No." My voice drew their gazes. "Grimoires are usually warded. It was worth trying."

"What now?" asked Edward.

"I don't know." I pressed my fingers to my temples, thinking. I walked to the door and back. How I needed Maria! Yet there was no time. Antoinette—Eleanor—might appear at any moment.

"Jane."

I stopped and looked at Edward.

"I believe in you."

The very words Maria had said to me before I left Thornfield the first time.

*I've come this far on my own. Maybe I am enough.* Edward seemed to think so. This man who had been dealt such a heavy hand of sorrow still somehow managed to believe in me. How I loved him. How I wanted to *save* him.

"This is nothing I've trained for," I said. "It's the darkest of magic. But I think there must be a way."

He took a step toward me. "There is something darkness can't survive, and you have more of it than anyone I know."

"Light," murmured Poole like he was answering a riddle.

*Not fire, but light.* And not just any light.

*Maybe I am enough.*

"Dr. Poole," I said, "retrieve the book."

He grabbed the ash shovel and stuck it into the flames, then dumped the book out onto the hearthstones. Sybil gave a half-hearted growl as the flames continued to lick over the cover a moment before burning out. Poole touched it tentatively, then picked it up and brought it to me.

"Let me," said Edward.

I didn't like the idea of him touching the book, but if this worked—*blessed sun and moon and stars, please let this work*—he should be the one.

"Yes," I said, and Poole handed him the book.

"Hold it steady, Edward."

He tightened his grip and raised the book.

Reaching the palm of my hand underneath it, I drew a spiral with the tip of a finger.

*"Light within,"* I said in my strongest voice, *"shine without."*

My spirit-light flared over my palm. As Edward lowered the book, the flame rose to meet it. *"Curse of Eleanor Montagu be broken! So mote it be!"*

Silver light enveloped the book, but as with the hearth fire, it did not burn.

Yet after a moment, an even brighter silver traveled along the edges of the cover.

"Let go of it, Edward."

He drew back, but the book remained suspended in the light. Thick drops of silver dripped down until the whole thing shone, like it was coated in mercury. The mercury began to bubble.

Beads of silver smaller than elderberries rose like steam from the grimoire until there was nothing of it left. My spirit-light flickered out, spent, but the beads kept rising. They plinked against the rafters like tiny hailstones.

Suddenly they remembered gravity, diving into our hair and clothing and striking the floor, where they rolled hither and thither, disappearing into cracks between floorboards.

Then the cottage window shattered.

# "This Romantic Fantasy"

Glass fragments sliced through the air as we all crouched to the floor. The table under the window flew suddenly across the room, dumping pots and dishes on the floor and smashing into the shelves on the opposite wall.

Poole crawled under the dining table, and Edward retrieved his hawthorn club from the floor, where it had been blown in the blast. Then he threw his arms around me protectively.

I felt powerless with the cottage breached, my spirit-light spent, and my staff gone. Scanning the floor around my trunks, my eyes lit on something I'd completely forgotten.

"Edward, let me go!" I said, squirming out of his arms.

Crawling to the item that had caught my eye, I tucked it under one arm and scooted back to him. I reached out and broke a long thorn off the club, accidentally piercing my thumb in the bargain. I'd not repent it this time; it would only make the magic stronger.

"Be ready," I said to Edward.

His eyes went wide, gaze sweeping over the floor around us. "Jane! *My vision.* You—"

I put a finger against his lips. "You believe in me."

His eyes still wide, he nodded.

"George, dear, come out, come out . . ."

We couldn't see her, but her voice rang clearly through the open window. Frigid air filled the cottage.

"Show yourself, Eleanor," I called.

A ghoulish head slipped slowly into view. "Boo!" she cried, then let out a peal of shrill laughter.

"Good *god*," muttered Edward, shuddering.

She moved in front of the window. "How clever of you to sleuth it out, Miss Aire. The good doctor never saw it coming, did you, dear?" She scanned the room, looking for Poole. "Poor smarmy, smitten George."

"Very impressive spell work," I said. "How many years had you waited for someone like Dr. Poole to come along?"

She smiled, revealing she'd lost a tooth since last night. "Oh, ages. But I was in no particular hurry. The dead are very patient." She sighed. "It *was* clever, wasn't it? A grimoire that was also a trap and a curse. And now you've destroyed it."

"The book served its purpose, I suppose."

"Heavens, yes, and poor George too! I always thought it would be a Rochester who found it, making my revenge all the sweeter. But the Rochesters are such cold fish. The book knew what was best." A frown of annoyance twisted her rotting lips. "Though even *my* magic won't hold this body together for long. George took too long in working up his nerve, didn't you, my love?"

Poole made a sound between a moan and a whimper, but she fixed her gaze on *me*. "No matter. I've got an even cleverer plan. One that will make us *such* a cozy little family. Impress me again, Miss Aire. What am I thinking?"

"That you might have a chance at redemption if you relinquish your claim on Antoinette's body and join the rest of the Montagues on the other side."

"*Fie*, do you actually *believe* in redemption?"

"I do, in fact."

"But be *serious*! Tell me what I have in mind."

I had finally fit all the pieces from the last several days together. I only hoped it wasn't too late. "Very well. I'm guessing it has something to do with taking my body instead. You've tried twice now, I believe."

Edward uttered a noise that almost sounded like a growl.

Eleanor laughed. "Nearly there, Miss Aire! Honestly, until recently, I only hoped to be rid of you by whatever means necessary. I was extremely vexed at your arrival and subsequent meddling. But alas, you fell in love, and upon your return to Thornfield, it occurred to me it would be very wrong to waste such a *fresh* body, though perhaps not as perfectly formed and pleasing as the angelic Antoinette. A mote earthy and plain for my tastes, yet not unattractive, and certainly a quicker and more active mind—and a vastly less saccharine disposition."

I was too preoccupied with my own plan to deliver a satisfying reaction to this. When Eleanor spoke again, she was cross and impatient.

"See here, you can't stay in there forever. I suspect that you have very little food or water. A bachelor, a widower, and an unmarried schoolmistress—it's all highly improper, and soon you'll be swimming in your own filth. Your little magics can't hold out against power that has fermented for centuries. This romantic fantasy of yours and Edward's has come to an end."

So my protective spells were holding together. It was small consolation, because she was right about all of it. She hadn't even mentioned the broken window and dwindling supply of fuel for the fire.

"I'm prepared to offer you a deal," I said.

The shock of everyone, inside and outside the cottage, was palpable. "*No*, Jane," Edward murmured urgently.

"We will end this right now," I continued. "I'll invite you in here among us, and you can carry out the plan you have in mind. Edward and Dr. Poole will *assist* you."

She eyed me appraisingly. "In exchange for?"

"When you have what you want, you let both of them leave Thornfield."

"You can't trust her!" warned Poole.

But Edward had gone quiet. He was no fool, and he knew that I wasn't either. I had a hunch that Eleanor had no intention of harming Edward, at least for now. He was the current master of Thornfield, and she would need him alive to shield her from discovery. And if she was powerful enough to force him to *marry* her—in my body—she could become mistress of Thornfield openly. *Such a cozy little family.*

But she didn't know how well I understood her plan.

Or so I hoped. The seconds that ticked by before she responded were the slowest ones of my life.

"How charming!" cried the abomination, clapping her hands together—though the sound was more of a dry thud. "And well played, my dear—you have proven that romance is alive and well."

"We have an agreement?"

*"Jane,"* protested Edward convincingly, "let it be me instead!"

"And become a flesh-and-bone Rochester?" said Eleanor. "Over my dead body." The creature let out a giggle. "Miss Aire, we have an agreement."

"Dr. Poole, get up," I ordered.

He shuffled up from beneath the table, his gaze flitting uncomfortably between his monster and me.

"Please go and open the front door," I said.

He hesitated, and Eleanor grumbled, "*Move*, George."

He jumped at the edge in her voice and then did as I'd instructed—unbolted and opened the door.

"Now take the broom and sweep away the salt," I said. This time he complied immediately.

I let the silence build a moment, then said, "Eleanor Montagu, won't you join us?"

In the second or two that she couldn't see us, walking between window and door, I cast a desperate glance at Edward. I held up my hand, hoping he'd understand: *Watch and wait.*

She came slowly into the cottage, her head moving in that odd, jerky way as she took stock of her surroundings. I knew she would be wary—likely even suspecting a trap—but she'd made it clear she saw my power as no threat to her. Bringing her into the cottage was risky, maybe unnecessary, but I wasn't sure exactly what was going to happen. I'd get one chance at this.

"You've a comfortable witch lair here," she observed. "I once dried herbs here myself."

"Indeed?" I said faintly. My heartbeat was frantic.

"Lined the shelves with all my pretty poisons." She frowned. "How that chit Katherine figured it out, I never discovered. Brighter than she looked."

She glanced at Edward, her expression somber for once. "I assure you Thomas's death wasn't personal, though the Rochesters always hated me. You see, my family *built* Thornfield. The real crime was that I should be forced to marry and become, along with the estate, the property of my husband. How little things have changed."

I wondered whether she was thinking about Antoinette—how she'd married, practically on her deathbed, to protect family property.

Eleanor now walked to the table, and I remembered Sybil on the floor near the hearth. I willed her to keep still.

"This will do," the lady said, laying a hand on the table. Her gaze drifted down to the floor. With her foot, she shifted aside a shard of teapot, revealing the small kitchen knife beneath. She smiled and bent to pick it up.

*Now or never.*

She seemed to hear my very thought. The moment I pulled the poppet from under my arm, her eyeless sockets were on me. Expression taut with fury, she chanted a few words in Latin—the opening of a baneful spell.

Sybil let out a perfectly timed yowl, breaking Eleanor's chant. Her gaze raked around the room, searching for her feline foe. The witch's head stilled as she spied Sybil on the quilt by the fire, and I felt the magic building in her.

I raised the bloodied thorn over the poppet—the one I'd made from the charm bag containing Antoinette's hair—and stabbed it through the heart.

Eleanor let out a shriek to wake the dead, and it was answered by a hundred crows. The poppet jerked in my hands, but I held on tightly, keeping the thorn in place.

*"Body be blessed, return to your rest! Spirit retire, consigned to the fire!"*

The body of Antoinette Rochester froze in place. Then her knees buckled, and she slumped to the floor. Before I'd even started breathing again, she began to disintegrate.

Suddenly, a shadow erupted out of her. It whipped into the rafters like a swarm of bees, wailing and shrieking, and then swooped directly at us.

"Now, Edward!" I cried.

He raised the hawthorn branch—witch's ally, blessed by fairies—and swung it through the shadow.

Wind ripped through the cottage, blasting in each of the four directions. The shadow wafted wildly, like a sheet loosed from a line by a storm, and when the wind turned south, it swept the shadow right into the hearth. Flames flashed out, swallowing the spirit and licking high up into the chimney.

Then both wind and fire snuffed out.

Sybil let out another hiss, followed by a sleepy groan. Then she laid her head back down on her paws.

Edward dropped the thorn branch and pulled me roughly into his arms, squeezing the breath out of me. "Jane!" It came out almost a sob.

"Is she truly gone?" called Poole, who crouched near the open door. He looked like a man who'd escaped the gallows.

"Dr. Poole," Edward called without looking at him, "go and saddle your horse."

Poole hesitated, not sure he'd heard right. Edward turned his head to glare at him, and finally he muttered, "Yes, sir," and left us.

Edward buried his face in my hair, laughing—it was a happy but ragged and weary sound. "I don't know what I've done to deserve you."

I wound my arms tightly around his waist. "Something awful, I'm sure, but we do seem to make a good team."

We had almost made it back to the hall. Early-morning light filtered through the trees, and though the path was slick with frost, the clear sky overhead prophesied another fine October day. I held Sybil against me with one arm, while the other held tightly to Edward to keep from slipping.

"You are quiet, Jane," he said as we rounded the end of the north wing. "Will you tell me your thoughts?"

I looked at him. The knot on his head was almost gone, the cut now closed and clean. "I'm not sure that I will. You would think them strange. And possibly impertinent."

His eyes crinkled at the corners as he laughed. It was one of my favorite things about his face. "I would be satisfied with nothing less."

"As you like," I said. "I was thinking that in coming here for the first time from Lowood, I had believed *myself* to be the greatest hazard I would face."

He nodded. "Indeed you *are* terrifying, as I believe I've told you. But I suppose that's not what you mean."

"Not exactly, no. I was afraid that my inability to conform to the idea of what a woman should *be* out in the world, as instilled in me by Mr. Brocklehurst, would be my downfall. And Lowood's as well."

"You believed—correctly—that you would fail to be docile. And that would lead to you getting the sack."

"Precisely. Yet had I succeeded in subduing my nature—"

He stopped abruptly and looked down at me. "I would be dead now, or worse. But I am not dead, and moreover I have a life before me that is worth living, and for that I will forever be grateful to you."

The intensity of his gaze stirred up the winged creatures in my belly and robbed me of speech. He touched my cheek. "You are cold. Let us make ourselves warm and comfortable, and then we'll talk more."

Inside the manor, the first thing Edward did was shed his jacket, fold up his shirtsleeves, and get a blazing fire going in the great fireplace. While I settled Sybil on the rug in front of it, he crossed to the other side of the hall and returned with the portrait of Eleanor Montagu, tossing it directly into the flames. We stood watching it bubble and blacken. Though nowhere near as dramatic as the grimoire transmutation or the spirit banishing, it was nonetheless satisfying.

We were going to the kitchen to see what food we could find when there came a knock on the door. I fetched my staff from the foot of the stairs, and Edward took an old sword down from the wall. Then he slowly opened the door. George Poole stood sheepishly outside, his horse saddled and cropping grass on the lawn. He asked whether there was anything he could do for us, which took courage and made me think better of him.

We let him inside and bade him wait while we each wrote a brief letter: I wrote to Maria, informing her that all was well and promising a longer missive would follow, and Edward wrote to Mrs. Fairfax in Hay, asking if she would contact the other servants and determine who might be willing to return. We gave him the letters and sent him away.

Then we foraged for breakfast and soon found ourselves settled comfortably on the rug in front of the fire with a wedge of cheese, days-old bread we'd toasted (burned) on the fire, blackberry jam, pickled onions, stale almond biscuits, and a bottle of claret. As far as I was concerned, it was a feast.

When we'd eaten our fill, warmed by the fire without and the claret within, Edward fixed his eyes on me.

"The time has come."

I brushed crumbs from my lap, my hand slightly trembling. "Very well."

He raised an eyebrow. "You honestly do look like you're about to get the sack. You must know we're beyond all that now."

I gave him a nervous smile. "Are we? It's only that I have no idea what you intend to say to me, so I have no idea how I will respond."

He made a gallant effort to suppress his amusement at my expense. "That is indeed a muddle. Perhaps try to *think* less. If only for a moment."

"I'm afraid you're not the first person to give me that advice. I shall give it my best effort."

He acknowledged this with a nod. "Now, Jane, I well know that you have a life outside of Thornfield. I know that Lowood and your work are important to you. More than anything, I wish you to be happy. Yet now that you've defeated Thornfield's shadow, I find I cannot help but hope you might find happiness with *me*."

I knew of course that he intended to speak of his feelings, yet this caught me completely by surprise. Was it marriage he was proposing? I believed him too honorable to mean anything else by it, yet how could this be?

"I can see that you're thinking, Jane."

I caught myself just as I was about to call him "sir" again. "I know, and I'm sorry, but I must. Both of us must. Recall that I have no legitimate family or status. Recall that I am a *witch*, a thing many disapprove of, and indeed not something I would be willing to give up. We would be rejected by your ladies Ingram and likely by everyone you know. I could not bear to be the cause of that."

"Hang the ladies Ingram!" he said with force. "And anyone else who might think themselves too good for my wife, whom I would not wish to change in the slightest, even had I any hope of doing so." He took a deep breath, and his features softened. "But maybe you hesitate for another reason. I'm well aware that I am not the handsome and dashing young fellow you deserve."

Now it was my turn to speak out. "What I *deserve* is a respectful, kind, and intelligent man. As for handsome and dashing, the philosopher has rightly stated that the perception of beauty is specific to the perceiver."

A smile tugged at his lips. "You can't mean you think me handsome."

"Can I not? But what about what *you* deserve? I am plain, sir. Most days I have dirt on my hands—quite often my face. And in case you've forgotten, I am not even fully human."

The smile took over his features. "You've left off my favorite of your many advantages. You disagree with, laugh at, and openly defy me."

"And you consider this an omen of future happiness?"

He let out a burst of laughter, and he took hold of my hands. "I shall take your dirty face and raise you a school of witchery, for there is an abandoned structure not far from here. I believe you inspected it yourself one day after rudely following me on a very private errand. It can easily be set to rights, and in fact we may soon want it for another purpose."

My heart was full. Too full for thinking, or speaking.

"Jane, take time to think about it if you will, but I love you most desperately, and I must know: Is there the remotest possibility that you will marry me?"

Very seriously, and rather wickedly, I said, "There is not the remotest possibility."

I let his face droop only an instant before leaning closer to him, until my lips almost touched his ear. "By which I mean to say, *the possibility is not remote*."

After which I was pulled into his arms, scolded for impishness, and thoroughly kissed.

# *Epilogue*

## *(Rochester)*

The ceremony was conducted in my family's chapel, which had been made whole again for the specific purpose of the ceremony. Jane's students attended, and her friend Maria Temple. And Mr. Brocklehurst of all people. Jane wore a lilac dress with cream lace and carried butter-yellow primroses. Her mother came, too, in the form of Sybil, sunning herself on the threshold of the church while we exchanged our vows. The way Jane smiled at me as she spoke . . . her hands in mine . . . my lips against hers . . . it filled me with a joy like none I'd ever known.

A week before the wedding, the great hawthorn stump had sprouted leaves, and Jane came to me in tears. She had seen her mother take her true form again.

A month *after* the wedding, I watched Jane welcome the first students to the Thornfield School for Witches.

One year and fourteen days after the wedding, the restored church bell rang out again, honoring the birth of Marion Sybil Rochester. People say she has her father's eyes, her mother's smile, and a voice that makes them think of spring rain on green leaves.

# Acknowledgments

It makes me so happy that you have this book in your hands right now. *Jane Eyre* was my gateway classic novel. After that, I ran through the other Brontës, Jane Austen, Anthony Trollope, Ann Radcliffe, and many more. But Jane was always special to me, and once, on a trip to New Orleans, I bought an old version of the novel with beautiful woodcut illustrations.

**(Spoilers below.)**

The original book comes very close but never quite includes any real magic (except for love, which is of course the strangest magic of all). Rochester teasingly refers to Jane as fairy, elf, witch, and sprite, but we know she is not actually any of these things. At one point, the question came to me: What if she was? And what if Rochester was brooding and charming without having locked his wife in the attic and lied to Jane about it? What would that story look like? So I read my woodcut *Jane Eyre* again and ordered a truckload of witchcraft books. (That whole journey released something truly wonderful and wild in me, but that's a story for another time.)

**(End of spoilers.)**

All that was the easy part. Admittedly—and adorably—I had this idea that retelling *Jane Eyre* was going to be a lark. Fun, not too taxing. I mean, someone else had already done the heavy lifting, right? And that first draft was indeed a fun little exploration, unburdened by the knowledge of the heavy lifting that was to come. So I must begin as I often do—by thanking Beth Miller, who works with my fabulous agent, Robin Rue, at Writers House. I'm sure I've thanked Beth in every book, and she deserves it because she is a wonderful editor, but this book in particular would not now be in your hands without her kindly critical eye and brilliant suggestions. I must also thank Writers House intern Amanda Mullett, who also read for me and contributed terrific ideas.

Heartfelt thanks to Robin, always, for her enthusiasm for me and the book but also for the many emails and phone calls it took to come to a final decision about who would publish the book.

Thank you to Lauren Plude at Amazon and editor Lindsey Faber for loving the book and making me feel like a rock star. Thank you for helping me make the book even better. (Through some kind of editorial sorcery, Lindsey even managed to get me to put my own biggest fear as an author right down onto the page.) Thank you to my copyeditor, Stacy, for close and careful attention to the manuscript (and for wayward-comma wrangling).

My love and gratitude to Debbi Murray, who has somehow been a first reader for more than a decade now. (Check out her amazing artwork at debbimurray.com.) Thank you also to Donna Frelick, writing peer and friend, for reading an early draft. Thank you to Jason, for talking me down from anxiety or up from the blues, as applicable, and for springing for the good bubbles.

I want to shout out to the witchy Instagram community. I learned so much from you all, and just being a part of the community helped keep me going. Three individuals in particular I want to thank by name:

- Bianca-Rose of @belladonnabooks, for her encouragement and herbal expertise (and excellent fiction recommendations). Also for generously reading and commenting on an earlier draft of the novel.
- Susan Ilka Tuttle of @whisper_in_the_wood, and author of

*Green Witch Magick* (2021), for her many teachings and gorgeous magical aesthetic. Also her botanical offerings; if *Salt & Broom* had a signature scent, it would be either Harvest Moon whipped body butter or Witch perfume.

- Sarah Justice of @tinycauldron and managing editor of *Witchology Magazine*. Her class on cottage witchcraft was tremendously inspiring and helpful.

In addition to the folks above, there are a few other key resources I want to acknowledge:

- Various books and writings by Maia Toll, which reawakened me to the fact the world is full of magic.
- *Hedge Witchcraft* (2012) by Harmonia Saille, the first how-to book on witchcraft I ever read and a perfect beginner book.
- *The Complete Herbal* (1653) by Nicholas Culpeper, a resource my witchy Jane would certainly have known well.
- The website and Instagram account for Bane Folk, a small company that creates salves and essences from "baneful" plants.
- The delightful *What Jane Austen Ate and Charles Dickens Knew* (1993) by Daniel Pool, which saved me from having characters doing things before they were invented.
- Most of all, the brilliant and ageless original by Charlotte Brontë.

In the writing of this book, I strove to create a relatable and aesthetically enjoyable version of witchcraft for my fictional Victorian England. I also strove to lay a sensitive and accurate foundation via the book's brief references to the real-world history of witchcraft. I researched to the best of my ability, but I am certain the book is not without error, and I hope I may be forgiven in those cases where I have gotten something wrong.

# *About the Author*

Sharon Lynn Fisher writes smart, twisty, passionate tales—mash-ups of fantasy (or sci-fi) and slow-burn romance set in lush and atmospheric worlds. Her books have been praised and recommended by *Booklist*, *Kirkus*, *Publishers Weekly*, the Historical Novel Society, and *RT Book Reviews*.

A city mouse who was dragged by her country-mouse-aspiring family to an acreage just outside Seattle, Sharon is mom to two brilliant teens, two ridiculous goats, an orange cat, and a fluctuating number of poultry. When she's not writing, you'll find her wandering the woods looking for mushrooms and fairies.